"Who touches you, Ariel?" Jarad asked. His voice sent a low sensuous shiver down her spine. She tried to look away, but he used his other hand to capture her cheek and turn her face back to his.

"Who?" he repeated, more firmly.

Ariel said nothing, unsure what he was asking her. Was he asking if there was a man in her life she hadn't told him about? He had to know that she would never have let him near her if that were true. She wasn't starved for affection, either, if that's what he was thinking.

Either way, she had no intention of answering him. That was far too personal a question. She had no intention of baring her soul to a man again and leaving herself vulnerable. As far as she was concerned, the conversation was over. She pulled away from him, starting to rise.

With a hand on her arm, he pulled her back, bringing her onto her knees in front of him. Startled, she turned her face up to his. A second later, his lips were on hers. His tongue was bold, slipping through her parted lips to sample the sweetness of her mouth. His fingers massaged her back, her shoulders, her scalp through the thick tangle of her curls. He slanted his mouth over hers, and she moaned, inflaming them both.

With his hands and body and his mouth he was sending her a silent message: *Now someone does.*

## BOOK YOUR PLACE ON OUR WEBSITE AND MAKE THE ARABESQUE ROMANCE CONNECTION!

We've created a customized website just for our very special Arabesque readers, where you can get the inside scoop on everything that's going on with Arabesque romance novels.

When you come online, you'll have the exciting opportunity to:

- View covers of upcoming books

- Learn about our future publishing schedule (listed by publication month and author)

- Find out when your favorite authors will be visiting a city near you

- Search for and order backlist books

- Check out author bios and background information

- Send e-mail to your favorite authors

- Join us in weekly chats with authors, readers and other guests

- Get writing guidelines

- AND MUCH MORE!

Visit our website at
http://www.arabesquebooks.com

# SPELLBOUND

## *Deirdre Savoy*

ARABESQUE
BET
BOOKS

BET Publications, LLC
www.msbet.com
www.arabesquebooks.com

ARABESQUE BOOKS are published by

BET Publications, LLC
c/o BET BOOKS
One BET Plaza
1900 W Place NE
Washington, D.C. 20018-1211

First Printing: December, 1999
10 9 8 7 6 5 4 3 2 1

Printed in the United States of America

To my mom and dad,
Dolores and Eugene Savoy,
for teaching me to see the world
as a wondrous place.

To Bi and Christy Burnett,
for teaching me to love the island.

To my husband, Frank LaMantia,
for teaching me to believe in myself.

And to my grandmother, Ethelind Farr Reid,
for teaching me that all things are possible
and good things come to she who waits.

## Acknowledgments

Special thanks to my "readers"—Elyse, Joyce and Sharon—for their unflagging devotion and shameless praise. To Gwynne Forster for her infallible advice and incredible support. And to my agent, James Finn, a miracle worker who believed in my story when, sometimes, I didn't.

This book wouldn't have been possible without them.

# One

Ariel Windsor stood at the railing of the *Islander*, the oldest of three ferries that made their way between Woods Hole, Martha's Vineyard and Nantucket. Despite her fatigue from the torturous five-hour drive from New York, the splendid view before her took Ariel's breath away. The sky above was a cloudless azure that melted into the clear blue waters at the horizon. On either side of her stood the bluffs of Woods Hole. Their riotous display of greenery was uninterrupted, save for the stately homes that dotted the cliffs—grand mansions, which Ariel thought only enhanced the beauty of the scene before her. In less than an hour, she would be home.

Although she rarely spent more than a couple of weeks on the Vineyard each summer, she still thought of the little island off the shores of Massachusetts as her home. New York was where she lived, worked, where she had gone to college. This place was in her blood.

This time it was Jenny's wedding that beckoned her to the island. Her cousin Jenny, who used to say marriage should be against the law. That is, when she wasn't daydreaming about what the perfect man would be like. That was the trouble with her family. Hopeless romantics, all of them—head-strong and impulsive and downright crazy. Un-doubtedly, the upcoming wedding would rival any illustrious one with its abundance and splendor. She wouldn't be surprised to find the Vineyard Symphony playing the wedding march.

Still, she was looking forward to having everyone together again: Jenny the soon-to-be blushing bride; Dan, her fiancé; Gran, the crusty old family matriarch; and Charlie, Gran's salvation after Grandy died. Then there were her parents. Steve and Diana Windsor were on an extended cruise through the Caribbean. They would be flying home the day of the wedding.

Ariel sighed, running her fingertips along the railing. Now that Jenny had succumbed to the du-bious merits of marriage, Ariel knew her entire family would turn their attention to her, expecting her to be next. She was the only one who could go next. There were no Ludlow women behind her. No other Ludlows period.

What a laugh! At twenty-seven, she'd had only two halfway serious relationships, and they had both been disasters. She'd never felt the grand sweeping passion that her friends talked about. She didn't want to. That sort of lack of control only got people into all sorts of trouble. As a psycholo-gist, she'd seen exactly what love could do to a person. She could do without that kind of misery, thank you.

The still familiar blast of the ferry's horn sig-naled that the *Islander* was setting sail. Ariel glanced around her. The deck wasn't crowded. Only a few passengers had forfeited the shade of the lower deck for a seat out in the warm July sun. Ariel loved the feel of the sun on her face and the wind wreaking havoc with her hair as she stared out at the ocean, though she wished for a pair of shorts and a T-shirt instead of the lightweight slacks and sweater she wore. Resting her elbows on the railing, she shut her eyes against the brilliant ball hovering over her.

The small ship rocked in tune with the ocean, lulling her into a hazy nostalgia for the island that had been her childhood home. The clay cliffs of Gay Head, the little lagoon by the State Lobster Hatchery, the Old Sailor's Graveyard—all her special places.

Ariel opened her eyes, letting out a long contented breath. Coming here was like a respite from everyday life. The air was cleaner, the stars shone brighter, the grass was greener—there was grass period. She smiled at her own attempt at humor.

And while she was at it, a moonlit stroll on the beach on the arm of one of Jenny's "perfect men" couldn't hurt either.

The sound of a deep, masculine voice startled Ariel from her thoughts. She looked in the direction of the man who'd spoken. Her first thought as her gaze wandered over him was: Here is a man used to being in control. She didn't know what made her think that, but her mind was soon preoccupied with her second thought, which was "Whoa!"

She had to close her mouth first to be able to form the words. "Did you say something?" she asked.

"I'm sorry I startled you," he said. He smiled a disarmingly pleasant smile and shrugged, as if in apology. "After a few minutes staring at the ocean, I start talking to myself."

She couldn't help noticing how close he came

to the fantasy man she'd been daydreaming about.
But this man with the tight-fitting jeans and muscular bronzed arms was certainly very real. And besides that, he was handsome, too—a strong,
straight nose, and sculptured jaw, set in a chocolate
brown face. His eyes were a deeper brown, fringed
by lashes long enough to make any woman jealous.

She smiled back. "I know what you mean. I tend
to daydream myself."

"What a pair we make," he said, laughing. "I'm
Jarad Naughton."

She shook the hand he extended to her, his
hand feeling warm and strong against her own. She
didn't usually try to strike up friendships with
strangers. This one didn't seem dangerous—except, perhaps, to a girl's heart. She was about to
give her name when he added, "I did mean what
I said about your eyes, though. They are very lovely
and very unusual."

She snatched her hand back, narrowing her eyes
on him, eyes the same sea-green color as every
other woman in her family. If that wasn't the quintessential New York pickup line, she didn't know
what was. She'd heard more than her share of such
lines due to her eye color. It was a sore point with
her anyway, since most people she met swore she
must be wearing contacts. "My, how original," she
said, her voice full of sarcasm.

He had the nerve to laugh. "I suppose I deserved that. I'll try to be more creative in the future."

*Yes, he's attractive, and he knows it, too.* He leaned
against the railing as if it were his little ferry and
he was nice enough to let everyone else ride on
it. What did you say to a person like that? She'd
never been any good around charming men. She

never managed to say anything that didn't sound rude, obnoxious or downright stupid.

She turned her attention to a seagull flying alongside the boat. Where had this man come from anyway? It was unnerving to look up and find the flesh-and-blood equivalent of a man you'd been fantasizing about standing next to you. It made her feel as though she'd conjured him up from thin air. Maybe he'd go away just as easily.

She could feel his presence next to her as he moved closer, turning to face the ocean as she was. She could feel his eyes on her, watching her, though he was trying not to be obvious about it. He was making her nervous, which was an odd feeling. She'd been in the same room with convicted sex offenders and they didn't inspire this much reaction in her.

"So, what's a nice girl like you doing on a ferry like this?"

She couldn't help but smile as she turned to face him. He was persistent, she'd give him that. "If you must know, I'm visiting my grandmother. What about you?"

Why had she asked him that? She was trying to get rid of him, not encourage him, as if he needed it. Yet, some small part of her felt flattered by this man's attention. There weren't a whole lot of handsome, charming men beating down her door in New York.

"Some friends of my parents invited me up." He turned to look out at the water. The coast of Martha's Vineyard was coming into view. "I haven't been up here since I was a kid. I didn't realize until now how much I missed this place."

The wistfulness in his voice made her smile. That's how she felt, too. "Are you staying long?"

She looked up at him through the sweep of her lashes.

"I haven't decided. The people I'm staying with will probably be too busy to pay much attention to me." He cocked an eyebrow suggestively. "Maybe you could give me a tour."

It was impossible to tell if he was serious. At least it was impossible for her. Either way, she wouldn't be accompanying him anywhere. She was here for Jenny's wedding, not to go frolicking around with handsome strangers. Annoyed at herself for wishing that might be a possibility, she snapped, "You don't give up, do you?"

"I don't know what you mean," he said, but she could see that he did.

"You," she said dryly, "are trying to pick me up."

"Who me? I'm just trying to be friendly. As I remember it, islanders are supposed to be very friendly people."

Seeing his smile, she could imagine what kind of friendliness he had in mind. She felt a feathery chill steal up her spine at the prospect. She really must need a vacation if she was going to react to every bit of innuendo she heard. She was supposed to be immune to such things. "Vineyarders," she corrected, "usually are."

"That means you should be nice to me—a poor, lone man traveling to your hometown . . ."

She groaned inwardly as he left his words hanging there. She supposed the faint trace of a Vineyard accent gave her away. Then she made the mistake of looking up at him, right into his eyes. She had to admit there was something very appealing about this man. It went beyond her silly fantasies, beyond his good looks. And his eyes. She could get lost in those eyes. She swallowed down the lump that had risen in her throat.

Frowning, she wondered what it was about being on this island that always made her revert into a teenager. The last time she'd thought about men with mesmerizing eyes, she'd been about thirteen, discussing the latest teen idol with Jenny. She was a sane, rational, grown-up woman now.

Shrugging mentally, she turned her attention to the harbor coming into view. The boardwalk leading to the Steamship Authority building was crowded with cars, bicycles and pedestrians waiting their turn to board the ferry. It was Sunday afternoon, time for the weekend masses to return to civilization. Beyond that, she could see the town square and police administration building, decorated with rows of colorful flowers.

To the left of the dock, children wearing snorkeling masks were diving for coins thrown into the clear green waters by passing tourists. Nearer to the beach, swimmers splashed each other, laughing.

This is how she remembered the island. A lovely trip back to a simpler life than existed most other places. Here, her only worries were what bathing suit to wear, which boat to take fishing, or what flavor frappé to order at Mad Martha's ice-cream parlor. So she did have one romantic weakness. Even sensible people were entitled to one.

"So beautiful," she mused.

"Yes."

Turning to look at him, she realized he was looking at her, not at the harbor. Surprised, she looked away from him, feeling heat rise in her cheeks. He reached out and stroked an errant tendril of hair behind her ear.

The ship was moving into the harbor, but whoever manned the helm hadn't aligned it correctly within the slip. The starboard side banged against the pilings, jolting both of them. She grabbed for the railing to steady herself. At the same time, the stranger's arms came around her protectively. His hold on her wasn't tight, but she could feel the heat of his body, smell his cologne. His breath fanned her cheek as she instinctively turned to face him.

"I'll have to remember to thank the captain," he said huskily.

She just stared at him, or more precisely, at his mouth, wishing she could think of some witty exit line, something clever to say before getting the heck out of there and back to her car. What did he intend to do? Kiss her? In the middle of a crowded deck? But there was no one there but them. All the truly sensible people had already gone back to their cars.

"Any chance I'll see you again?" he asked.

Ariel shook her head, feeling his grip on her tighten.

"Then I'll have to settle for this," he said. Ariel's eyes automatically closed as his head lowered toward hers. It was a surprisingly tender kiss he bestowed on her, making her unable to think, unable to move.

Then the blast of a car horn sounded, startling her. She pulled away and ran to her car like Cinderella leaving the ball. Once inside, she started the engine, strapped on her seat belt, laid her head on the steering wheel and sighed.

She ought to have her head examined. She had had her head examined as part of her training. Obviously, it hadn't done her any good.

If she were honest with herself, she'd have to admit she had wanted that man to kiss her. That complete and total stranger who could have who-knew-what disease. True, he had initiated the kiss, but she could have left when she'd thought to do so. She could have pushed him away. She didn't have to stand there and enjoy it.

Her only saving grace was that she hadn't really kissed him back. She was too stunned to do much of anything. Revving her engine, she pulled off at a far greater speed than necessary.

There was a clinical term for women who behaved as irrationally as she had that afternoon.

Nuts.

A half hour later, Ariel pulled her car into the drive in front of the home that had been in her family for quite a few generations. Surrounded on three sides by a grove of oak trees, the stately manor house had remained unchanged since the time of Ariel's youth. The exterior was the same dove gray and white wood it had always been, with darker gray covering the eaves and roof.

On the fourth side lay the ocean, calm and majestic. Ariel drank in its salty aroma as she parked her car in the garage. She could hear the sound of feminine laughter coming from the back of the house.

Walking along the white stone footpath, she followed the sound, stopping to pick up a small red ball lying under the rosebushes that ran along the side of the house. Gran took great pride in the flowers which exploded in riotous pinks, yellows and oranges around her. Ariel retrieved the ball, careful not to prick herself on one of the thorns.

"Well, child. Stop smelling those flowers and come over here and give your old Gran a hug." Isabel Ludlow stood a few feet in front of her, wearing a pale blue dress. Her thick gray hair was pulled back in the same bun that Ariel had never seen her without. She seemed a little thinner than Ariel remembered, her almond-colored skin might show a few more lines, but she was nearly seventy now.

"Gran!" Ariel cried, running into the open arms of the older woman. Despite her age, Gran still gave the bear hug that had knocked the wind out of Ariel as a child. Old woman, indeed!

"It's so good to see you child," Gran said, releasing her. "Turn around and let me look at you."

Ariel did as she was told, knowing this was all part of the homecoming ritual. "You're too thin." That was the same pronouncement Gran always made.

"I am not. You're just not happy unless you have something to complain about."

"You're darn right. When you get to be my age, there isn't a whole lot left to do but complain."

"I refuse to listen to this any longer. I have never seen you with nothing to do. Between your garden and your charity work, I doubt you have a moment to yourself."

Lifting the paper bag at her side, she presented it to Gran. "Look what I brought."

"Mmm," Gran purred, as the smell of the cookies wafted up to her when she opened the bag. "I think you need these more than I do, but I'll be more than happy to eat them just the same."

"Oh, Gran," Ariel said, placing an arm around the older woman's shoulders.

"Welcome home, dear." Gran planted a warm,

moist kiss on her cheek. The two women walked toward the house arm in arm.

They'd gotten about ten feet when Ariel saw a large Irish setter headed straight for her. He succeeded in knocking her to the ground, and began licking her face in long wet wipes. "Help," she cried, laughing.

"You've got Dudley's ball." Ariel heard Jenny's voice before she could see her cousin through the haze of russet fur.

"Get this thing off of me."

Ariel glared at Jenny, who offered her a hand up, laughing heartily. "When did you get that mangy mutt?" Ariel asked, swiping at the dirt and grass that Dudley's large paws had deposited on her clothes.

"Don't talk about Dudley like that." Jenny ruffled the fur on the setter's back. "We rescued him and his siblings after his mother got hit by a car. Besides, Dudley means well."

Hands on hips, Ariel stared up at her taller, more voluptuous cousin. "So did Torquemada. And we all know what happened with him."

"All right, all right," Jenny conceded. "I give up. I'm no match for you when you get on a roll."

"It's about time you admitted that," Ariel teased as she took a seat at the white wrought iron table next to Gran.

Jenny took the seat to Ariel's right. "So, how are things going for our resident sex therapist these days?"

"I am not a sex therapist," Ariel said for perhaps the millionth time. Ever since Ariel told Jenny about her taking over a workshop on human sexuality from a colleague on maternity leave, Jenny had started in with this sex therapist business. Ariel would bet the board of the private school where she was the staff psychologist would love to hear about that!

Jenny leaned close so that Gran wouldn't hear what she said. "What a pity!"

Ariel pursed her lips before letting out a heavy sigh. "Besides, I should be the one asking questions, considering I was summoned here to be your maid of honor, of all things. When did you decide marriage wasn't a sin, Jenny?"

"I never thought it was a sin, exactly . . ."

"Just a crime punishable by a life sentence."

"Somehow, I remember you sharing that sentiment."

"I still do. I'm trying to figure out why you defected on me."

Jenny placed a hand on her heart and sighed affectedly. "True love."

"Ah, the ruin of many a great woman." She meant that sincerely. "How is Dan anyway?"

"Calm as a cucumber. It's disgusting. I'm the one with a serious case of the jitters. He's been complaining all week about how I'm driving him nuts."

"You could have just lived together." Ariel cast a devilish wink at Jenny. They both knew how opposed Gran was to live-in arrangements. It was one of those subjects Gran could lecture on for hours.

"Young women," Gran said with a snort.

For a moment, Ariel feared Gran might launch into one of her diatribes about the proper behavior for Ludlow women. Luckily, Mrs. Thompson, Gran's housekeeper and companion, came onto the patio. She wore a red-and-white checkered shirtwaist dress. It made a sharp contrast to her nut-brown skin and black hair. The tray she carried was laden with her delicious seafood salad, fresh fruit and a variety of crackers. Ariel heaped her plate high with the tasty concoction, sighing with delight after sampling a forkful.

Ariel leaned back in her chair. "This is even better than I remembered it."

"Thank you, darlin', and welcome home," Mrs. Thompson said, deliberately exaggerating her West Indian accent. "How ya been?"

It seemed everybody was in the mood to give her "the treatment." Normally, Mrs. Thompson's speech was as plain as the rest of theirs.

"I cleaned yer room, ya know. But I no bringing no heavy bags up them stairs, now."

"I'm sure I can handle it, Emma. I only brought my duffel bag, anyway. And I'm certainly big and strong enough to handle that."

"Strong, maybe," Jenny interjected.

"I was quite capable of carrying the thing out to the car by myself this morning.

"Don't get testy, runt," Jenny said, laughing.

"Emma's about to become a grandmother," Gran said when she'd gone back inside. "I'm not sure she likes the idea, though she's looking forward to seeing the baby."

"When is her daughter due?"

"The day of my wedding, of course," Jenny said. "I hope she doesn't have to miss it."

"I hope not. I'm sure she's been looking forward to it." Ariel finished her meal and laid her napkin on the table.

"Speaking of people missing the wedding, have you heard from your parents yet?"

"I got a fax from them yesterday," Ariel told Jenny. "They're coming, but only for the day. They'll have to take a late flight back to the ship."

"I'm surprised you haven't run out for a swim,

yet," Mrs. Thompson told Ariel when she returned to collect the dishes. Ariel's love of the ocean was not usually affected by anything.

"Yes," Gran suggested. "Why don't you two girls go for a swim. I have to find out what happened to our missing houseguest."

*What missing houseguest?* Before Ariel could ask the question, Jenny issued the childhood battle cry, "First in the bathroom!" Jenny disappeared through the open French doors.

Ariel took off right behind her, knowing that if history proved true, she didn't stand a chance of getting there first.

"Come in here, young man," Isabel Ludlow scolded. "We were really getting worried about you."

Jarad stood in front of the Ludlow house, poised to knock. The door had been pulled open before he'd gotten the chance. "I'm sorry Isabel. I got lost."

"I can believe that. We never could send you out anywhere by yourself without having to send out a search party an hour later." Gran ushered him into the house, closing the door firmly behind them. "And what is this Isabel nonsense? Have you gotten too grown to call me Gran?"

"No, Gran," he said, embracing her. "How are you?"

"Hanging in there, as you young people say. You've become quite a handsome devil, haven't you?" She patted his cheek affectionately.

"Thank you," he said, groaning inwardly. At least she hadn't tweaked his nose. Yet.

"Come on outside, and we'll have a talk."

Jarad dutifully took her arm and escorted he
toward the back of the house. She looked exactl
as she had, what was it, fifteen years ago? No,
had to be more than that. Perhaps she was a b
grayer, a little thinner. But to his young mind, sh
had merely belonged in the category "Old Folks.

Once they were seated at the wrought iron fur
niture at the back of the house, Gran looked u
at him, smiling. "It's too bad your parents couldn
make it," she told him. "But it's good to see yo
again."

"It's good to be here. Even if I did see half th
island in one afternoon."

"Where are my manners?" Gran asked, rising
"You must be hungry. Let me find you somethin;
to eat."

Jarad stood as she departed. Looking around, h
shoved his hands in the front pockets of his jeans
Aside from the new patio furniture, the house and
grounds seemed exactly as he remembered them
He'd spent three weeks here every summer from
the time he was eight until the year he'd turnec
sixteen, when he'd flatly refused to come anymore
His parents had claimed they wanted to get hin
out of the smog and congestion of L.A. Thinkin;
back on it, they'd probably just wanted some tim
alone.

Ironically, he had exactly three weeks to spend or
the island before having to begin promoting his lat
est film. In many ways, it was the work he was mos
proud of, but he'd had a devil of a time shooting
it. Every Murphy's Law of movie-making plagued th
production, including a record-breaking cold snap
in the small Southern town where the film was shot

His best friend Sam complicated things most o
all. Known to the rest of the world as Samantha

Hathaway, he'd cast her in the female lead. She and her male co-star had confounded everyone by actually falling in love. He didn't begrudge his friend her happiness, but for the first time, he felt the lack of someone special in his own life.

He found himself looking at Sam and knowing he wanted more to his life than a bit of notoriety and a few dollars in the bank. Seeing the chemistry between his two stars made him wish for a little chemistry of his own.

Thankfully, he'd been at his parents' house watering the plants the other morning when Isabel Ludlow called. He'd gratefully accepted her invitation to serve as emissary for the Naughton family at her granddaughter's wedding. Maybe a few days enjoying the peace and beauty of the island would help him put things back in perspective.

The image of one particular example of island beauty flashed in his mind. The woman he'd met on the ferry coming over. He'd never even gotten her name. He'd been standing by the railing, minding his own business, enjoying the heat of the sun and the salty spray of the ocean. He hadn't noticed her at all until the couple that had been standing between them moved away from the railing.

Her face had been turned up to the sun as her curly black hair swirled around her face, disturbed by the sea breeze. The wind had blown the thin material of her clothing snugly against firm breasts, taut legs. Her lips had been parted in a smile so innocently sensuous it had sent a shiver up his spine.

Then she'd opened her eyes, the most striking green eyes he'd ever seen. He'd assumed she must have been wearing contacts. Eyes just did not come in that color. Not naturally, anyway. Still, he'd had the urge to tilt her face toward him to get a better look at them.

Of all the bodily parts to get stirred up about. He should have known he was in trouble if a woman's eyes were all it took to get him going. He would have been better off if he'd followed his first impulse and gone to stand at some other part of the ship. Out of harm's way. He hadn't trusted himself not to do something stupid, like speak to her so she'd have to open her eyes to respond.

Then he'd heard himself murmur that inane comment, which thankfully, she hadn't really heard. *What lovely eyes.* That one definitely belonged in the Pickup Line Hall of Shame. Usually, he had a bit more finesse than that. He usually didn't go around kissing women he'd barely met, either. But when he'd found her conveniently tossed into his arms, he'd felt a powerful urge he hadn't bothered to resist.

Well, what did it matter, really. He would probably never see her again. Martha's Vineyard was small, but not that small. And in his present state of mind, that was probably for the best.

He pushed thoughts of her from his mind when Gran returned a moment later, carrying a glass of iced tea and a plate of seafood salad.

"The girls should be back any minute." Gran settled herself in her seat. "You probably don't remember them. They were such little things the last time you were here."

He did have a dim memory of two dark-haired little girls, one much smaller than the other.

"Jenny's the one getting married, the brunette. She'll make such a beautiful bride. She's wearing the same dress her mother wore. And Ariel is a psychologist in New York."

"Any wedding bells in her future?" he asked, mildly curious.

"I'm afraid not." Jarad thought she sounded almost apologetic. "She's quite a handful."

He wondered what she meant by that but figured he'd find out soon enough.


"I thought you told me no one but kids and grandmothers were going to be on the beach." Ariel looked down at herself, feeling half-dressed in one of Jenny's bikinis that had shrunk in the wash. Every time she moved, some part of her threatened to expose itself. After the mad dash to the upper floor, neither of them were inclined to go back down to the car for Ariel's bag. It wouldn't have been so bad if half the island didn't seem to be out on the beach, including several gawking young men looking directly at her.

"So, I lied." Jenny was spreading suntan lotion over her honey-colored skin. Unlike Ariel, she had a tendency to burn whenever she was in the sun. "It's better than staying up at the house listening to Gran complain that her grandchildren don't need her anymore. She's been driving me crazy with all her talk about me leaving the nest."

Gingerly, Ariel lay on her stomach, trying to move as little as possible. "I know what you mean," Ariel said. "She still calls me, 'my child.' " Ariel did such a perfect imitation of the older woman that they both burst out laughing.

"I have to admit, it's going to be weird living at the hotel at first. This is the only home I've ever known."

Ariel remembered fondly the little bed-and-breakfast in Oak Bluffs Dan inherited two years ago. Actually it was a big old house his uncle had converted into twenty-two separate rooms.

"So, it's true love, eh? I always thought you and Dan were perfect for each other, although you tried to tell me that I was suffering from delusions at the time. You're so lucky to have found such a great guy."

"He is pretty terrific," Jenny said, smiling dreamily. She handed Ariel the bottle of suntan lotion. "Put some of this on my back, will you."

Ariel complied, thinking of similar times in their teens when they'd sneaked off for an afternoon away from everybody else. On those days, they'd swim and talk for hours, usually about boys and love—an emotion Ariel had already been sure she was incapable of. Or at least true love as they imagined it to be—perfect and unconditional.

"The real question is, is Dan the PC you've always dreamed about?"

"I can't believe you of all people remember that." Jenny stared out into the distance, looking thoughtful. "Is Dan my Prince Charming? Yes, but not in the way we meant back then. Dan isn't perfect by any means," Jenny said, making a comical face to emphasize her point.

"But he's perfect for me, if you know what I mean. He's so supportive and loving. You know, he's the one who encouraged me to expand my catering business beyond just baked goods, and helped make it possible for me to do it. I don't know what I would do without him. And I love knowing he feels the same way about me."

"This all sounds disgustingly blissful," Ariel said, feeling an unwanted wave of sentiment flood through her. "I might be jealous if I weren't a con-firmed bachelorette."

"You don't fool me one bit, Ariel. Your bach-elorettehood or dom or whatever it is, will remain confirmed only as long as it takes you to find the right man."

"Don't start that. You're beginning to sound like Gran."

"Well, she's right. I used to say the same thing, if you'll recall."

"That's different."

"Oh, really. It's only different because it's you we're talking about."

"No. I don't think there's a man alive who could put up with me for the rest of his life. I'm difficult. Isn't that what you and Gran keep telling me."

"I think you do it on purpose."

"Do what?"

"Try to scare the pants off every man you meet."

"That's nonsense. Why would I, why would any-one want to do that? Haven't you heard? In New York the women are practically killing each other over the few decent men there are. Why would I want to scare anyone off?"

Jenny gave her a "you've got to be kidding" look. "For one thing, it keeps them at a nice, safe distance. For another, it keeps you in control. They're always on their guard because they never know what you're going to do next. You're a psy-chologist. Tell me you don't know how to get peo-ple to do what you want them to do."

"A certain amount of deviousness is sometimes necessary in the practice of psychology, but if you are suggesting that I go around manipulating peo-ple to get my own way, that is absolutely untrue."

"Prove it."

"What?" Ariel sat up and looked at Jenny.

Jenny sat up and stared back. "I said prove it. You've been telling everyone since we were kids that you had no intention of getting married, how you'd never be crazy enough to fall in love with anybody, and certainly no one would ever fall in love with you. Well, I say that's a lot of baloney. I say you're just afraid to find out what might happen if you did give some guy a chance."

"That is ridiculous. And I have given plenty of men plenty of chances."

Jenny held up her index finger. "You gave one guy one chance, and it was a long time ago."

Ariel gritted her teeth. She should have known Jenny couldn't resist mentioning Peter. She'd gone against Jenny's advice in seeing him. She never would have gone out with him at all if he hadn't been so persistent. Jenny had been right, though. Peter turned out to be a total jerk.

Jenny wasn't exactly right, either. There had been another man in her life, but the less said about him, the better.

"It's not my fault all the men I meet are wimps, idiots, or have too much ego for their own good." She added that last one remembering the man she met on the ferry.

"More likely, that clinical brain of yours is busy analyzing the guy to death." Jenny put her index finger to her temple, affecting a philosophical pose. "He looked at himself in the mirror three times last year, he won't do—must have narcissistic tendencies. He works long hours—he has a compulsive personality." Jenny waved both hands downward. "Please. No one can stand up to that kind of scrutiny."

"So tell me, Ms. Know-It-All, what are you suggesting I do?"

"Let me fix you up with someone while you're on the island."

"What?" Ariel nearly exploded. "What on earth for?"

"A test. A psychological experiment, if you will."

"An experiment," Ariel echoed, disbelieving.

"Yes, an experiment. Here's the hypothesis we're going to prove: Ariel Windsor is completely capable of loving and being loved when she leaves herself open to it."

"You have definitely gone off the deep end this time. Give me one good reason I should go along with this."

"Let us examine your situation logically. You should appreciate that. First of all," Jenny said, raising one finger. "Left on your own you have worse taste in men than Lorena Bobbitt."

"Thanks a lot. You're really going to win me over to your ideas by insulting me."

"Second point,"—Jenny held up two fingers on her left hand, laying the index finger of her right hand across the two—"What you need is a nice strong man with a sense of adventure, maybe even a little dangerous—not the stuffy intellectual types you think are so wonderful.

"Third, you are only going to be on the island for three weeks. Hardly enough time for anything serious to happen. A healthy case of lust should suffice." Jenny quirked her eyebrows suggestively.

"Has anyone ever told you you have a one-track mind?"

"Dan doesn't mind."

"I didn't think he would."

"You're trying to get me off the subject," Jenny chided.

"No, I'm not. I just can't believe you're suggesting I use some poor man for the purposes of . . . what? Testing the waters?"

"You got it!"

"That hardly seems fair. What does he get out of it?"

"Your company. You can be a fun person to be around when you set your mind to it. I like you."

"Thanks, but no thanks." Dangerous men were, well, dangerous, upsetting to one's peace of mind. "How about if I promise to be as sweet as Jell-O to the next slightly dangerous man I meet in New York?"

Jenny laughed, scoffing. "I just think you're chicken."

"That's not fair," Ariel protested. Jenny knew her weakness. From childhood, she'd had a disconcerting disability to back down from a challenge, especially one involving the word "chicken."

Jenny merely shrugged, apparently unconcerned with her own fairness or lack thereof. Ariel gritted her teeth, knowing that behind the show of nonchalance lurked a will of pure steel. Jenny would only pester her until she finally agreed.

"All right, all right, you win," Ariel conceded. "Bring on the Adonis." Again, she was reminded of the man she'd met on the ship. She doubted Jenny would come up with anyone to rival him. "We'll see how long he lasts in the ring."

"No."

Shading her eyes with her forearm, Ariel looked up at Jenny. "No?"

"No. There are conditions to this experiment. You have to promise to wait and see how things turn out. None of your usual analyzing, psychologizing and criticizing. You have to give the guy a chance. You have to be nice to him. Are we agreed?"

"I've already conceded to you, conditions and all. I promise to be nice."

"Good. Now," Jenny said, fanning herself. "All this talk about men is making me perspire. Let's go in the water."

A few moments later, Ariel dove under the surf, reveling in the tender touch of the ocean all around her. She loved the way the water looked and tasted and smelled. She resurfaced a few feet away from Jenny, easily swimming back to meet her.

Ariel dove under again, grabbed Jenny's legs and pulled her under, just as they used to when they were children. When they came up, both were slightly out of breath. "Was that fun enough for you?" Ariel asked. Jenny merely laughed.

The sun ducked behind a cloud for the fourth time that afternoon, and Ariel felt a chill run through her. "What do you say we find out what Mrs. Thompson is making for dinner. It's getting cold, and I'm starved."

"You always did have a healthy appetite, string bean," Jenny said, splashing her with water. "That's for dunking me."

"I guess we're even then." Ariel swam for the shore.

After toweling off, the two women headed back toward the house. Ariel's curiosity turned to surprise, then to utter amazement, as she realized who the attractive man sitting next to Gran was.

"You know that little experiment we concocted

back on the beach?" Jenny said as they grew closer. "I think I've found the perfect specimen."

"Oh?" Ariel said, dreading the worst.

"Yes." Jenny said, pointing. "Him."

# Two

He should have known that that particular shade of green eyes could only have come from one family. They were glaring at him again as Gran introduced their owner and her companion as her two granddaughters.

Yes, she was a handful, but not the way Gran had implied. The softness of her golden skin, the feel of her lips under his, were already imprinted on his senses. He had the feeling she was teasing him now in that tiny bathing suit she almost wore. Her hips swayed provocatively as she moved closer to him.

"It's good to meet you Mr. Naughton." Jarad shook the hand she proffered to him, somehow able to keep the amazement he felt from showing on his face. She was pretending never to have met him. Of all the asinine games he'd seen people play, this had to be the most asinine one yet.

"Likewise." That at least sounded civilized, though he wasn't feeling particularly civil. He was annoyed, angry maybe. He could understand her being surprised to see him. He could even understand her being upset with him for having kissed her. He had to admit that wasn't the brightest of moves.

What he couldn't understand was this . . . this charade. He was right about her. She was trouble. So why did he feel so disappointed?

"Do you know what we're having for dinner, Gran?" she asked. He supposed he'd been dismissed, as she turned her back to him.

"I hear it's something special in honor of your homecoming."

"Oh, good. What time should we be ready?"

"Seven should be fine."

"We'd better get going," Jenny said. "We all know how long it takes you to get ready for anything." He noticed Jenny practically push her through the door.


"Okay, out with it," Jenny said as they walked through the black-and-white checkerboard-tiled foyer.

"This just isn't my day, my week, my lifetime, that's all." Ariel put one hand over her face and sighed exaggeratedly.

"What are you talking about?" Jenny asked.

"I met Jarad on the ferry coming over here. Except I didn't know who he was visiting." They'd reached the bottom of the stairs and Ariel paused for a minute on the first step. "I was so surprised to see him, I didn't know what to say."

"Oh, I see what the problem is now." Jenny waved a finger at her as they headed up the stairs. "He came on to you, and you did your Little Miss Priss routine."

"That isn't important now." Ariel pursed her lips. "The important thing is that he's obviously here for your wedding, which means I have to put up with him for at least six days."

"Wrong. His parents are old friends of Gran's. She invited him to stay as long as he liked. As far as I know, he'll be around for a while."

"You knew he would be here all along, didn't you? You made that bet with him in mind."

"I cannot tell a lie, I did. I can be pretty devious too when I set my mind to it."

Jenny sounded rather pleased with herself. She had a right to, Ariel thought ruefully. Ariel had certainly been fooled.

"Now I find I have a head start," Jenny continued. "It's obvious he likes you already, so my part is taken care of."

"What made you think of him, if I may be allowed to ask?" They were standing outside Jenny's room on the landing. Ariel's hand rested against Jenny's door, preventing her from going inside.

"I don't know. He doesn't seem like the type to be bullied around by the likes of you. Besides, he's absolutely gorgeous. If I weren't getting married in six days . . ."

"Jenny, you are incorrigible. And you are getting married in six days."

"A girl can dream can't she?"

"Looks aren't everything."

"Add to that fame, money . . ."

"What fame? What money?" What on earth was Jenny talking about.

"My, you do lead a sheltered life down in New York." Jenny brushed past her, going to Ariel's room and opening the door. "Jarad Naughton, film director?"

Ariel shrugged as she followed her cousin into the room. "Never heard of him."

"Tsk, tsk. *Ebony* magazine just did a whole story

on him. America's Hottest Young Filmmaker, and all that. His father is Bob Naughton, the writer."

"Just my luck." Ariel slumped into one of Jenny's chairs. "The famous son of a famous man. He's probably got an ego the size of the Taj Mahal, too."

"Must you be so melodramatic? He didn't seem that bad."

"Jenny, if you value our friendship at all, you have to call off this silly experiment." Fun was fun, but this was ridiculous.

"Nothing doing," Jenny said playfully. "You said I could pick anyone I wanted."

"Jenny," Ariel said in her most reasonable tone. "In the first place, this whole thing is ludicrous. In the second place, I can't understand why this is so important to you. I'm happy with my life the way it is."

"If you're as happy as you claim to be, you wouldn't be hanging around here for an extra two weeks on the pretext of keeping Gran company while I'm on my honeymoon. You'd be rushing back to New York the minute the ceremony was over."

Jenny knelt in front of her and took Ariel's hands in hers. "I care about you, Ari. I want you to be as happy as I am. You never will be if you keep insisting on being so blasted serious about everything.

"And don't give me that infuriated look of yours. For once you are going to have to do as I say. If it will make you feel any better," Jenny said, rising, "I'll let you take a shower first."

"How magnanimous of you."

"See you at dinner," Jenny said before disappearing through the bathroom.

"Ooh," Ariel groaned before storming off toward the bathroom herself.

The warm spray of the shower felt exhilarating against her skin. Too bad her mental state wasn't in the same glowing condition. She had walked right into Jenny's trap. Now she had no clear idea how to get out of it. Once Jenny latched onto an idea, she could be extremely persistent—or incredibly stubborn, depending on how you looked at it.

"Damn," she exclaimed, toweling herself dry. It was obvious Jarad was still interested in her, after the purely lustful way he'd appraised her in Jenny's pre-shrunk bikini. The very last thing she needed right now was some sex-starved man following her around like a puppy. No. She doubted he was starved of anything, especially female company.

Why did that thought bother her so much? The hint that she would be just another in a long line of women? If she submitted to this ridiculous experiment of Jenny's, that is. True, she had toyed with the idea of having a summer fling. So what? That didn't mean she intended to do anything about it.

She went to the closet and grabbed the first thing she found, a body-hugging sleeveless red mini-dress Jenny had convinced her to buy the last time she was on the island. She glared at it disapprovingly, then put it on anyway. She didn't care how she looked. The whole experiment idea was preposterous.

He was a charmer, she reminded herself, as if she needed to. He would make her tongue-tied and awkward and stupid if she didn't watch it. He'd already made her stupid. Why else would she have pretended not to know him? She'd planned to say it was nice to see him again and explain

how they met. It was a half-truth. She wasn't glad
to see him, but it was the polite thing to say. Those
other words poured out instead.

She sat down at her dressing table, vigorously
brushing her hair into some sort of order. If anything, she felt more like the guinea pig than the
scientist. What did she really have to gain by going
along with it? He was probably a self-centered, ego-
tistical moron under all that charm, anyway.

She flung down her brush, realizing it wasn't doing any good. The brief exposure to the salt water
had made her hair downright frizzy. She snapped
open the case housing her makeup brushes. She
worked with them mechanically. Her mind wasn't
on what she was doing.

And Jenny expected her to . . . to . . . She
wasn't sure what she was supposed to do. See
where things lead? What did that mean? Sit around
and wait for something to happen? She'd never
been much good at waiting. Or sitting around doing nothing. She walked back to the closet and
slipped on a pair of red shoes. Jenny really had
lost her mind this time with her romantic imagin-
ings.

Catching her reflection in the full-length mirror
on the back of her door, she stopped mid-stride.
Without even trying, she realized she looked absolutely gorgeous, if she did say so herself. Her skin
was more golden, her eyes were luminous. Her
trim figure was outlined by the clingy fabric. The
high heels made her legs look longer, sleeker, sex-
ier.

A slow smile formed on her lips as a plan started
to coalesce in her mind. If Jenny wanted a healthy
case of lust, she'd have one. Maybe, it just wasn't
going to be Ariel who suffered from it. Taking a

calming breath, she opened the door and headed down the stairs.


Jarad glanced down at his watch. Seven o'clock, and except for the six place settings laid out on the white tablecloth, the dining room was empty. Obviously, the Ludlow family hadn't changed. They never did anything on time. Dinner at seven more likely meant seven-thirty, quarter to eight. He was about to take the nearest chair to wait when he heard a booming male voice behind him.

"That's my chair you're about to sit in, young man." He turned to see a man who looked familiar entering the room. He appeared to be in his late seventies, his short hair gone mostly white. He had a body like many of the old sailors he'd met: burly, robust, though a little thick in the midsection.

"You're Old Charlie," Jarad said with affection, then realized how insulting it must have sounded. "I'm sorry. That's what I used to call you, isn't it?"

"Don't worry about it, son." Jarad shook the hand Charlie extended to him. "I'm still old, m'name's Charlie. I guess it fits." He clapped Jarad warmly on the back. "And you're Bob Naughton's boy. Good to see you again. How is the old man?"

"Fine. He and Mother are on vacation. I know they'll be sorry to have missed the wedding."

"No need to be." Charlie sat, motioning for Jarad to do the same. "The bride is beautiful, the women cry, the father goes broke. Except in this case. Poor little Jenny's parents died when she was a baby. It took some doing, but I talked Isabel into letting me foot the bill. I know she can afford it, but a man's supposed to pay for the wedding, you know. Isabel's a widow. She needs someone to look after her."

Charlie was still the exuberant man he remembered, if a bit provincial. He wondered how Jenny and Gran felt about being considered poor and little, and a widow in need of supervision.

"Don't look like that, son," Charlie said, laughing. "It's just man talk. You know you can't say hello to a woman these days without being told you said it wrong." Jarad smiled. He had noticed that himself recently.

"I figure, when the men are alone, we should be able to say whatever we damn well please. Hey, I'm not fooling anyone. Isabel can take care of herself, you, me and those two girls upstairs. I'm in love with that crazy woman, have been all my life. She wouldn't marry me fifty years ago, won't marry me now. Says we're too old for that nonsense. Men are never too old for what counts."

Charlie winked devilishly, and Jarad had no doubt what he meant. "Have you seen Jenny and Ariel, yet?" Charlie continued. "They must have been babies the last time you were here."

"I saw them this afternoon. Actually, I met Ariel on the ferry coming over." He'd said that on purpose, just in case she tried that stunt again of pretending not to know him. That irked him beyond reason. It also made him determined to find out what she was up to.

"Watch out for that one." Charlie sounded serious for the first time. "She's the last of a dying breed."

That was too cryptic a statement to leave alone. "Come again?"

"Ludlow women. She's the last one to be married off." Charlie leaned closer. "Six days is all it takes."

"All what takes."

"For you to fall in love with them."

Jarad burst out laughing. He quickly subsided when he saw the disapproving look on the other man's face. "You can't be serious, Charlie."

"Oh, I'm very serious indeed. It happened to me. I met Isabel down at the dock one day. I was bringing in my boat and she was walking by with a girlfriend. I took one look at those big green eyes and forgot the ring I saw on her finger. Six days later, I was begging her to marry me instead of that fiancé of hers. She wouldn't hear of it, though."

Jarad had noticed the effect Ariel's green eyes had on him. Their color had startled him at first. Murky toward the center and clear at the edge, you could read almost any emotion into them. It made him want to know what she was thinking, and maybe to protect himself from her.

That was an odd thought. What could a barely five-foot woman do to him that he would need protection from? He must outweigh her by at least ninety pounds.

"You don't believe me, but you can ask Dan. I think that's him I hear coming."

A few seconds later, a man about his own age appeared in the doorway. Tall, dark-skinned, good-looking, he supposed, dressed in a dark blue jacket and gray pants.

"Come on in here Danny," Charlie called. "I'm telling Jarad here about Ludlow women and he thinks I'm pulling his leg."

"Good to meet you," Jarad said, shaking his hand.

"Same here." Dan sat down across from him. "What's this old fogy been telling you?" Dan smiled warmly at Charlie.

"You watch your mouth, young fellow. I tried to warn you about the same thing. You thought I'd gone senile."

"I did." Dan folded his arms in front of him, leaning his elbows on the table. "But you were right." Dan paused a moment as if to collect his thoughts. "About two years ago I inherited this bed-and-breakfast from my uncle, so I came out here to see what shape it was in. I was hoping to sell it if it was in good condition and get myself back to Connecticut.

"The first morning, Jenny walked into my office and demanded to know what my plans were. She was catering the breakfast rolls and muffins and all that, and told me she had a right to know if the change in management would mean a change in suppliers.

"I took one look at those green eyes of hers, and suggested we have dinner to discuss it. She said she didn't date her customers and walked out, claiming she had a valid contract, and a little wine and candlelight wasn't going to change that."

"And six days later . . ." Jarad said. That was the next line, wasn't it?

"Six days later, a mutual friend had a party on his yacht. I'd seen her a few times between that first day and the party, even got to 'apologize' for what I'd said, but I'd never seen her like she was that day. She was wearing this tiny striped bikini, sitting cross-legged on a lounge chair, talking to—it must have been about five or six men. I was too far away to hear what she was saying, but they were mesmerized and so was I.

"I walked up to her, and damned if I know what made me say this, but I told her she was going to marry me."

"What happened then?" This was too outrageous to be believed. This must be the standard joke played on unsuspecting male visitors. Charlie and Dan hadn't had any time to rehearse.

"She told me I was becoming a nuisance. She said she wouldn't tolerate sexual harassment and would report me to the authorities if I didn't leave her alone. It took me six months to get her to go out with me, and another year and a half to get her to marry me. She's a very stubborn girl. Of course, I never did leave."

"The curse of the Ludlow women," Charlie said pensively. "It's funny, they think you're the one that's crazy. They don't even realize what they've done to you. The spell works just the same."

"You make them sound like a coven of witches." Jarad almost choked when he heard that "curse" business. Just how gullible did they think he was? And what did that make Dudley? Their familiar?

"Just about. Isabel's family originally came from Salem, you know. I hate to tell you this, but Ariel's the worst of the lot. Stubborn as a mule, headstrong, thinks she knows more than anyone else alive. And that mouth of hers. Keener than a lobster's claws. Do you feel anything yet?"

Sure he was attracted to her. He'd have to be the Rosetta Stone not to feel something. He doubted he'd be making any protestations of love by the end of the week. He'd only met the woman a few hours ago. And he had a word for her, all right, but it wasn't witch. This word started with a "B."

What was he thinking? Of course he wouldn't.

This was a game the three of them were playing. Charlie had said it himself: While the women were away the men would play. They just hadn't told him the rules. What was his next response supposed to be?

"I did notice what you said about her eyes . . ." That should get them going again.

"It's always the eyes," Dan said ruefully.

"The worst of it," Charlie said, "isn't that you fall in love with them. The problem is convincing them that they love you."

"Ssh." Dan seemed to listen for a moment. "I hear them coming."

Jarad laughed to himself. Yes, this was the same crazy family he had visited year after year so long ago. The people might change, the circle might expand, but the spirit was the same—pure lunacy. He could use a little of that right now. Especially since he was going to be madly in love in the space of six days. Whoever thought that one up was a genius.

Arriving in the dining room, Ariel found everyone else already seated. "Am I late?" she asked, glancing at the clock.

"No. The rest of us are starving," Jenny said.

Gran was seated at the head of the mahogany table, with Jarad seated to her left. Jenny sat to Gran's right with Dan by her side. Charlie sat across from Gran. The only remaining chair was between Charlie and Jarad. Ariel could guess whose idea the seating arrangement had been.

"Sit down, dear," Gran said. "Mrs. Thompson will be bringing in dinner in a second."

Jarad rose gracefully to hold her chair for her.

He looked especially handsome in his black suit, the white of his shirt accentuating the darkness of his skin. A tiny shiver stole up her spine as his hand brushed her bare arm.

"Thank you," Ariel said, reaching for her wine. She took a deep swallow for courage. There was no time like the present for putting her plan into action.

"How are you, Ariel?" Charlie Peterson asked. Ariel had never doubted her liking of Charlie. He was still a warm, bubbly man despite his years. He and Gran had been friends practically forever. After both spouses died, the friendship intensified.

"I'm just fine, Charlie. I see the years are treating you well."

"The years are fine," Charlie said slyly. "It's the decades that do me in."

"Now Charlie, what trouble are you starting down there?" There was more humor than censure in Gran's voice.

"Go on, Isabel. Spoil my fun." Charlie did such a perfect imitation of a little boy being scolded that they all burst into laughter.

Mrs. Thompson brought dinner in, looking a little puzzled as to what all the laughter was about.

"Don't mind them, Emma." Gran patted the other woman's arm. "I think they're just giddy from hunger."

The first course was a delicious lobster bisque, Ariel's favorite soup. She was dismayed, however, that her and Jarad's arms kept touching one another. She hadn't noticed before that he was left-handed.

Charlie remarked, "Jarad tells me you met on the ferry. How's that for coincidence."

"Yes," Ariel said. She looked up at Jarad and

smiled sweetly. "Sorry I didn't recognize you on the patio." She turned her attention back to her soup. "The sun was in my eyes." That was an out-and-out lie, but they all seemed to accept it. All except Jarad, who gave her a coolly assessing look that almost made her drop her spoon.

As was usual for the first night of one of Ariel's visits home, Gran started reminiscing about the days when both Ariel and Jenny lived under her roof. At least that's what Ariel thought at first. Soon she realized that she was the focus of this stroll down memory lane.

There was the time she climbed the clay mountainside at Gay Head and nearly scared all of them to death. And the time she broke her arm playing football with the boys. Then there was the time she and Jenny and some other kids decided to visit the West Side cemetery in the dead of night. There was a picture frame on one of the graves that one of the boys dared her to open. She did so, and several very big, very ugly bugs crawled out. They'd scared her so badly she'd run thirteen blocks before anyone could catch her.

There were other stories, but those were the ones that seemed to intrigue Jarad the most. That made them the ones she most resented being told in front of him. She resented the whole thing really. All of this was for his benefit, she realized. Was this some misguided attempt at matchmaking on Gran's part? Jenny couldn't have told her about their experiment. Jenny merely shrugged when their eyes met. At least she wasn't imagining the whole thing.

Charlie even told a story about the time he'd tried to teach her how to sail and she'd accidentally knocked him out of the boat. She barely remembered that happening; she couldn't have been more than six years old at the time. Jarad seemed to like that story best of all, laughing with Charlie about how the only person to succeed in knocking him out of any boat at any time was a three-foot little bit of nothing. She would get Charlie for that.

"So, Jenny," Ariel said when she couldn't stand any more of it. "Tell me more about this wedding we're having. You haven't told me what I'm supposed to do yet."

Jenny swallowed her last mouthful of broiled flounder. "Tomorrow we go and get you fitted for your gown. The shop says they can have it ready that evening if we get you there before ten o'clock. We have the wedding rehearsal tomorrow night, and Friday's the wedding."

"That sounds simple enough, but what do I do?" Ariel was perfectly aware of the responsibilities of the maid of honor. She'd read an etiquette book. She didn't want the conversation to stop. She didn't want to give anyone the opportunity to tell any more stories unless someone else was the brunt of them.

"Since I'm not having a flower girl or bridesmaids, all you do is walk down the aisle first. Then Charlie will escort me down the aisle. You hold my bouquet, things like that. The minister will tell you all that at the rehearsal tomorrow."

"I know," Ariel said, wringing her hands under the table. "I'm just nervous, I guess. This is the first wedding I've ever been in." At least that was partly the truth. She was nervous about the wedding. She wanted everything to be perfect for her cousin.

"Tell me, young man," Charlie interjected. "How's the movie business treating you?"

"Not bad. Glad to take a break from it, though."

"What movies have you worked on, Jarad?" Ariel slanted a look up at him. She couldn't have cared less, but the conversation was finally drawn to a topic other than herself.

"That depends on what you mean. I actually started out as an actor—a very bad one. I've done a little producing too. But directing is my real love."

Jarad went on talking about the movies he'd directed at Jenny and Gran's insistence. They were so attentive to him, it was a wonder Dan and Charlie didn't call a strike. Apparently, she wasn't the only one susceptible to charming men.

Soon Gran and Charlie excused themselves to go for a walk, admonishing the young folks not to stay up too late.

Going for a nice, relaxing walk sounded like a perfect idea to Ariel. Her nerves were jangled, and aside from a few quizzical looks from Jarad, she didn't seem to be having any effect on him at all.

But sitting so close to him during dinner was having a profound effect on her. She'd never been so conscious of another person's movements, not even during therapy sessions when she monitored her patient's body language for clues to what they were feeling.

And she had to admit she was curious about him. He was so readily accepted by her family, which harbored the typical Vineyard reticence toward anyone but their own.

Jenny told her that he used to spend summers on the Vineyard in this very house. How was it she didn't remember him at all? She had memories dating back to the time she was three years old.

Certainly she was older than that the last time he was here.

There were other questions about him circling around in her mind, but those were better left unanswered. Curiosity like that was bound to get her into trouble. To hell with her plan. It was time for sensible little Ariel to go to bed.

Before she could excuse herself, the others decided to continue the evening in the sitting room. She couldn't get away now, not without looking completely ungracious, or worse, giving the others a reason to question her motives. Besides, she'd promised Jenny to be nice to him. She had no choice but to go along.

A fire was already roaring in the fireplace when they got there. The room had been Grandy's study when he was alive. Consequently, it was a very masculine-looking room with dark paneling, tan leather furniture and a massive bar in the far corner of the room. Bookshelves lined one long wall. It was from her grandfather that Ariel acquired her love of books and reading.

Jenny and Dan had claimed the small love seat adjacent to the longer sofa Ariel was sitting on. Jarad served as bartender. Ariel watched as he poured white wine for her and Jenny and two fingers of Scotch each, for himself and Dan.

Usually, Ariel was pleased that she came from an intelligent, literate family, where conversations came easily and laughter was frequent. There had been many similar lively discussions in that room. Tonight, as their discussion ranged from the latest bestsellers to politics to the state of American education, she wished they'd all shut up. Jarad was sitting so

close to her on the sofa that she could smell his
cologne, feel his breath fan her skin. She wondered
if he was purposely trying to unnerve her, to make
her uncomfortable with his presence. He didn't have
to sit that close to her. It was a large sofa.

She was relieved when Dan finally rose to bid
them all good night—until Jenny volunteered to
walk him to the door. Suddenly she was alone with
Jarad.

Quickly, she stood, ready to make her escape.
"I'm very tired. I think I'll turn in." Ariel stretched
languidly to prove her point.

"Wouldn't you like another drink?" Jarad walked
over to the bar and poured himself another Scotch.
"We could have a . . . talk."

There was a decidedly sensual air in the way he'd
asked the question. And in the hesitation in his
voice before he'd said "talk." It was a dare if she
ever heard one.

"All right, why not?" she said, trying to sound
cavalier. She was going to start having to think of
herself as weak-willed little Ariel if she kept this
up. "White wine with seltzer, please."

She walked over to the bar to collect her drink,
and sipped deeply. If she didn't know better, she
would swear it was all seltzer. That didn't make
sense. Weren't men supposed to get you drunk to
take advantage of you? Jenny was right. She didn't
know squat about dangerous men.

Jarad picked up his glass and turned to her.
"Perhaps you could explain a few things to me.
Like how a setting sun could be in your eyes when
you were facing east. The sun does still set in the
west, doesn't it?"

Jarad took a gulp from his glass, waiting for a
reaction. She'd been so attentive to him during

dinner. They all had. At first he'd thought they were setting him up for practical joke number two. Then . . . nothing. They all went to bed without so much as a second glance at him.

He watched her set her glass down on the bar. He doubted she weighed one hundred pounds, but she wasn't fragile. Graceful, yes. Proper, definitely, especially now when she was slightly tipsy and her Vineyard accent was strong. It was similar but not as stressed as a Cape Cod accent, more delicate. She was delicate, with long, slender limbs, a tiny waist and huge green eyes that were doing something wicked to the pit of his stomach.

"It's very simple," she said. "I was just surprised to see you here, I didn't know what to say. You have to admit it was an incredible coincidence."

"Yes it was." But that didn't explain why she had been smiling at him so magnificently during dinner. "Some people might call it kismet."

His voice was low and husky, and a sensual smile played at the corner of his lips. If this was the turn the conversation was going to take, it was definitely time for her to get out of there. The fact that she'd been able to maintain any sort of equilibrium tonight was nothing short of a miracle. There was no point in testing her resolve any further.

"If our little 'talk' is over, I'm going to go to bed." Without waiting for a reply, she walked over to the sofa to slip the shoes back on that she'd discarded earlier.

"Aren't you going to kiss me good night?"

"No." Not if she had any sense she wasn't. She turned around to face him, surprised to find he'd followed her across the room. "You tried that on the ferry. It didn't work the first time."

"How do you know? I'd barely touched you when

you ran off to your car." His hands went to her shoulders, massaging them. It was a delicious, delicate caress that sent a flood of heat coursing through her.

"I did not run off," she protested, even though she knew she had. "I was parked in front. There was a ship full of angry passengers waiting to wring my neck."

She took a step backward, but there was nowhere to go. The sofa was behind her. She could imagine how they'd end up if she slipped and landed there.

"Besides," she continued, "I'm not the little girl that everyone's been telling you about anymore. I know what a woman is supposed to do when a man she wants kisses her."

Her voice took on a sultry quality. "She's supposed to melt against him and put her fingers in his hair and sigh longingly against his lips. If it's a particularly good kiss, she might even tremble a little. At the very least, she kisses him back. I didn't do any of those things."

She'd hoped to wound his ego with her provocative words, but it had the opposite effect. His smile broadened as his hands slid down her arms to settle on her waist. They left behind a trail of fire on her heated skin.

"As you said, there wasn't time. I think we owe it to ourselves to try it again."

"I told you on the ferry. I'm not interested." That didn't sound terribly convincing, even to her own ears.

"Prove it."

That was the second time today someone had dared her to prove something to them, and frankly she was getting sick of it. At least Jenny hadn't had such an incredibly smug look on her face when she'd said it. Did he think every woman in the world was dying to be seduced by him?

Well, she had spent the better part of the evening trying to get him hot and bothered. Whose fault was it that her plan worked better than she had expected?

She crossed her arms in front of her. "What exactly do you expect to gain by this?"

"I get to have my way with you."

"What?" He couldn't be serious.

"I get to have my way with you. I'm sure you've heard about these things, even in such remote places as Martha's Vineyard."

Oh, yes, she'd heard of it. It was near impossible to think about anything else. But with all these people in the house, "having his way with her" was at best an idle threat.

"And if I win, I get to—"

"Have your way with me," he interjected.

"To be left alone." She couldn't believe she was actually going to submit to this. "Is that a promise?"

"Scout's Honor." He lifted one hand to make the obligatory sign.

She let out a sigh. "Go ahead." There was a side benefit to this madness. Jenny couldn't fault her if he avoided her of his own free will. "You don't welsh on your bets, do you?" she asked, just to be sure.

"I won't have to. You're susceptible to me."

*And you're terribly arrogant.* She watched his lips descend toward hers. She held herself still, arms at her sides, teeth and lips clamped firmly shut. That would teach him.

That's what she thought before his mouth touched hers. His lips were not sweet and gentle

as they had been before. This was an urgent, passionate kiss that demanded a response. She
couldn't give him one, nor could she pull away;
then he would win by default. How on earth had
she gotten herself into this mess?

He was turning her, she realized, dipping her low
once her back was away from the security of the sofa.
Then he let go of her. He caught her again, but not
before she shrieked and clutched his shoulders.

He pulled her up against him roughly, her
breasts flattened against the hard wall of his chest.
One hand tangled in her hair, the other pressed
her hips firmly against his own. She could feel him,
hard and urgent against her belly.

That was her undoing. The fingers at his shoulders gripped him more tightly as she arched
against him. She let out a little moan as he deepened the kiss. His tongue flicked against hers, hot,
moist, intoxicating.

When he finally pulled away, he looked down at
her as her eyes slowly flickered open. There was
something about them, he admitted, feeling suddenly agitated. He stroked a lock of that curly
black hair behind her ear.

"It occurs to me I haven't asked you if you welsh
on your bets."

Ariel simply stared at him, his words taking a
moment to register. She pushed away from him
with her hands on his chest, annoyed at herself for
her easy acquiescence, annoyed at him for the
amusement she saw in his eyes. She didn't succeed
in budging him an inch. "T-that wasn't a fair kiss,"
she said finally.

"Why not? Your arms went around my shoulders.
That's got to be close enough to my hair."

"I thought you were going to drop me," she protested. How clever of him! He was using her own criteria to defeat her.

"You sighed against my lips."

"That was not a sigh." She closed her eyes, mortified when he looked at her questioningly. She couldn't believe she'd actually moaned when he'd touched her. "It doesn't count."

"You were trembling," he whispered against her ear. He ran the tip of his tongue along its rim, setting off a whole new tremor.

"You scared me," she said breathlessly, as his lips dipped to the side of her throat.

"You kissed me back."

His breath fanned her skin, tickling her. What could she say to that? There was no denying it; she had definitely kissed him back. She had no choice but to concede. "No, I don't welsh on my bets," she said.

"Good," he said, raising his head. "Go to bed, Ariel. I'll see you in the morning." He kissed her on the forehead before he turned and walked out of the sitting room.

Ariel stood there a moment, feeling stunned by his sudden departure. She didn't know what she'd expected him to do, but leaving her standing there with her senses all whipped into a frenzy wasn't it.

She wrapped her arms around herself, still able to feel the imprint of his lips on hers, the touch of his hands through the thin material of her clothing. In all honesty, she couldn't say she would have offered much resistance if Jarad had tried to carry through on their bet. Right now, she wasn't at all sure what she wanted.

Jenny had accused her of being manipulative, but in this game of cat and mouse, she was definitely the mouse.

It only went to prove Gran's old saying about trying to "fix" people: Whenever you set out to dig a grave, dig two.

# Three

Ariel awoke to the sound of birds singing outside her window. She rose to open the curtains, and issued a resounding "Shut up!" Brilliant sunshine streamed through the open curtains, nearly blinding her. If her guess was right, it was about 8:30. She had less than a half hour to get ready before they had to leave for the fitting.

Twenty minutes later, after the horn of the brown Mercedes had called for her three times, Ariel hurried down the sloping staircase toward the front door. She slid easily over the leather upholstery covering the backseat of the car.

"It's about time," Jenny said, pulling out of the circular drive and heading toward the main street of Oak Bluffs township. The rows of quaint little shops turned to roads spotted with houses, and finally to the main road populated with tall trees.

Despite Jenny's constant chatter, Ariel couldn't fight off her fatigue from the trip the day before or the drowsiness that claimed her due to lack of sleep.

"Wake up, sleepyhead." Both Gran and Jenny were peering back at her over the tops of their seats.

"I wasn't sleeping." Ariel enjoyed a brief stretch in the confines of the car.

"You were snoring," Jenny confirmed. "But never mind that. I've picked out the perfect dress for you. Wait until you see it."

Ariel was truly impressed with her cousin's taste once she tried on the princess-length gown made from a luxurious pale pink satin. On the hanger, it looked like any other gown with a sweetheart bodice. Yet it fit Ariel's slender curves perfectly.

"I love it," Ariel cried. "It's gorgeous." A shawl and matching shoes and bag were produced to complete her outfit.

"I have to confess. I do have great taste, don't I?" Jenny beamed triumphantly.

"And so modest, too." Gran shook her head as she surveyed the two young women. "Come on, now. We have a busy afternoon ahead of us."

Ariel hated to get out of the dress, even for a moment. The strapless gown and high-heeled shoes made her look inches taller. The tight-fitting bodice accentuated her modest figure, making her appear more voluptuous. She had little time to consider her reflection. The store attendants had already begun to unbutton the gown.

The couturier promised to have everything delivered later that afternoon, and by twelve o'clock they were back at the house. Mrs. Thompson had fixed them all sandwiches, declaring that the kitchen was off limits.

After lunch, Jenny went to the bed-and-breakfast to see Dan. Gran and Mrs. Thompson were busy overseeing the workers that arrived to wax the floor and polish the mirrored walls in the huge ballroom where the reception would be held.

Ariel was left to wander the big house alone. She

wondered where Jarad was, but wasn't crazy enough to go and look for him. Nor was she about to spend the day hiding in her room. This was her house. She could go anywhere she liked.

After changing into a loose-fitting tank top and shorts, she finally decided to go out on the patio to read. She'd started a novel by one of her favorite authors, and was anxious to finish it. She sat down in one chair, propping her feet up on another. A half hour later, she was so engrossed in her book she barely heard the door to the patio slide open.

"Hi."

Ariel nearly jumped two feet in the air. Jarad was standing over her, holding two tall glasses of iced tea. He was wearing a short-sleeved red-and-white striped shirt and a pair of white shorts that bared a long stretch of lean, muscular legs.

"Mrs. Thompson told me you were out here," he said, handing her one of the glasses.

Why did he keep saying things to which there was no obvious response? Ariel put down her book and dropped her feet to the ground, allowing him to sit. She couldn't get up and leave him there, which was what she wanted to do. Gran would never understand her being so rude to one of her house guests without some explanation. She was stuck with him. She took a sip from her glass. "Thank you."

He picked up her book, surveying the cover. "Somehow I didn't expect a sex therapist to go in for murder mysteries."

By the grin on his face she knew he knew she was no such thing. "I'm not a sex therapist," she felt obliged to say anyway. "I fail to see why Jenny insists on telling that to everyone."

Jarad shrugged. "I'm sorry to hear that." His smile became more suggestive. "It might have made collecting on our bet more interesting."

It had been too much to hope he'd forgotten about that. "You had your chance last night."

"I knew you'd try to worm your way out of this. To the victor belongs the spoils—when he decides he wants them."

It was impossible to tell if he was serious or not, but either way she didn't like it very much. She was not about to sleep with him simply because he'd won that stupid bet. She didn't want to be teased for going along with it in the first place, either.

"Do you suppose you could tell me when that might be?" she said sarcastically. "I'd like to put it down on my social calendar under the heading 'Thankless Tasks.' "

He seemed to consider it a moment. "By the end of the week, I guess. I haven't got anything planned for Saturday night." He ran a finger along her bare forearm. "Don't worry. I'll be gentle."

Her lips parted slightly as a frisson of electricity traveled along her skin. She could imagine what making love with him would be like, if last night was any indication. That was the problem. Her hormones had gotten a taste of something they liked and were screaming for more. She was not going to be ruled by a few little chemicals running around in her bloodstream.

"There is a word for men who force women to do things against their will."

"Who said anything about force?" He picked up one of her hands and brought it toward his mouth. "When I make love to you, I promise, you're going to want it as much as I do."

She snatched her hand away moments before it reached his lips. How could she be so attracted to such an arrogant, insufferable man. She should know better.

She was more relieved than surprised to see two dark-haired little girls appear at the end of Gran's lawn. Neither of them looked to be older than six; both were dressed similarly in T-shirts and blue shorts.

"Can Dudley come out and play?" one of the girls asked as they approached her chair.

Ariel shrugged. She wasn't aware Dudley was in the habit of receiving guests. "I guess so, but I don't know where he is."

Dudley was scratching at the door behind her before she'd finished her sentence. She got up to let him out, hearing Jarad talking to the girls. She couldn't hear what he said over the sound of Dudley's barking, but she did recognize the sound of girlish giggling in response.

The minute she got the door open, Dudley bolted out to run helter-skelter around the yard. The two girls ran after him, shrieking and laughing and falling all over each other. It wasn't hard for Ariel to remember a time when chasing a dog around the yard was the greatest fun in the world. Soon both she and Jarad were laughing with them.

"I've got an idea," Jarad said rising. Ariel's head snapped around to watch him bound off in the direction of the garage.

Now was as good a time as any to make her escape. She grabbed her book and turned to leave. Jarad was back before she'd taken a single step. He was carrying a green Frisbee that looked as if it had seen at least one world war.

"Where are you going?" he asked, stepping between her and the door.

"I'm a bit tired." She raised her hand to her mouth to cover a feigned yawn. "I thought I'd take a nap before dinner."

"I wouldn't have kept you up last night if I'd known you were going to spend the whole day sleeping." He touched a finger to her cheek. "What you need is some exercise." His eyebrows quirked suggestively.

"Don't start that again."

"This time I'm talking about Frisbee. Come on." He took her hand, leading her to where the girls were sitting having a conversation with Dudley. Ariel trailed behind him like an errant child. She had no desire to play anything, but the girls' presence would prevent any more talk about that stupid bet.

"Who wants to play Frisbee?" Jarad called in his best camp counselor voice.

"We do," the two girls cried simultaneously.

They organized into teams, Jarad and Dudley on one side, Ariel and the girls on the other—a lopsided arrangement at best. Every time Dudley caught the Frisbee, he scurried around the yard until someone, usually Jarad, caught him.

The girls, sisters who lived two houses down, loved this. In the space of a couple of hours Jarad had become their hero. When they left, they asked him if he'd like to play with them again tomorrow. He said he'd have to see, ruffling each dark head before they scampered off.

Watching him, Ariel let out a sigh. She was surprised how good he was with them. She'd been studying him during their game. She couldn't help it. She noticed he threw the Frisbee making sure they could catch it. He only threw it to her occasionally, and then it was usually over her head. The girls loved that best of all.

Her eyes wandered over his tall, sinewy body as he walked toward her. She'd also noticed how graceful his movements were, how naturally athletic he was. She pushed those thoughts from her mind and tried to think of Dudley. The girls hadn't even said good-bye to him. Poor Dudley was friendless once again.

"So what will we do now for fun?" Jarad grasped a lock of her hair and gave it a tug. She stepped backward, out of reach. She would have a much easier time maintaining her equanimity if he'd only stop touching her. "I'm going to get ready for dinner."

"It's early, yet. We could go on playing. You can have Dudley this time."

She shook her head. "Thanks, but no thanks." She started back toward the house. "I don't think Dudley's speaking to either of us," she called over her shoulder. She turned back to face him. "Not after you stole his girlfriends."

She heard his wicked, wicked laugh behind her. "What can I say? I'm irresistible."

"I could resist you," she said under her breath. The Frisbee whizzed by her, landing in the grass a few feet in front of her.

"I am not going to play Frisbee with you," she said, turning around to face him.

"Okay, stick in the mud," he called. "Just throw it back to me." She did so, only to see the infernal thing whiz by again.

Of all the juvenile pranks. "Cut it out." She stomped her foot, hands on hips.

"Okay, okay," he said, laughing. "Just throw it back and I'll leave you alone."

No wonder he laughed, she thought. No one paid attention to women stomping their feet anymore. She needed a more direct approach. She picked up the Frisbee, throwing it as hard as she could. So, her aim was a little off and it hit him in the stomach. Close enough. Hearing his sharp exhalation of breath as she started toward the house was all the gratification she needed.

Then she heard him growl. Or she thought it was him. She looked over her shoulder to see Jarad coming straight at her looking like some large animal that had spotted his prey—her.

Whether he actually meant to do her bodily harm wasn't apparent, but she wasn't waiting around to find out. She took off toward the house, which was only a few feet away. She would have made it if she hadn't tripped over one of Dudley's toys left lying in the grass. Her arms flew up in surprise as she felt Jarad grab her waist and turn her so that she landed on her back. He landed soundly on top of her, moving swiftly to capture her wrists that lay above her head on the grass.

"Well, Ariel Windsor," he said, looking from her face to her throat to the swell of her breasts peeking out from the scooped neckline of her shirt. "I've finally got you where I want you."

She glared up at him, trying to free her wrists from his grasp. There was nothing juvenile about the way his body covered hers. His eyes twinkled mischievously, as if to say she wasn't going to get away that easily.

"Very funny," she said sarcastically. "Now get off me, you big oaf! I can't breathe."

He shifted, putting more weight on his knees.

"That wasn't a very nice thing you tried to do to me."

"I didn't try to do anything to you. I'm just a poor, weak little woman unable to throw a Frisbee straight." She batted her eyes at him exaggeratedly.

"You were doing fine before."

Damn him, and that self-satisfied look on his face. "You're hurting me."

"No I'm not. I'm barely touching you." He loosened his grip on her nonetheless. "You're just mad at me for proving you have no self-control."

She had plenty of self-control. She hadn't kneed him in any sensitive areas, which is what he deserved. "And you are suffering from delusions of grandeur. Do you think every woman you meet is going to fall all over you?"

"Just the ones with no self-control. Tsk, tsk, tsk, Ariel. Didn't anyone ever tell you not to make a bet you can't afford to lose."

"Ooh," she groaned, finally able to free her wrists. She pushed him off into the grass, scrambled up and inside the door, locking it behind her. She stalked down the hall, nearly colliding with Jenny who was coming out of the kitchen.

Jenny stepped back, wondering what had gotten Ariel so steamed she didn't even notice where she was going. Then she heard a knock at the patio door. She turned to see Jarad there, a Frisbee in his hand and a sheepish look on his face. It wasn't a what, it was a who. Imagine, sensible little Ariel steamed up over a who!


After pacing around her room for a few minutes wondering who he thought he was to tease her like that, there was a knock at her door. It was Jenny.

"I just wanted to remind you that dinner is going to be early because of the rehearsal. I'm sure you forgot about it."

Ariel had forgotten about the rehearsal, but not for the reason Jenny was implying. It had merely slipped her mind. "Don't start, Jenny," she warned. She seemed to be doing a lot of that lately. Warning people about their bad behavior.

"Who me? You know I would never start anything. You certainly couldn't accuse me of that."

"No, never. What time is dinner, anyway?"

"Don't change the subject."

"I didn't know we had a subject."

"The subject of you and Jarad. This is the first opportunity I've had to find out what is going on between the two of you. Where did you disappear to after the rest of us left the sitting room? Don't tell me you went to bed because I checked your room."

"Boy, you really are a snoop."

"Only for the sake of the experiment, of course."

"Of course." Ariel flung herself into one of the wicker chairs. "If you must know, we were in the sitting room . . . talking."

"I'll bet." Jenny sat down on the bed, crossing her arms in front of her. "About what?"

"Things."

"You may as well just spill it," Jenny said with a wave of her hand. "You wouldn't be so secretive unless something happened."

Ariel pursed her lips and stared at Jenny. "What happened is that my whole family went berserk last night. Did you think either of us were too stupid to know what was going on?"

"That wasn't my fault. Gran came up with that idea on her own. You should be glad she didn't tell him about the time we entered the boat race in Menemsha. She told Dan that story the first time he came to pick me up."

"Well, I would appreciate it if you would call off the dogs. I'm quite capable of doing my own matchmaking—"

"Oh, are you now?"

"You didn't let me finish. I was going to say if I wanted to be match-made."

"That's a rationalization if I've ever heard one. No wonder you're a psychologist."

"Why must you be so persistent?" Ariel said, but she really meant stubborn.

"Because you are being deliberately obtuse. This is my experiment. I have the right to know how the tests are proceeding."

Ariel pushed a lock of hair behind her ear. "If you must know, we sat there discussing our theories on how all present members of one family could go insane at once. We decided it must be some form of mass hypnosis imposed on you before we arrived. We considered going to each bedroom and snapping our fingers to see if you'd revive. Then we decided it was better to let you sleep."

"All right," Jenny said, rising, looking offended. "I see you're not going to confide in me. I am your only cousin, you know."

"That isn't going to work."

"I know. It hasn't worked since we were about twelve."

"If ever." Ariel straightened in her chair. "Besides, there's nothing to confide." Except the fact that Jarad intended to seduce her by the end of the week. She certainly couldn't tell Jenny that.

"Nothing to confide," Jenny echoed, standing at the door.

"Only that I think you're wasting your time. Jarad is the most overbearing, intolerable man I've ever met. We've got nothing in common except being alive. Why you want me to have anything to do with him is beyond me."

Jenny shrugged, smiling mysteriously. "Dinner's at five-thirty," she said, before disappearing down the hall.

Ariel closed the door then headed off toward the bathroom. After a long, soothing shower, she put on a white halter dress with a full skirt that fell almost to her ankles. That was the trouble with being short—you had to hem everything. She hadn't had a chance to do anything with this one. She tugged on a pair of open white sandals with high heels. The higher the heel, the longer the dress, the taller you looked. Short people's fashion lesson number seventeen.

Sitting down at her dressing table, she began brushing her hair. She had used a deep conditioner after shampooing, and it seemed to be doing its job. Her curly hair formed into a presentable mass without too much fuss.

She didn't bother with a lot of makeup, just a thin coat of red lipstick. Pausing at her full-length mirror, she surveyed her appearance. She didn't look half bad, despite the length of her hemline. She felt floaty and feminine and surprisingly calm. She wasn't going to let anything upset her, not Jarad's juvenile sense of humor, not Jenny's insinuations, not anything.

She stepped into the hall, walking past what she referred to as the Ossie Davis Hall of Fame. A series of portraits of the various generations of men who had married Ludlow women that spanned the entire length of the hall.

Grandy's portrait occupied the place of honor at the center. If you didn't look at the features too closely, it was difficult to tell the men apart. Each portrait was painted to commemorate the fiftieth birthday of its subject. Each man wore a black suit and tie, or a reasonable facsimile for that period. Oddly, they were all standing in the same pose. Each had a full head of salt and pepper hair and the same lean physique. Ossie Davises the lot of them—at least that's how they seemed to her. In another year her father's picture would join their ranks.

Descending the stairs, she wondered if that's why Gran wouldn't marry Charlie. He was more of a Rosie Grier.

At dinner, everyone seemed subdued. Subdued for the Ludlow family. A light but steady rain beat against the windows, emphasizing the quiet of the room. If someone didn't say something livelier than "Pass the salt," she was going to scream. At least Mrs. Thompson had abandoned all that fancy food for some good old fried porgies and corn bread.

The minister and Dan and his entourage arrived almost simultaneously, all of them complaining about the unexpected shower. After all the umbrellas were put away, they decided to hold the rehearsal in the large foyer, where everyone would be lining up to enter the garden anyway.

The ceremony would be very simple and very beautiful, Ariel imagined. She could picture Jenny floating down the aisle in her white satin gown to meet Dan. She felt a lump rising in her throat. Good lord, she was getting as bad as Jenny.

Lifting her eyes to the portrait of Grandy on the landing above, she drowned out what the minister

was saying. It was a shame Grandy wasn't here to
see this. He did so love any occasion for pomp and
circumstance, especially one in which he was involved. If he'd been alive, he'd be the one walking
Jenny down the aisle, not Charlie.

Then a large, dark shape moved into her field
of vision. Her eyes refocused until the paintings
were merely a backdrop. He wasn't an Ossie Davis,
either. Nor would he become one with age. He was
more of a Sidney Poitier: tall, very masculine,
proud.

Their eyes met, and even at that distance, they
burned through her like red-hot lasers. There was
such a look of intense desire in them it made
something in her go very still. She'd seen that look
in men's eyes before, but never directed at her.
Seeing it now amazed, titillated and scared the holy
heck out of her.

She turned her attention back to what the minister was saying. Otherwise, she might have run for
dear life, right out the front door onto the nearest
ferry.

She'd never thought of herself as the type of
woman to arouse grand passions in men. Was that
what she was doing to Jarad? She doubted it. She
was sure he'd only dared her to kiss him out of
some purely male need for conquest. It was probably all a game to him. He must be used to crazy
families with marriageable daughters by now.

Twenty minutes later, the rehearsal was over. The
rain had stopped as unexpectedly as it had begun.
While Jenny and Gran made their good-byes, Ariel
slipped out the patio door and headed for the
beach. She would never be able to sleep in the
mood she was in, wound up like a spring ready to
pop. Walking on the beach was a childhood ritual

for relieving tension. After a half hour or so she'd be back to her normal, rational self.

The full moon hung low in the sky. It seemed to rest on the water's surface way out on the horizon, spreading a blanket of light across the waves. The warm water lapped over her feet as she walked along its edge, stopping only to collect some of the colorful stones she spotted with her flashlight. When she'd gathered more than she could carry in one hand, she started back, carrying them in the hem of her skirt. She would inspect them more closely later. Some of them would make nice additions to her collection.

Standing on the balcony to his bedroom, Jarad watched the solitary figure on the beach. What had started out as a harmless flirtation on the ferry had really taken an unexpected turn. Not only had he kissed her on the ferry, heaven only knew what possessed him to make that bet with her last night. He'd been thinking about how lonely his life had been, but that didn't make him so hard up he had to throw himself at the first attractive woman he met.

She made him feel hard up with that sharp tongue of hers. She aroused him, period. Out in the yard when he'd grabbed her, his only thought had been to protect her from falling. But when he'd landed on top of her, she'd wriggled underneath him so provocatively. All he could think about was having her in that same position, only in his bed. Luckily, she'd pushed him off before he made even more of a fool of himself.

If he didn't know better, he'd swear she had cast a spell on him, like Charlie said. Ariel and this island, and the full moon that seemed to rest on the water, way out on the horizon. That was as good an explanation as any for his uncharacteristic behavior. He laughed to himself, shaking his head. Whatever the reason, he only knew he found her the most alluring, the most desirable woman he'd ever met.

Did she know what effect she was having on him? He doubted that. She thought he was merely flattering her when he told her how lovely he thought she was. Didn't that woman ever look in the mirror? He saw how she'd turned away from him during the rehearsal when he couldn't keep the desire he was feeling for her out of his eyes. Was it so difficult for her to believe that he wanted her?

Or, maybe that was the problem. She did know. Maybe there was someone else, someone she didn't want her family to know about. No. If that was true she'd have thrown that in his face by now.

He watched her stoop to pick up something in the sand. She looked as alone as he felt. He wondered if she would welcome his presence on the beach. Probably not. She obviously wanted to avoid him, if that afternoon was any gauge.

Maybe she just wasn't interested, like she'd told him countless times. Something in him rebelled at that thought. He'd never had to chase after a woman in his life. Maybe that was what was so intriguing about her. Here finally was a woman who wasn't impressed with him, his job, his money or his family. Was he so shallow that his ego couldn't take a little rejection?

He knew that wasn't true. But he also knew he'd never sleep knowing she was down there by herself, possibly as lonely as he was. If she didn't want him there, she'd have to tell him that herself.

\* \* \*

Ariel walked along, not watching where she was going, enjoying the cool breeze and the pungent scent of the ocean. It was amazing how she'd managed to clear her mind of all worrisome thoughts with a simple walk along the coast. It had always been like that, a strange sort of self-renewal.

She had never been disturbed by anyone on these walks. In a way, she thought of this beach as being hers at night. She was quite alarmed when she heard footsteps in the grass leading onto the beach. So alarmed, she let go of her skirt and the stones tumbled all over her feet. An outgoing wave immediately took a number of them out with it.

It didn't take her long to discern to whom the tall, masculine body striding toward her belonged. Every pore agreed it was Jarad, long before he was close enough for her to see his face. Who else made her so nervous she couldn't pick a few simple stones out of the sand?

He stopped a couple of feet in front of her. She could see his sneakers, but she refused to look up at him. She was intent on saving as many of her stones as she could. Many of them had become embedded in the sand.

He squatted down beside her. "What are you doing?" he asked.

Ariel turned the flashlight so it shone right in his eyes. That would teach him to sneak up on people. "I am collecting the stones you made me drop."

"I'm sorry. I didn't mean to startle you." He was grimacing, holding a hand in front of his eyes. "Would you put that thing down?"

She did, feeling sufficiently avenged. "That's

what you said the last time, if I remember correctly."

He laughed. "You mean on the boat?"

"On the ship. Ferries aren't boats, they're ships." She'd found all the stones she was ever going to find. She stood and put them in her pockets this time. The hem of her skirt was damp and clinging to her calves. "I'm going inside," she announced.

"So soon?" He stood up quickly, brushing the sand from his jeans. "It's early, and it's beautiful out." He made an expansive gesture with his hands. "And it deserves two people to fully appreciate it." One of those hands came to rest around her waist. "Come on. We could take a walk."

She stepped away, out of his grasp. "In the first place, I've already had a walk. In the second place, I came out here to be alone."

"You looked lonely," he said softly. "I was watching you from my balcony." He nodded in the direction of the house. "I thought I'd come out here and rescue you."

"Rescue me from what? I like being alone. Sometimes I prefer it."

He laughed again, a rich melodious sound that made her want to bean him with the flashlight. "To being with me, you mean."

"You could put it that way." Especially when her head felt all cloudy and strange, and her knees were in outright rebellion.

"You have to be the meanest woman I've ever met." His voice was full of amusement.

"How do you expect me to be when you've spent the entire afternoon making fun of me?" She turned her back to him, staring up at the stars. "Why did you really come out here, Jarad? Decided you couldn't wait until Saturday to collect payment?"

"Would you forget about that damn bet!"

She snapped around to face him. "Why should I? You haven't. You spent all afternoon reminding me about it. If it's so important to you, go ahead. You'll have to forgive me if I don't join in."

She saw him moving closer to her on the sand. He couldn't possibly be taking her offer seriously. Maybe she should have learned her lesson about trying to get back at him last night. Though the hands that rose to cup her shoulders were gentle, she couldn't hold back a tremor that shivered through her body. Was that fear—or something else?

"Not on a bet," he said simply.

She opened her eyes, searching his face in the dark. He'd spoken those words so seriously and his gaze on her was so intense that it sent another tremor through her. This time she was sure it wasn't fear.

"Jarad . . ." The word slipped out on a sigh. She had no idea what she wanted to say.

"I wasn't making fun of you this afternoon. I was trying to get you to lighten up. You looked so serious." He let go of one shoulder to stroke the side of her face. "I don't think I've ever seen anyone look serious playing Frisbee before."

"Oh," she said, averting her gaze to his chest. If her face had borne any expression at all it was because she'd been observing him. The first part of any psychological experiment was observation. Some part of her had been cooperating with Jenny's experiment all along.

"Then why did you make that bet with me in the first place?"

"I don't know. You were driving me crazy. First you pretended never to have met me on the ferry. Then, if I'm not mistaken, you were flirting with me."

Blushing, she turned her face from his. He hadn't been mistaken. She hadn't thought he'd noticed.

"I was trying to . . ."

She glanced up at him. "Teach me a lesson?"

"No. To find out what you were up to." She could barely make out his smile in the dim moonlight. "And, you wouldn't have kissed me otherwise."

She smiled, too. No, she wouldn't have kissed him last night. She probably shouldn't have. She had the feeling that it set something in motion that she didn't have any control over. Experiments had a way of running their own course, with no respect for the will or the expectations of the researcher.

"Does this mean we've called a truce?" Jarad asked, his hands settling on her waist.

"Yes," she nodded. She'd had enough of fighting for one day.

"Then perhaps you could answer a question for me?"

"I guess so," she said, wondering what he could possibly want to know.

"Why do you have a bunch of rocks in your pockets?"

She laughed. "They're not rocks, they're stones. I collect them."

"You collect stones?" he said, laughing.

"Stamps are so boring." She was following him down the beach, she realized. He was leading her along with a hand on her arm. "I had some really good ones, too, until you made me drop them."

He retrieved the flashlight from where she'd dropped it in the sand and turned it on. "I suppose it's my duty to help you find some new ones. What do you look for in a stone?"

"I don't know. Something unusual. The color, or the shape. I know 'em when I see 'em."

"How about this one." Jarad bent and picked up a large, oddly shaped stone. It's circumference was oval, but its bottom was flat and the top domed. He held it in his palm, shining the flashlight on it so she could examine it. Its smooth gray surface was mottled with swirls of indigo and purple.

"It's perfect," she said. She put it in her pocket with the others. "You have very good taste in stones."

He smiled, as if to say, "Of course."

They continued down the beach, stopping occasionally when Jarad bent to look at one stone or another. He dutifully examined each one before handing it to her for her perusal.

He'd found several more for her by the time they decided to turn back. His pockets were beginning to fill, too.

"What are you going to do with all these rocks . . . I mean stones?"

"If I get enough while I'm here, I'll start another terrarium."

"How many do you have?"

"Fourteen. Or I've made fourteen. I had to give some of them away."

"I can imagine." He stopped, picking up another stone. He examined it a moment, then threw it away. "How did you get started with all this."

"It's kind of silly, really." She wasn't sure she

wanted to share such a personal story with him. He'd probably laugh at her childhood sentimentality. But she also didn't want to end the camaraderie that had built up between them.

"My parents had a little jewelry store in Edgartown when I was a kid. I always heard them talking about this or that kind of stone. I thought they meant regular stones, like you found on the beach. I started collecting them and giving them to my father. He never told me he couldn't use them, so I kept it up.

"When I got a little older, he bought me this rock polishing kit so I could make my own little jewelry. He soon regretted it, because the noise from the machine kept everyone up at night. I actually did make a few pairs of earrings. Gran even wore hers once." She shrugged. "I told you it was silly."

Jarad turned her around to face him. She looked soft and shy, almost vulnerable. "I don't think it's silly. It's kind of touching." Even in the dim moonlight her eyes looked curiously luminous.

The wind stirred wispy tendrils of hair about her face. He smoothed them back with the palm of his hand. Then his fingers tangled in her thick black tresses, tilting her head back. She looked incredibly lovely, looking back at him through the thick fringe of her lashes. Her hands were at his shoulders. He wasn't sure if they were there to act as encouragement or restraint. He decided to kiss her anyway. The worst that could happen is that she'd run back to the house and never speak to him again.

But she didn't run. She practically melded right to him. Her arms wound around his neck as if they belonged there. He hugged her to him, feeling surprised and elated and oddly triumphant. And he felt a desire more powerful than any he'd known stirring inside him. How could she have gotten under his skin so quickly?

He pulled away, watching as her eyes slowly flickered open. She smiled. He'd half-expected her to tell him to unhand her in that proper way she had. But she didn't. She smiled. He let out a very pleased sigh.

"Now, isn't that better than fighting?" he asked, lifting her and spinning her around.

"Yes," she laughed. About four-hundred eighty times better.

"What's so funny?" he asked, setting her down on her feet.

"Oh, nothing." She looked over his shoulder in the direction of the house. *Now hear this, Jenny Douglas, you hopeless romantic. You wanted an experiment, you've got one. But for God's sake, please don't be wrong.*

# Four

Ariel woke to the feel of something wet across her face. She swiped at the intrusion. It couldn't be Jarad, she thought in her dreamy state. He wouldn't slobber like that. Sitting up, she laughed sleepily at her own humor. When she opened her eyes, she was face to face with Dudley. He licked her right on the mouth.

Wiping her face with the back of her hand, she shooed the dog from the bed. "What are you doing up here?" Gran must be up and out already, she realized. The minute Gran left the house Dudley ran upstairs where she forbade him to go. "Get back downstairs," she scolded. He only looked at her and wagged his tail happily. That dog didn't listen to anything she said.

She relaxed back on her pillows, replaying the previous night in her mind. She and Jarad had walked along the beach into the small hours of the morning—talking, gazing at the stars, laughing. He'd left her at her door with her pockets full of stones and a good night kiss on her lips. If nothing else, she had the romantic moonlit walk she'd fantasized about.

She showered and dressed in a T-shirt and shorts. The house was incredibly quiet. She didn't find anyone upstairs or in the sitting room. The only sign of life was Dudley, who followed persistently behind her. After getting a cup of coffee, she headed back up to her room to write out the postcards she'd bought in Edgartown the day she'd tried on her dress. She'd promised to send them to a couple of her friends who were envious of her trip up to the Vineyard this time of year. She took her time writing them out, when normally she would have scrawled a hasty message and been done with it.

She acknowledged that part of her reason for dallying was to put off seeing Jarad again. She'd resigned herself to the experiment last night, but in the light of day, she didn't feel comfortable with the idea of spending time with him. A sense of foreboding warned her that getting involved with him wouldn't be the simple summer fling Jenny suggested.

She shook her head mentally. She was being silly. She didn't believe in seeing into the future. It was her family, not fate, that was conspiring against her. Not only Jenny, but Gran, seemed to think a romance between them would be a marvelous thing.

As for Jarad, he didn't seem to expect any more from her than a pleasant companion to share the time he'd be on the island. He'd told her he was only staying until the beginning of August, less than three weeks away. What could happen in that short time that would be so terrible?

She picked up her postcards and put them in her purse. Whatever the future held, she couldn't hide in her room forever. It was almost noon, and her stomach was beginning to rumble. When she walked into the kitchen she saw Mrs. Thompson busily packing a picnic basket.

"Good morning, Ariel. Isn't it a lovely day?"

Emma Thompson practically glowed. Ariel poured herself a cup of coffee from the urn on the counter. "What are you so happy about, Mrs. Thompson?" And who was the basket for? Had Mrs. Thompson found some nice, eligible man to spend the day with?

"Nothing, dear." She tucked the thermos into the wicker basket. "I'm afraid Mrs. Ludlow and Jenny have already gone out for the day. You were sleeping so soundly, none of us wanted to wake you."

"Oh?" They'd summoned her to the island to help with the wedding plans, but they didn't want to wake her? Something about that was definitely fishy, and it had nothing to do with the contents of the picnic basket.

"Can I help you with anything?" Ariel asked. She was just sitting there while Emma was doing all this work.

"You can hand me two sets of the plastic dinnerware."

Ariel got the step stool out of the side closet so she could reach the cabinet. Times like these, she really hated being short. It was so embarrassing to have to stand on a stool to reach anything. She'd already found two plates and was looking for the cups when Emma sighed and started talking again.

"Such a nice young man."

"Excuse me?" Ariel peeked around the open cabinet door to see her.

"Isn't he a nice young man? That Naughton boy." Mrs. Thompson stared dreamily into space for a few moments, then returned to what she was doing. Oh, no. That Naughton boy had whammied her, too.

"Get a hold of yourself, Emma. I think he's a bit too young for you." Was that jealousy she felt? How ridiculous!

Mrs. Thompson waved a dismissing hand in the air. "You're just starting trouble."

"Not me." She found the second of the bright red cups and was about to climb down from the stool when something big and wet grabbed her. She shrieked, dropping the dishes, which clattered noisily against the floor. Jarad's arms were clasped tightly around her waist, and he was growling in her ear. Her feet were miles above the floor. "Put me down, you big idiot," she said between clenched teeth.

He did, and she turned around to face him. Seeing him dressed only in a pair of little black swimming trunks, she almost forgot she was mad at him. "What is your problem?" she demanded.

He shrugged, but the look he gave said he was looking at it. She glanced over at Mrs. Thompson, who practically had her head in the picnic basket. Ariel wasn't going to get any help from that quarter.

"I would appreciate it if you would restrain yourself." She bent and picked up the plates she'd dropped, for want of anything better to do.

"I'd better go get changed," Jarad announced. "Try to be ready for our picnic when I get back."

He was gone before she had a chance to protest. Or fling something at him. She looked back at Mrs. Thompson who looked like she was going to burst from trying not to laugh. "Go ahead, Emma," Ariel said, sitting on the floor, laughing herself. "Why didn't you tell me who you were packing the basket for?"

"I thought it was obvious."

It should have been. "I'd better get changed too," Ariel said, getting up. Her T-shirt was soaked and sticking to her. Her shorts weren't much better. What did he do—wet himself down with the garden hose before coming in?

She went back to her room, Dudley following behind her, despite any attempts to shoo him away. She wasn't having much luck with males of any sort today. But a picnic—that sounded like a wonderful idea. She hadn't been on a picnic in years.

Ariel tugged on a pair of blue shorts to match the blue and white shirt she'd just put on. Sitting at her dressing table, she set about tying her hair back in a ponytail. That done, she studied her reflection in the mirror. She had on only a minimum of makeup, but her eyes looked brighter than they had in ages, her skin smoother. Two days on the Vineyard had done that for her. She let out a happy little laugh.

She was tying the laces of her sneakers when she heard a knock at the door. She knew it was Jarad. "Come in," she called.

"Good. You're almost ready." Ariel looked up to find Jarad leaning against the door frame. He wore a pair of faded jeans and a tight-fitting polo shirt, looking handsome. "I thought it took you forever to get ready for anything."

She glanced up at him, wondering if he'd guessed correctly that he'd been the topic *de jour* when Jenny'd used that pitiful excuse to drag her off the day before. Probably. She turned her attention back to the task at hand.

"It wouldn't have taken me any time at all if you hadn't done your caveman routine in the kitchen." She finished making her second bow and stood up.

"I couldn't help it. You looked so cute standing on that little stool."

"I am not cute," she protested. "Why do tall people always think short people are cute? You don't hear short people going around calling tall people gargantuan all the time, do you?"

"No, but I didn't say you were cute. I said you looked cute. There is a difference."

"A very small one." She walked past him out the door, an airy expression on her face. Jarad followed her, and Dudley was a close third. Mrs. Thompson was no longer in the kitchen, but the picnic basket sat ready for them on the countertop near the door. Jarad picked it up, complaining that she must have packed the entire contents of the refrigerator in it.

He also insisted they take his car. Dudley howled mournfully once the two of them were inside. She had hoped to leave him behind. There was no telling what a dog that unpredictable might do. Seeing the animal's dejected look, she finally relented and let him climb into the backseat.

They parked near the gazebo in Oak Bluffs. It was a warm day, with a cloudless azure sky hanging overhead. Vineyarders and summer people alike were about in droves, walking, riding bicycles or mopeds, flying kites or splashing on the beach in front of them.

They spread their blanket near a group of young boys trying unsuccessfully to get a kite in the air. Ariel doubted there was enough wind for their heavy kite to fly. Jarad decided to help them, while she poked around in the basket. It did seem like the entire contents of the refrigerator. There was even a bone for Dudley. He took it and slobbered over it lavishly.

"You shouldn't be such a pessimist," Jarad said. He sat next to her on the little red-and-white checkered blanket. He pointed toward the triangular blue-and-white kite flying above them.

"I sit corrected," she said, handing him a plate laden with cold chicken, potato salad and a large hunk of Jenny's Portuguese sweet bread. They ate in silence, Jarad watching her and Ariel looking away every time their eyes met. She felt both more relaxed and more insecure in his company than she had before. After a while she put down her plate. Her appetite had fled, and there was no use trying to force herself to eat.

"What's the matter?" Jarad asked.

She was about to answer, "Nothing," when she noticed two pairs of dark, shapely legs standing behind Jarad. She looked up to see two cow-eyed girls, about sixteen, staring down at him. He didn't seem to notice they were there. "I think we have company," she said, nodding in their direction.

He looked around, grimacing when both girls issued a collective shriek. "It *is* him," the shorter one said, clutching her friend's arm.

He looked back at Ariel, shrugging sheepishly. She smiled her amusement, her eyes traveling from him to the girls and back to him again. The taller one stared at her with such animosity that she almost burst out laughing. That would never do. Sixteen-year-olds had such precious egos.

Jarad turned his attention back to them, while she busied herself putting things back into the picnic basket. There was really no need to, but it was easier to hide behind the lid than keep a straight face as the two girls sighed and giggled their approval of him. Apollo had descended from Mount Olympus and all was right with the world.

He handled them nicely, she thought, watching him. He was neither condescending nor rude, though she did notice the tension in his back when he turned to face them. It must get tiresome dealing with an adoring public, especially a sixteen-year-old one. If it bothered him, he hid it well. She would have to add the word "considerate" to her list of attributes for him.

The girls left after a few minutes, claiming their boyfriends were waiting for them at one of the souvenir shops and wouldn't understand being kept waiting because they were talking to Jarad.

"Ah, to be sixteen again," she teased when the girls were out of earshot.

"Don't you laugh at me," he warned. "I may be partially deaf from that first scream, but I heard you snickering behind the picnic basket."

"Me? I would never snicker. I was only keeping out of the way of the tall one. She looked like she wanted to snatch me bald. I don't think I'd look good without any hair."

"Be nice. Didn't you ever have a crush on anyone when you were younger?"

She considered it for a moment. "Not really. I tried for Jenny's sake. According to her, girls just weren't normal if they didn't."

"I see. How about now?" He leaned closer to her. "Feeling any strange romantic yearnings lately?"

"Like for America's hottest young director?"

"Don't tell me you read that," he said, shaking his head.

"Actually, I didn't. Jenny told me about it. She was quite impressed."

"Tell her not to believe everything she reads."

"You mean *Ebony* magazine lied when they said you were the next Spike Lee?"

"They never said that."

"Then what did they print about you that was so terrible?"

"Nothing, really. Just the usual glowing report."

"Shouldn't that make you happy?"

"In this business, you have to take your own publicity with a grain of salt. There's a saying that if you believe all the good the media prints about you, you've got to believe the bad as well. Some of the media are not too scrupulous about the trash they print."

"You mean the ones that intersperse stories about three-headed chickens with celebrity gossip?"

"Something like that. One in particular has found me fascinating of late."

"Are you trying to tell me you have a reputation?" She widened her eyes and put her hand to her chest in pretend shock. Of course he would. Even if it were undeserved. Handsome men on magazine covers sold almost as many copies as beautiful women. "Jarad Naughton, super stud. Something like that?" That was an exciting possibility.

"Close."

"And you did nothing to deserve this reputation?" she asked cynically.

"I didn't say that." He smiled cockily. "But if I'd been as busy as the papers claimed, I would have been too exhausted to get any work done."

"Isn't that part of the territory, being in the movie industry?"

"Pretty much. Though, for those of us behind the scenes, you generally have to do something unusual to become interesting. A few lucky people like me have notorious relatives to get them into trouble."

"Your father, you mean?"

"My mother, actually. She started an organization years ago that lobbied for better treatment of minorities and women, especially in the movie industry. You know, better roles, the end of the casting couch. Her ideas were not met with a great deal of enthusiasm, as you might imagine. This was back in the days when people thought feminism was a passing phase."

She sat back, resting her spine against the picnic basket. She wrapped her arms around her knees. "What did that have to do with you?"

He gave a noncommittal tilt of his head. "One day when I was about fourteen, I guess, she dragged me to one of these charity things. I'm sure she was trying to build my social conscience, but I couldn't have been more bored if I'd been in a coma. I remember sitting on this couch when this woman came over and sat next to me. She didn't pay any attention to me, but I was fascinated by her. I'd never seen anyone quite so"—he seemed to search for a word—"well-endowed before."

He chuckled, shaking his head. "I thought I'd done a good job of trying not to stare, but the next week my picture appeared in one of the papers under the heading, 'Like father, like son?' You see, my dad had been known to be a bit of a ladies' man before my mother knocked some sense into him."

"That's terrible. You were only a child."

Jarad shrugged. "I was there. I was fair game for those people who disliked what my mother was doing and didn't mind publishing embarrassing stories about her. It wouldn't have been so bad if one of the kids at school hadn't seen it and taped it to my locker. I was the school pervert after that."

"That must have been awful for you." She saw it every day, how cruel children could be to one another.

"Nah. At first it was kind of fun. Girls who'd never known I existed before were suddenly interested in me. And if you'd seen me at fourteen you would have understood what a miracle that was."

She couldn't imagine a time when the female of the species wouldn't have found him desirable. "What was the matter with you?"

"Nothing really, just awkward and shy and a little overweight. Typical stuff. I was sort of a bookworm. Until I discovered girls, I didn't care how I looked."

Thank heavens for that discovery, Ariel said silently.

"Then, a couple of months later," he continued, "I started getting bit roles in a few movies. You know how in mainstream movies there's always that one black kid hanging out with a group of friends. Half the time that was me. There was this one movie where I actually got to have a real scene, and after that it was like the rest of the media discovered me.

"By then, I'd shot up, slimmed down and gotten my first pair of contact lenses. There must have been someone at this one teen magazine who remembered the picture, because they started portraying me as some sort of teenage playboy, which couldn't have been further from the truth."

"Didn't the attention become tiresome after a while?"

"Very quickly. Once I realized that most of the girls who went out with me did so on the chance they'd meet someone famous or get their picture printed somewhere, I was heartbroken. I wasn't such a quick study in those days."

"That's so sad." Unconsciously, her hand reached for his, giving it a gentle squeeze. It surprised her how protective she felt about him.

"Not really. It brought me out of my shell. Otherwise I might still be a pudgy bookworm with a pair of glasses falling off my nose."

She laughed. "Today you'd be a nerd."

"Thanks a lot." He picked up a cracker, biting it in half.

"After all that, why did you decide to stay in the movie industry?"

"It wasn't a choice, really. Growing up in L.A., I was surrounded by all my parents' friends—writers, actors, producers, studio people. It seemed like the most important thing in the world.

"One summer, my father convinced a director friend of his to let me work on his set. My official duties were to keep quiet and stay out of the way. I was in heaven. Then one of the kids who was to be in a scene went home sick. He stuck me in instead. The rest, as they say, is history." He quirked his eyebrows comically, popping the rest of the cracker into his mouth.

Ariel watched him, her head tilted to one side, her eyes narrowed. She didn't know what to make of the man seated in front of her. One minute he was as arrogant as a Tudor king. The next, he was self-effacing enough to share with her an incident from his youth that couldn't have been pleasant for him. There were times when he looked at her and she felt warm and tingly and feminine. Then there were times, like now, when he seemed to have no more interest in her than he would his kid sister. He was an unusual man, full of contradictions.

There was one thing she did know for sure. Any man who could yell "quiet" and the world around him fell silent was used to having his own way.

Her assumption about him proved true a second later, when he rose up on his knees, rearranging her position to suit him. He laid his head in her lap, stretching his long legs in front of him. They extended at least a foot beyond the checkered material of the blanket.

"Don't look so grave," Jarad said, though his eyes were closed. "I assure you my precious juvenile psyche was not damaged. I know you sex therapists worry about that sort of thing, Oedipal complexes and all that."

"I am not a sex therapist," she said. But what to do with her newly freed hands? She placed them on either side of her, leaning back on them.

"That's too bad." He was smiling. "Then you'd know what you're supposed to do when a man you want puts his head in your lap."

"Jarad . . ." she warned, but he didn't seem to be in the mood to pay attention to her.

"You're supposed to run your fingers over his hair and make little contented noises." She didn't move, yet she admitted to herself the desire to do just that. So much for the convivial mood that had existed between them. Having his head nestled against her thighs proved more erotic than she'd imagined possible.

He reached back to grasp one of her hands, placing it on his head, dragging her fingers through his hair until they stayed there on their own. "That's better." He settled against her legs with a sigh. "If you're not a sex therapist as you claim, what is it you do? Listen to a bunch of buppies complain their parents didn't love them enough because they didn't get that bicycle they wanted on their eighth birthday?"

"No," Ariel said, shaking her head. She supposed that was most people's view of psychology today, thanks to the media and daytime talk shows. In her opinion, pop psychology had raised "feeling good about yourself" to a quest tantamount to the search for the Holy Grail.

"I work at a private high school in Manhattan."

"Private school? Sounds like a cushy job."

"Not really." Ariel couldn't blame him for thinking that. That's what most people thought when they heard where she worked.

"There's a myth in our country that having money solves all problems, but wealth and power are no insulation against pain. In some cases, it's worse for these kids because so much pressure to succeed is placed on them that failure of any kind can be devastating. Conversely, some parents are so busy with their own lives that they forget they have kids. The money's there, so the kids still have nice clothes and they don't starve, but they get no direction from the people that brought them into the world."

Ariel was silent for a moment, and she could feel Jarad's head shifting on her lap so that he could look up at her. She averted her gaze, looking up at the cloudless sky. She felt moisture gathering in her eyes, and with an ease borne of practice she blinked it away. She always got a little misty when she thought about the more difficult aspects of her job. Most of the kids at the school were happy, well-adjusted. But there were some kids whose lives were so sad it broke her heart.

"Ariel, look at me," Jarad said. His voice was little more than a whisper, but it carried a command just the same. When she didn't respond, he sat up, taking her shoulders in his hands. His fingers slid down her arms to grasp her wrists. "You are such a softy," he said.

"I am not."

When she finally looked at him, Jarad noted her eyes had reddened slightly and there was a defiant tilt to her chin that dared him to contradict her. It was in that moment he remembered her from so many years ago. She'd worn that same expression when he'd found her and asked her why she was crying.

With a voice full of as much disdain as a ten-year-old could muster, she'd told him she wasn't crying, and even if she was it was none of his business, anyway. He was only a guest in her grandmother's house and should take his nosy behind home if he knew what was good for him. She had given him grief even then.

He wasn't going to press her, partly because he remembered what she did to him the last time he'd tried that, and partly because he didn't want to upset her further. "Don't go getting in a huff," Jarad teased, stroking his hands over her bare arms. "What is left in that picnic basket for dessert?"

"We could go into town for some ice cream."

"You're on," he said, rising to his feet and extending a hand to her. With one firm tug, he brought her to a standing position. Another tug, and he brought her against his chest. He pressed a soft kiss to her forehead. "Let's go."

* * *

"Town" was about three blocks of stores along Circuit Avenue with a few offshoots on its side streets. A frappé looked suspiciously like a milk shake to Jarad. The pistachio one Ariel ordered at Mad Martha's was a bit too green for his liking. He ordered a chocolate ice-cream cone for himself with the multicolored jimmies Ariel insisted he get. Jimmies looked surprisingly like sprinkles. Vineyarders were a strange bunch.

They sat at one of the little tables in the ice-cream parlor, facing out onto the street, where they could keep an eye on Dudley, who wasn't allowed in the store. Jarad leaned back in his chair, taking in the scene around him. The small shop was crowded, mostly with families with young children or pairs of lovers huddled together. Out on the street, pedestrians strolled leisurely by, most holding hands and smiling. A far cry from New York, where everyone seemed intent on getting to their destination within the next ten seconds, or L.A., where everyone did as little walking as possible.

"I'd forgotten how peaceful it is up here. What made you decide to move to New York?"

"Pragmatics." She took a sip from her straw. "Martha's Vineyard wasn't exactly known for its wonderful school system. Once Jenny and I reached school age, we were shipped off to school in Boston, but we never really considered that home. Every chance we got we were back here.

"By the time I went to college, I wanted to be on my own. I went to NYU as an undergraduate, and I did my graduate work at Adelphi."

"Why didn't you come back?"

"I already had an apartment of my own, friends. I liked the work I was doing. Besides there isn't much call for high-priced psychologists on the island. Many people struggle to make it from one summer to the next. For them, therapy is a frivolity."

"And that's what's most important to you, your career? I wondered why Gran hadn't managed to marry you off yet."

"Gran hasn't managed to marry me off, as you put it, because I haven't wanted to be married off." She sat up, leaning closer to him. "Frankly, I am sick to death of hearing about weddings, engagements, honeymoons and anything else connected with marital bliss, including and especially my own!"

She flopped back in her chair, sighing. "Besides, I'm difficult."

"I've noticed." He took her hand, holding it lightly between his fingers. "And the men in New York have accepted your decision to remain unmarried off?"

"The men in New York don't have anything to say about my decisions."

"And I thought New Yorkers were supposed to have backbone. Just be thankful you don't live in California. You wouldn't get off so easily."

"I thought Californians were supposed to be laid back."

"We are." He winked at her. "But we'll try anything once."

"Oh, brother," Ariel said, giving him a droll look. "We'd better go get Dudley."

After clearing away their table, they headed toward the door. "What's next on the agenda?" Jarad asked.

Ariel shrugged her shoulders, looking up at him, not looking where she was going. She bumped into a man on his way into the store.

"Excuse me," she said, taking a step back, bumping into Jarad. His hands settled on her waist, steadying her.

"Ariel? Ariel Windsor?"

She looked up into the face of the last man she'd hoped to see on the island. Peter Allan Barton stared back at her, a smug expression on his face.

Ariel closed her eyes, wishing the sidewalk would open up and swallow her whole. Until that moment, she'd had no idea Peter was on the island, let alone in the same township she was. He usually favored the more affluent sections of Edgartown and East Chop.

Her eyes skimmed over him as he adjusted the leather satchel he carried on his shoulder. He looked the epitome of preppiness, with his short-sleeved polo shirt, white shorts and topsiders with the obligatory white socks. For maybe the hundredth time in her life, she wondered what she had ever seen in this man.

Despite the questioning note to his words, she had the feeling this meeting was no accident. He looked too pleased with himself for that to be true. What could he possibly want? He had to know she didn't want to see him.

She glanced back at Jarad. He gazed down at her, and already she could see the questions in his eyes. She would have to give him some sort of explanation, and for the life of her, she couldn't imagine what that would be. Here is the man I was almost stupid enough to give my virginity to? Even though she'd only known him a few days, Jarad's opinion of her was important to her. Not in this lifetime would she tell him that.

"What can I do for you, Peter?" Ariel asked, hoping her nonchalance wouldn't arouse Jarad's curiosity more than it already had been.

"I wanted to say hello to an old friend."

What universe was he living in that he could still think of them as friends? His gaze was anything but friendly as it raked over her, making her feel severely underdressed, despite the modesty of the outfit she wore.

"You look great, as always," Peter said.

"Thank you." The only thing she was grateful for was that he'd ceased his perusal of her and turned his attention to Jarad.

"Aren't you going to introduce me to your friend?" Despite the amicable tone of his words, there was a coldness in Peter's eyes when he looked at Jarad that Ariel found hard to fathom. He seemed to be deliberately antagonizing Jarad. As for Jarad, she could feel the coiled tension in him. Maybe Peter's focusing on Jarad wasn't such a good thing after all.

"Wait a minute," Peter said, before she had a chance to say anything. "I know who you are," he said, wagging a finger at Jarad. "You're a film director or something?"

"Something like that."

Peter turned to her, taking a step toward her. Instinctively, she inched back toward Jarad. She hoped he hadn't notice her reaction, but the tightening of his grasp on her waist told her he had.

"I hear Jenny is getting married Friday," Peter said, apparently oblivious to their exchange. "Please wish her well for me."

"Of course," Ariel said. But she had no intention of mentioning Peter to Jenny in any context. No one spoke for a moment, and Ariel foundered for something innocuous to say to extricate her and Jarad from the uncomfortable meeting.

She was relieved a moment later when she heard Jarad say, "We'd better get going."

Peter leaned toward her. "Maybe I'll see you again."

*Not if I see you first.* "Maybe."

With a shrug of his shoulders, Peter headed into the ice-cream parlor.

That was too weird for words, she thought, turning to watch Peter's departure. What had he hoped to gain by talking to her? Peter wasn't the type to do anything without a motive or two. An invitation to Jenny's wedding, maybe? That seemed like a somewhat logical guess. Many of their old friends would be there, and Peter wouldn't take being excluded lightly. He should have known better than to think Ariel would intercede on his behalf.

"Who was that?" Jarad asked, startling her out of her musings.

"Just someone I used to know," she said cryptically, then walked ahead of him in the direction of the car.

Jarad grasped her arm, pulling her to a stop. "Slow down, would you?" She turned to squint up at him in the bright sunlight.

"Are you going to tell me what that was about, or should I draw my own conclusions?"

"There's nothing to tell."

He stared down at her, a skeptical look on his face. She'd actually paled and drawn closer to him when that man had taken a step toward her. While it pleased him that she would look to him for protection, no one had a reaction like that to someone that they just used to know. Who was he to her? An old lover? If he hadn't been, he'd wanted to be—that much Jarad knew. He'd looked at her with such undisguised lust that Jarad had wanted to shake him to pop his eyes back in his head. Whatever they had been to one another, he'd obviously hurt her. Otherwise, she wouldn't have responded the way she did.

"Really? That's why you stalked off like that?"

She sighed dramatically, looking heavenward. "Okay, okay, we dated a few years back. No big deal. It was over a long time ago. I'd rather not talk about it, if you don't mind."

He did mind. He wasn't some stranger to her, at least he hoped he wasn't anymore. He'd thought they'd forged some sort of bond between them in the short time they'd known each other. He didn't expect her to recount all the gory details, but neither did he expect her to shut him out completely. Did she think him so callous that seeing her upset wouldn't affect him, too?

She turned away from him, raising her hand to shade her eyes. She glanced back in his direction, but not at him. "What are you doing?" he asked.

She stepped closer to the curb, to the spot where they'd left the dog to wait while they were in the ice-cream parlor. Lifting both hands in a gesture of exasperation, she said, "Dudley's gone."

Until two minutes ago, Dudley had been sitting at the curb, waiting obediently for them. Sighing heavily, he took one of her hands in his. "Come on. We'd better find him."

Twenty minutes later, they spotted him by the basketball courts, where a small play area was built into the grass. Several small children were spinning on the carousel a larger child was pushing. There was Dudley, chasing after them, salivating and barking and making a nuisance of himself.

"I'm really beginning to wonder about that dog," Ariel said, taking a seat on the bleachers facing the play area. Jarad sat on the row above and to the right of her. He leaned forward, resting his elbows on his thighs.

For a long moment, both of them were silent, as the group of children in front of them disbanded, running off together, laughing. Jarad wondered what Ariel was thinking about. Or whom.

He glanced down at her profile, seeing a smile lifting the corners of her mouth. If she seemed to have forgotten about the man from her past they'd bumped into, he wasn't going to be the one to bring it up again.

He leaned down, taking a strand of her hair between his fingertips. "I just realized that you've been holding out on me. You never did tell me why Jenny calls you a sex therapist."

Ariel shook her head and laughed. "You are going to be disappointed if you've been waiting for a juicy story.

"A friend of mine works for a program called Gateway. It's a screening agency that helps minority students get into private schools like mine. The schools are interested in diversifying their populations and Gateway reaches into the community looking to give scholarships to students who show promise.

"Every summer they give workshops for parents of new students, which are usually conducted by a friend of mine. She was all set to do them this year, too, but her doctor put her on total bed rest. She was seven months pregnant, and afraid she wouldn't be able to carry her baby to term. So when she asked me to fill in for her, I had to say yes. That, at least, was one worry off her mind.

"One of the topics this year is how to talk to your kids about sex. It's a shame to say that most parents still don't know how to talk comfortably with their kids about sex."

"I know what you mean," Jarad said dryly. "My father told me two words: 'Be careful.' I was about twenty-four at the time. Luckily, my mother was the sex educator in the family."

"My parents explained it all to me, but it was still confusing. And since children will make up things to explain what they don't understand, I came up with some interesting theories of my own."

"Like what?"

"I don't know." She toyed with her straw, looking away. "For one thing, no one ever told me that you didn't get pregnant every time you had sex. It seemed that the only way women knew they were pregnant on TV was that they fainted. I figured it must happen when people weren't aware, like when they were asleep."

"Takes all the fun out of it," Jarad claimed.

"I imagined that once you were asleep, the sexual organs acted like magnets or something that attracted each other."

"I've noticed that, too." He ran a hand along her bare shoulder.

"Jarad," she cried, playfully smacking him on the leg. She should have known this was one subject to avoid while he was around.

"Ow," he said, rubbing where she'd hit him. "These people you watched on TV must have had a ton of kids with their sexual organs attracting every night."

"Of course not. I thought all it took to thwart these impulses was to provide a . . . a barrier. I thought that's why couples on TV always wore pajamas to bed."

Jarad roared with laughter. "That's the most innovative approach to birth control I've ever heard."

She laughed too, remembering her childhood confusion. Then she added more soberly, "That's why it's so important for parents to talk honestly and openly with their children about sex and discuss more than just the facts.

"But you can't do that by trying to scare a child with fear of AIDS or getting pregnant. All they'll tell you is it isn't going to happen to them. You can't do it by telling a child to 'just say no.' Sex is a normal, healthy impulse which everyone is going to indulge in sooner or later. The more prudent approach, in my opinion, is to focus on when it's okay to say 'yes.' "

"When is that?" His voice was soft, low, compelling.

She cleared her throat, wondering if he meant in general or if the question was meant specifically for her. "When you find someone you care for who cares about you. When there's mutual trust. When you are responsible enough to protect yourself and your partner. And when you are willing and able to accept the consequences if things go wrong."

Ariel took a deep breath, letting it out slowly. "Not surprisingly, when kids give those factors a little thought, they usually postpone their first sexual encounters. It also helps if the kid has goals they want to fulfill that an unwanted pregnancy would interrupt, and a family that shows true affection for the child. Some kids are so desperate for physical contact they'll sleep with whoever comes along, just to be touched."

Jarad wondered if there was anyone in her life

who held her in that way, kept her grounded. He'd learned in the short time he was with her family that she didn't come home often. They visited her even less frequently. Apparently that was the way she wanted it, but he wondered if her family did her a disservice in giving in to her wishes. Emotionally, she was as closed off as a mine after a cave-in.

"Who touches you, Ariel?" he asked. His voice sent a sensuous shiver down her spine. She tried to look away, but he used his other hand to capture her cheek and turn her face back to his. "Who?" he repeated, more firmly.

Ariel said nothing, unsure what he was asking of her. Was he asking if there was a man in her life she hadn't told him about? He had to know that she would never have let him near her if that were true. She wasn't starved for affection, either, if that's what he was thinking. She'd never been one to tolerate too much physical closeness. An occasional hug from Gran or her parents was about all she could stand. Jarad had touched her more in the last few days than anyone else in her life.

Either way, she had no intention of answering him. That was far too personal a question. She was only willing to go along with Jenny's experiment to a point. She had no intention of baring her soul to a man again and leaving herself vulnerable. If nothing else, Peter's appearance had reminded her of how much havoc a man could wreak in her life. As far as she was concerned, the conversation was over. She pulled away from him, starting to rise.

With a hand on her arm, he pulled her back, bringing her onto her knees in front of him. Startled, she turned her face up to his. A second later, his lips were on hers. His tongue was bold, slipping

through her parted lips to sample the sweetness of
her mouth. His fingers massaged her back, her
shoulders, her scalp through the thick tangle of
her curls. He slanted his mouth over hers, and she
moaned, inflaming them both.

With his hands and body and his mouth he was
sending her a silent message: *Now someone does.*

# Five

Ariel was too overwhelmed by Jarad's overture to guess what was in his mind. Her whole body trembled in response to his kiss. "Jarad," she breathed when his lips ventured to the side of her throat.

"Hmmm?" Jarad raised his head and looked at her. He wore that sexy smile that made her insides quiver. He was breathing as heavily as she. She was kneeling, facing him. With a hand curved about the back of her neck, he brought her forehead down to rest on his. "What is it, sweetheart?"

Ariel dragged in a ragged breath. "I have to go." She tried to disentangle herself from his embrace, but he wouldn't let her go. "We'd better go find Dudley," she added. "Heaven knows where he's gone to now."

He shook his head as his eyes scanned her face. The irises of her eyes had darkened and her lips were puffy from his kisses. He touched a fingertip to the corner of her mouth, running it along her moist bottom lip. "Leave him alone. I'm sure he's found some cute little poodle to keep him company."

"You're probably right. Dudley is notorious for getting cute little poodles in trouble. Gran hasn't had the heart to 'fix' him. Besides, I have to go to Edgartown to pick up something for Jenny. I need to get back to the house to get my car."

"I'll take you where you want to go."

"N-No, that's okay. I'd rather go by myself." There was no way she was going to let him come along.

"That's ridiculous. Why should you drive all the way over there by yourself?"

"I'd just prefer it." She could imagine the comments he'd make surrounded by lace and satin in the little lingerie shop where she planned to pick up Jenny's garter.

"I thought we went through that last night."

"I'm not trying to get rid of you," she told him. "I didn't realize letting you kiss me a couple of times meant I was giving up my autonomy."

Jarad's jaw clenched. "Fine," he said, finally releasing her. "I'll take you home."

She stood, smoothing her clothes into place, watching Jarad precede her down the steps. She hadn't meant to snap at him. She hadn't meant to make light of what they'd shared, for in truth his touch affected her far more than she wanted to admit.

He had every right to be angry with her, but when he turned to offer her his hand to help her down the stairs, his anger seemed to have dissolved. "Come on," Jarad said, lacing his fingers with hers.

Once he'd collected Dudley and gotten them all in the car, he drove straight to Edgartown without getting lost once.

"You don't have to go in with me," she said as they pulled up to the curb.

"What if you have a big box to carry. Men are

supposed to lift and tote. That's what my mother told me."

"I won't. And I don't think we should chance leaving Dudley to his own devices again."

"Okay," Jarad said, deciding not to press his luck. "Holler if you need me."

He watched her as she got out and went into a doorway two stores down. There were several lacy negligees on display. No wonder she hadn't wanted him to go with her. What was she going to buy in there? Something sexy he hoped. He could imagine her in that black, lacy number in the window, all soft and yielding.

He scratched Dudley's ears absently, waiting for her to reappear. "She's something, isn't she, Dudley?" he asked, not noticing the dog gave no response. In some ways he wished he were the sort of man who would hold a woman to the promise of making love to him. Then he'd have some release from the tightening in his loins every time she looked at him with those witch's eyes of hers.

Did he do the same thing to her, he wondered. She'd trembled in his arms just now, but that didn't mean anything. She would have scrambled away from him the moment the kiss was over if he hadn't held on to her. But he wasn't fool enough to let her get away that easily. She was tiny, perfectly curved, and her skin was like silk to his touch. Not at all like his own hirsute, angular body. He was planning a hands-on, in-depth comparison study.

And more than that, there was Ariel herself: loyal to her family, supportive of her friends, dedicated to her students, feisty, sexy—and determined to keep him at arm's distance. He was falling in love with a woman who seemed to have room in her heart for everyone but him.

The irony of his situation didn't escape him. After years of being pursued by women, he was now cast in the opposite role. He'd always viewed women's overtures with amused detachment. They all seemed to want something from him, most often a part in whatever project he was working on. Or the women who couldn't care less what he did or who he was, never bothering to notice more than his looks. Jarad wasn't a vain man, but he knew women found him attractive. The worst were the complete strangers who'd proposition him, thinking they knew him because they'd seen his picture somewhere.

He couldn't remember one woman who'd been interested in him, Jarad, the man. At first that knowledge had been disheartening, but after a while he'd realized that suited him fine. He'd never been the heavy commitment type. Not until Ariel. Something about her drew him to her like a sailor to a siren's song. But his little enchantress ran from him every chance she got. Last night was the only time she'd endured his company without running away.

He wasn't going to let her get away that easily. He wanted her in so many ways, he was a little frightened of the depth of emotion she sparked in him. He also knew that he couldn't rush her. That would spoil everything. He'd only now gotten her to accept his teasing without bristling. She would come to him in her own time. She'd told him that this afternoon. She needed to realize that he cared for her, that she could trust him. He was a patient man. He could wait for her.

A moment later, the car door opened, and Ariel

slid in next to him, shooing Dudley out of the way. He'd been so lost in thought he hadn't noticed her approach. She had the tiniest little package with her.

"All done?" he asked, suddenly feeling very testy.

"Yes."

He looked at her, sensing the wariness in her. "Is everything okay?"

"You aren't going to say anything about me going into the lingerie shop?" She slanted a glance up at him.

"I hadn't planned on it, but I can improvise something if you'd like."

She smiled, and Jarad felt his heartbeat quicken.

"Thank you," she said. Then she leaned over, cupped his face in her palms and kissed him. It was a brief kiss, but he sat there stunned for a minute afterward. It was the first time she'd ever touched him without his prompting. "What was that for?" he asked.

"For not teasing me. That's why I didn't want you to come with me," she confessed.

She was blushing. He liked that. She could go on and on about sex, objectively, that is. The thought of him seeing her pick out lingerie made her blush. What a contrary woman.

And she hadn't been trying to push him away, not in the way he'd thought. She had him so confused, he didn't know what to make of that information. She settled back in her seat and smiled. "I guess we should get going."

She wanted him to drive now, when he could barely think? "Where to?" he asked, pulling away from the curb.

Affecting an upper-class British accent, she said, "Home, James." Jarad looked at her in complete confusion. Ariel giggled from the irony of it—a director having no sense of direction! "Make a right at the next corner," she told him, then dissolved into laughter again.

The dining room seemed too empty that night with Charlie, Dan and Jarad missing. That's what Emma Thompson thought as she brought in dinner for the ladies. She wasn't sure which of them looked the most forlorn. Bachelor parties did that to women, she wasn't sure why. She remembered her own long face the night of her Vincent's party, God rest his soul. She supposed even in this modern day and age, some things didn't change.

And Ariel's face was hanging just as long as the others'. It would take a man like Jarad Naughton to set her pulse racing. Emma laughed her hearty West Indian laugh as she went on about her work. Sooner or later there was going to be another wedding.

"What are you so happy about, Mrs. Thompson?" Jenny asked.

"Nothing, dearie. You all enjoy your dinner." Mrs. Thompson could barely get out of the room before another wave of laughter took her.

"She's been like that all day," Ariel said, cutting into her roast beef.

"Poor Emma," Gran said. "It must be the pressure of becoming a grandmother. Some women have the strangest reactions to it."

Later on, Ariel and Jenny relaxed in the sitting room. Gran declined to join them, feeling she'd better keep an eye on Mrs. Thompson.

"What do you suppose men really do at bachelor parties?" Jenny propped her feet up on the coffee table. "You hear all this nonsense about women popping out of cakes, but that's not what really goes on, is it?"

"You're asking me?" Ariel continued her search for something interesting on TV with the remote control. "They probably get drunk and do disgusting men things, I guess."

"Disgusting men things?"

"You know, things no woman in her right mind would let a man do in front of her. Like smoking gross cigars and belching without excusing themselves and telling dirty jokes. Disgusting men things. Just be glad they're all staying at Dan's bed-and-breakfast tonight. That way none of them has to drive around in the dark when they're through drinking each other under the table."

There wasn't a thing worth watching on television. Ariel flicked it off and put the remote on the table.

"When you get married, I'm throwing you a bachelorette party. What's sauce for the goose is sauce for the gander."

"Only if there are dancing boys. We've got to have dancing boys."

"What are you so happy about? Jarad is at that bachelor party doing God knows what with the rest of them."

Ariel's eyes widened and her shoulders came up. "What do you want me to do? I tried my pitiful look during dinner for your and Gran's sakes. I'm sorry, I just couldn't keep it up."

Ariel did feel happy. She'd spent a lovely day with a man she realized she was beginning to care about. He'd shared with her past incidents that weren't particularly pleasant. Hearing it, she understood he trusted her. His simple admission had touched her heart.

What was she protecting herself from, anyway? He was a nice man, he had a good job, he liked his mother. He hadn't even teased her as she'd thought he would. What more could she ask of any man who was the victim of her and Jenny's romantic experiment?

She wondered how this would all turn out, if when it was over she and Jarad could manage to be merely friends. Probably not. She smiled to herself, remembering his reaction to her kiss in the car. He'd been so surprised by her overture it almost made her laugh. But his arms had come around her and he'd kissed her back so sweetly. It thrilled her to know he was susceptible to her, too.

"You're smiling," Jenny said accusingly.

"It isn't a crime." Ariel covered her mouth to hide the now irrepressible grin.

"But it is a sign."

"What are you talking about?"

"The first sign of love. Don't you remember them? First comes smiling, then sighing, followed by loss of appetite and constant daydreaming, then glowing. By the time your toes start tingling, you're hooked."

Ariel snorted one of Gran's snorts. Although Jenny had had her share of episodes in which those signs were duly noted and counted, Ariel had never bothered with such nonsense. It was all cultural suggestion, anyway. There was little scientific foundation for such things.

"You are being ridiculous. Are you going to do that every time I smile?"

"Only when I know you're thinking about *him.*"

"I was not thinking about Jarad," she lied.

"I forgot one. Sleeplessness. It fits in there some-where between sighing and glowing. It's been a long time since I had to remember these things."

"I think you're suffering from bachelor party de-mentia or something. Are you sure you don't have a fever?"

"Say what you want, but I am the one who knows about love here. For two days you were storming around here telling me what a terrible person Jarad was. Now there's a sappy grin on your face a mile wide. I suppose a walk in the moonlight can change a girl's perspective on things."

"Jenny Douglas, you were spying on me."

"Only a little. And only for your own good." Jenny put her feet on the floor and leaned toward her. "You know I'm only teasing you about the smiling and all that. I'm just glad you've taken my advice. It proves there's a first time for everything."

And a last. That was absolutely the last time she was going to think about Jarad and smile.


Ariel descended the stairs the next day, dressed in a pair of khaki shorts, an old T-shirt and a pair of boots that should have seen their last days a long time ago. On her head sat her father's old fishing hat, which dangled lures along its crown like charms on a bracelet.

She couldn't imagine anyone missing her today, at least not this early in the morning. All the ar-rangements for the wedding were in place. Gran and Mrs. Thompson would probably never notice she'd left the house. Jenny would probably sleep late after worrying herself half to death over what Dan and the others were doing at his hotel.

Ariel hadn't slept well herself. She hated to admit it, but after a while, Jenny's anxiety had gotten to her, too. Ariel knew Jenny's worries were unfounded. Dan wasn't foolish enough to do anything reckless. For one thing, he was a solid, dependable, no-nonsense kind of man. For another, Jenny would kill him.

But unlike Jenny, Ariel had no claim on Jarad, no say in how he spent his time. She reminded herself that she didn't want one. This was only an experiment, and she'd be a lot better off if she just remembered that.

When after a fitful night her eyes popped open at five in the morning, she'd decided now was as good a time as any to escape for a relaxing day of fishing. Better that than sitting around wondering when Jarad would get back.

Besides, she was used to spending most of her time alone. She lived by herself and most of the women in her circle of friends had husbands or boyfriends who kept them occupied. Here, with so many people around her constantly, she missed the solitude.

Inhaling deeply, she headed toward the kitchen. Who could be up at this early hour brewing coffee, she wondered as she tugged on an old khaki vest. It was too early for Mrs. Thompson to be up. Dawn had not yet begun to make an appearance in the morning sky.

Standing in the doorway, she surveyed the empty kitchen. The lights were on, but the only sound in the room came from the dark fragrant liquid dripping slowly into the pot. Anyone could have started it. Hearing a noise behind her, Ariel started to turn. Before she'd moved an inch, an arm closed around her waist and a hand came over her mouth, stifling the scream that rose in her throat.

"It's me," Jarad whispered against her ear.

"You?" She pulled out of his embrace and turned to face him. "I thought you'd still be at Dan's." Looking him over, she realized he must have been home long enough to change clothes. He wore a pair of shorts and a tank top, not the casual jacket and slacks he'd had on the night before.

"I didn't feel like staying." He led her over toward one of the stools and sat down.

"Why not?"

With his hands at her waist, he pulled her forward until she stood between his thighs. Her hands rose naturally to rest on his shoulders. "I missed you," he said.

She looked into his face for any hint that he was teasing her. He wore a lopsided grin on his lips and a glassy look in his eyes that reminded her of what he'd obviously spent the night doing. "You're drunk," she accused.

"Who, me? Never." He leaned forward, resting his forehead against her breastbone. "Did you miss me?"

As he spoke, his warm breath fanned the valley between her breasts. In response, her nipples hardened, and a wave of heat spread through her belly. She pushed against his chest, seeking to end the intimate embrace. He didn't budge. "You haven't been gone long enough for me to miss you."

"Don't be mean to me, Ariel. My head is killing me."

"Poor baby." Despite the sarcasm in her voice, she cradled his head in her palms, rubbing her thumbs against his temple. "That's what happens when you overindulge."

"I didn't. Really. Just a couple of beers and Charlie . . ."

A terrible thought occurred to her. "You didn't drink anything Charlie gave you, did you?"

"It seemed impolite to refuse."

Ariel looked heavenward, gritting her teeth. God only knew what Charlie put in that home brew of his that had been known to terrify more than a few men's livers. She would have warned Jarad if she'd thought there was a possibility of Charlie trotting that stuff out.

"You didn't, um . . ." She tried to find a polite way to ask the question.

"What? Pass out? Puke my guts out? No, but I wanted to. I used to think Charlie liked me."

He sounded so pitiful, Ariel bit her lip to keep from smiling. Of course Charlie liked him. Charlie usually reserved his "brew" for old friends who were used to the stuff or as an initiation of sorts for new ones. Since he was still standing, Jarad had obviously passed.

"You don't have any aspirin do you?"

"I've got something better." She stepped out of his grasp, going to the cabinet beside the refrigerator. "You stay there and relax." She gathered her ingredients and added them to a tall glass of orange juice. Ignoring her advice, Jarad had moved to stand on the opposite side of the counter from her. She passed the glass to him. "Here you go."

His gaze went from her to the glass and back to her again. "What's this?"

"Something to make you feel better." With a sweet smile on her lips, she gestured with her hands. "Drink up."

She watched as he reluctantly brought the glass to his lips and drank. A second later, his eyes squeezed more tightly shut, a testament to the bitterness of the drink. He set the empty glass on the counter with a shudder.

"What was in there?"

"That's a Ludlow family secret."

"You can keep it."

Ariel laughed. That was the idea. Gran had mixed a similar potion for her and Jenny the one night the two of them had overindulged at a neighborhood party. Gran had offered them the "family hangover remedy" the next morning.

Later, Ariel found out it consisted mainly of juice, a couple of other vile yet edible ingredients, and the contents of two aspirin capsules. But that morning, she and Jenny had decided that if that was the cure, it wasn't worth it to have the disease.

Ariel took Jarad's glass, turning to rinse it off in the sink. "You didn't drive back did you?"

"Nah, I walked."

An image of Jarad wandering around in the dark came to her mind, and she suppressed a giggle. "How long did it take you?"

He grinned at her. "Only an hour."

An hour for a ten-minute walk. "Pathetic." She stretched out the first syllable for emphasis. Ariel crossed her arms in front of her. "What else did you guys do last night?"

"Sorry, can't tell. I'm sworn to secrecy."

Jarad used his index and middle fingers to cross his heart, touched them to his lips, then held them in the air. She'd seen Charlie and her father use that gesture countless times. Good God, he really was one of them now.

"Is that some sort of fraternity hand signal?"

"What?"

"Never mind." Ariel turned away from him, toward the refrigerator, shaking her head. "Pathetic," she repeated. She opened the door and rooted around for the package she'd left there.

"And what are you supposed to be?"

Ariel glanced over at Jarad, who watched her with his head propped up on his hands. Her fingers went to the brim of her hat, tugging it farther down on her forehead. She'd forgotten what she'd put on that morning, how she must look. "I'm supposed to be going fishing."

"Fishing? It's only five-thirty in the morning."

"That's when the fish are out."

"Who's going with you?"

"Me, myself and I. We make a great team." She resumed her search, finding what she was looking for on a lower shelf.

"I'll go with you."

Ariel straightened, holding the package in one hand. The other hand she placed on her hip. "You? You'll be lucky if you manage to stay in the boat."

Seeing his disgruntled look, she continued. "I'll be fine. This isn't New York or L.A. It's Martha's Vineyard, for goodness sakes. I'm a big girl. I even bait my own hooks." She spoke the last sentence with a suggestive smile on her lips, taunting him.

"What with?"

"This." She tossed the package of fresh squid onto the counter, smiling broadly when Jarad's complexion momentarily turned the same gray color as the fish.

"You're enjoying yourself, aren't you?"

"Serves you right, you men and your primitive bonding rituals."

"What's the matter? Afraid we men got wild and

woolly during our primitive bonding ritual last night?"

She glanced up at him, then returned her eyes to her task. The man was too perceptive by half. Either that or she'd started wearing her feelings as obviously as the tattered old hat on her head. Worse yet, he seemed amused by the situation.

Resting both hands on the counter, she leaned toward him. "Even if you did, you don't owe me any explanations. You're free to do whatever you want."

He took one of her hands in his. "Am I really?" he asked. "Free to do anything I want?"

His voice was a sexy whisper, and his gaze an inferno. There was no doubt in her mind that he meant to do anything to *her*. Her mind flooded with images of Jarad doing exactly as he pleased with her. A powerful wave of sexual yearning washed through her. How could he affect her so strongly, when he was barely touching her? What would happen if he ever really put his hands on her?

Ariel licked her dry lips, willing something intelligible to come out of her mouth. She pulled her hand from his, wiping her damp palms on her shorts. "I'd better go find the fishing um, uh stuff," she said finally. She turned and hurried from the room, hearing Jarad's husky laughter echoing behind her.

Jarad watched the horizon as Ariel steered her boat toward a little inlet nestled between two towering bluffs on either side. The rising sun cast a blanket of gold and crimson on the waters way off on the horizon. The earth here looked to be more

clay than soil. The hills' reddish cast took on a
deeper hue in the early morning light. High above,
houses dotted the cliffs, some of which seemed so
precariously perched as to be in danger of slipping
down into the water. There were no other boats
around as far as he could see. They were completely alone.

His gaze slid to Ariel. She swung the boat in a
wide arc to face the way they came. He'd actually
talked her into taking him fishing. The indignities
he had to subject himself to, to be with this
woman. He hadn't picked up a fishing pole in he
didn't know how long. Probably since the last time
Charlie dragged him into a boat so many years ago.
At least the pounding in his head had quieted to
a dull ache, thanks to that witch's brew she'd given
him.

He turned his face toward the cliffs, hiding his
smile from her. She'd been worried about what he
was doing last night. That surprised him and
pleased the hell out of him. She'd bid him good-
bye as he was on his way to Dan's hotel as if she
hadn't had a care in the world. She'd told him to
have a good time. She'd laughed and told him not
to do anything she wouldn't. He'd joked back that
he was sure not to have any fun then. She'd
shrugged her shoulders as if she didn't care, walking away from him without even a good night kiss.

She *had* worried.

Which had to mean she had some feelings for
him, some proprietary urge toward him. He had
no intention of telling her last night had been one
of the tamest evenings he'd spent in a long time.
The highlight of the festivities seemed to be playing practical jokes on him.

He enjoyed the camaraderie of the men, many

of whom offered him their condolences for getting involved with Ariel. Quite a few of them told stories of being shot down by her in very unflattering ways. Knowing her, she probably didn't realize any of these men were interested in her in any way other than friendship.

He wondered why she'd let him in the little bit that she had. Why was he different? He'd turned the thought over in his mind as he'd walked home last night, not coming to any conclusion.

"We're here," she announced, cutting off the engine.

"Where's here?"

"It doesn't have a name. Just someplace I like to come."

He watched her slide from her seat, going to the tackle box on the floor at the back of the boat. She crouched next to it, opening the lid.

Even from where he sat, the musty odor of the contents of the box reached him. "What do you have in there?" he asked. "Are you trying to catch fish or scare them away?"

She glanced back at him, her nose wrinkled from the smell. "I haven't cleaned this thing out in a while. Lucky for us, fish like stinky stuff." She pulled out the package of diced squid and shut the lid.

"Ready?" she asked him.

"For what."

"Anyone on my boat has to bait their own hook."

There was a taunting smile on her lips that raised the corners of his own mouth. "What makes you think I'm afraid of a little squid?"

"The look on your face when I tossed it on the counter."

"You surprised me, that's all. The last time I saw squid it was cooked, on a bed of lettuce, and covered in marinara sauce."

She gave him a scoffing look, then slapped a slimy bit of fish into his palm, tentacle side down. His gaze went to her face, which bore the most innocent of expressions. He knew she didn't believe him when he said he hadn't drunk too much. She was purposefully trying to turn his stomach. Well, it would take more than a little raw fish to accomplish that.

He didn't enjoy fishing anywhere near as much as she seemed to, but he wasn't totally inept either. He looked up at her to discover she'd already cast her line. Her little red and white bobber floated above the water a distance away. She slid her pole into a holder at the side of the boat, then turned to him, hands outstretched. "Want me to do yours?" she asked.

"I can handle it." Moving to the side of the boat, he clicked off the safety holding the line taut, flicked his wrist and sent his line flying over the water. Not a perfect cast, but decent at least. It didn't travel even half as far as hers did, but it did land in the water, and for that he was profoundly grateful.

Ariel glared at him, clearly amazed. He sat back in his chair, propping his feet on the railing, as she narrowed her eyes on him.

"You didn't tell me you'd been fishing before," she accused.

"You didn't ask."

She gave him a sour look and took her own seat. "Then you are responsible for your own fish from here on."

"Yes, ma'am," he said, offering her a mock salute. "You're the captain."

She gave him another sour look, then propped her feet up on a cushioned storage bin at the side of the boat. She picked up her rod, fiddling with the reel.

"What do we do now?" he asked.

"Wait for the fish."


Jarad waited and waited, but no fish was forthcoming. He'd gotten a couple of nibbles, but each time he reeled in his line, it was to find some fish had cleverly eaten his bait without managing to get hooked.

He'd just finished reeling in his line to find a garden of seaweed on the other end, when Ariel said, "I've got another one."

Jarad picked up the net. The only thing he seemed good for this morning was snaring her fish in the net as soon as she got them close enough to the boat for him to do so. He bent over the side and scooped up the foot-long flounder she'd caught. It flipped around wildly, splashing them both with water.

"Your fish, ma'am," he said, holding the net out to her.

"Thank you," she said, but she didn't look at him. He had laughed at first when she told him the garbage bag was "for the fish," but she'd done a good job of filling it. In the past two hours, she'd reeled in porgies, flat, walleyed flounder, black mollies and an angelfish with beautiful, delicate fins. Twelve in all, counting her latest catch. He held the bag open for her to toss the fish in with the others.

"Do you want to change sides?"

The expression on her face was almost apologetic. Jarad shook his head as he sat back in his seat. He didn't want her feeling sorry for him. Not when he couldn't care less if he caught anything or not. He enjoyed simply being with her, drifting on the calm waters of Nantucket Sound.

He wondered what the folks back in L.A. would say if they could see him now, sitting comfortably in an old boat none of them would deign to set foot on, savoring the company of a woman they would consider inconsequential, since she wasn't in the business and didn't hope to be.

He did have a few good friends, people he'd known since youth, with whom he could be himself. But even among them, there was no one with whom he could imagine spending such a day. A day with no one to impress, no clever repartee to come up with, no deals to be made, picked apart and discussed endlessly. No need to talk at all, he realized, glancing over at Ariel. She smiled back at him. She was the only person he knew that he felt content to just *be* with.

He wondered if she would fare as well in his world, and he immediately knew the answer. She would hate it. She would hate the phoniness and duplicity of many of the people there. She would hate the flashiness and the strain of having to be "on" all the time. No matter that she lived in New York, he knew, in her heart, she was a small-town girl who'd hate living her life in the fishbowl that was L.A.

Jarad cast his line again, if only not to arouse her suspicions as to what he was truly thinking. He propped his feet against the railing, settling back in his chair. He grabbed the hat from her head, using it to cover his eyes. "Wake me if I catch anything."

"Don't you dare go to sleep on me." She snatched the hat back, putting it on her head. "I wouldn't be able to wake you if Shamu were on the other end of your line."

He opened his eyes, swiveling his head to look at her. "Are you implying—again—that my mental state is not what it ought to be?"

She laughed. "It's your drunken state I was referring to."

He didn't suppose it would do him any good to protest his innocence any further. Instead, he grabbed her, pulling her sideways onto his lap, trapping her hands between their bodies. "If I'm as inebriated as you claim, you'd better watch out. Isn't alcohol supposed to lower a person's inhibitions?" He ran his hands down her sides, letting them settle on her hips.

"I'm afraid that only works well with women."

He knew she was trying to sound clinical, detached. Yet her voice was breathy, deep, very sensual. "Really?" he asked. He slid his hands up her sides, until his fingers touched her rib cage and his thumbs rested just below her breasts.

She nodded. "In men it tends to have a—um—deflating effect."

"Not this man." He saw a challenging glint come into her eyes in response to the arrogance of his statement. He welcomed the challenge. He wanted to push her, provoke her, until all the passion she tried to hide from him came spilling forth. He wanted to see the look in those incredible green eyes of hers when that passion overtook her.

His thumbs lifted, grazing her nipples. He felt a surge of satisfaction when her eyes fluttered closed and a soft moan escaped her lips. "Want to put that theory of yours to the test?" he teased. Not giving her time to answer, he covered her sweet mouth with his own. He felt her shiver as his tongue touched hers, and her hands wound around his shoulders, pressing him closer.

With his thumbs, he drew lazy circles around her engorged nipples. He nearly lost it when she moaned into his mouth and arched against him. God, he wanted her, but not now, not here. When he made love to her, he wanted to do it properly— in a soft, warm, welcoming bed. He forced himself to pull away.

Her eyes flickered open, and her gaze fastened on his face. For a moment, she seemed to be studying him. He'd just begun to wonder what she could possibly be thinking, when a broad smile lit her face.

He ran a thumb along her moist lower lip. "What are you grinning about?" he asked.

"I think you'd better reel in your line."

Jarad was suddenly aware of a soft whirring sound and turned in the direction Ariel indicated. The tip of his fishing rod dipped toward the water. Something pulled on the line, carrying it further and further away. He might actually have caught something.

With Ariel still on his lap, he grasped the rod. Whatever he'd hooked was either very large or very determined. Laughing, Ariel wriggled around on his lap until her back was pressed to his front. Her hands closed over his as she shouted directions that were completely unnecessary. He got caught up in her enthusiasm, laughing as he turned the reel over and over. With an arm around her waist, he leaned over the side to bring the fish on board. He leaned back, holding it up for her inspection. She took one look at his "catch," ducked under his arm and scrambled back toward her seat. "Get that thing off my boat," she demanded.

Jarad looked at her, puzzled. "What's wrong with my fish?" He looked at it, turning it back and forth on the line. "It's not too small is it?"

"Throw it back," she screamed.

"I catch one lousy fish and you want me to throw it back?"

"Lousy is right. Don't you know what that is?"

As if to give a clue to its identity, the fish made a hissing noise, drawing more air into its body. Startled, Jarad dropped the line, and fish and pole went crashing to the floor. Ariel shrieked, leaping onto her chair, looking like the proverbial woman terrified at finding a mouse in her kitchen.

Still hooked on the line, the fish thrashed and hissed and enlarged itself until it was absolutely huge.

"Get rid of that thing," she screamed.

He didn't want to touch it either. With its glassy fish eyes and swollen body and pointy teeth, it seemed to be grinning up at him like a black and yellow demon. He picked up the pole, letting the fish dangle from the line until he could get it over the side of the boat. Using Ariel's knife, he cut the line, releasing the fish back into the water.

When he turned back to her, she was still up on her seat, leaning against the windshield. One of her hands lay on her chest, which rose and fell rapidly under her palm. Looking at her, he started to laugh. Not in a million years would he have expected such a reaction from her.

He went to her, wrapping his arms around her waist. He lifted her down from her perch, pulling her into his lap as he sat down in his seat. Breathing heavily, she trembled against him. "Where's my big, strong fisherwoman?" he asked, stroking her back. "Don't tell me you're afraid of a little fish?"

He felt her relax against him. The hand on her chest rose to brush her hair back from her face. "Nine million fish in the sea," she muttered. "And you have to catch a blowfish."

"I thought it was cute."

"How like a man to appreciate something that can puff up to twice its original size." She pushed against his shoulder. "Stop laughing at me. I hate those things."

"I wonder what the good Dr. Freud would have to say about this little aversion of yours."

"Freud had a big mouth."

He laughed, giving her a squeeze. "I guess that about does it for fishing today."

She nodded. "I have to be getting back, anyway."

"Why? You have a hot date I don't know about?"

"Sort of. I have to make some phone calls."

"What for?"

"Jenny never had a real shower since she only gave us a month's notice that she and Dan were getting married. She claimed she didn't want one since she and Dan have everything they need." She shrugged. "I thought I'd invite a few of our girl-friends over tonight for a little get-together."

"I see. A primitive female bonding ritual."

"At least a shower serves a useful purpose. If staying up half the night and giving yourself a hang-over serves any useful purpose, I'd love to hear it."

"How about giving the poor guy one last night of freedom before the ball and chain goes on?"

Ariel rolled her eyes at him. "You men like to pretend women drag you to the altar kicking and screaming, but everyone knows men benefit more from marriage than women. Studies have shown that the two happiest groups of American adults are married men and single women. Ever wonder why that is?"

"Not lately. So, you're against marriage?"

She shrugged. "I wouldn't go that far. It's a problematic institution, that's all. If half the marriages in this country end in divorce, a whole lot of people are doing something wrong."

"And a whole lot of people are doing something right."

Ariel looked up at him, a wry smile on her lips. "Don't tell me you're one of those cockeyed optimists who always thinks the glass is half full."

"I don't worry about the glass. I drink straight from the bottle."

Ariel gave him a disgusted look. "Don't remind me."

Choosing to ignore her comment, he turned back to their earlier subject. "Isn't it a little short notice to be inviting people over?"

"Probably, but they'll come."

Ariel wiggled her way off his lap, unknowingly torturing him. He knew her well enough to know there was more to the story than she was telling him. "How can you be sure?"

She didn't answer him for a long time, fussing with the fishing poles. "Growing up, I was always included with the girls because Jenny saw to it that I was. I wasn't exactly a girl's girl, if you know what I mean. When it came to talking about boys or clothes or whatever we used to talk about back then, I didn't have a clue. If I'm calling everyone together, they'll come, if only out of curiosity."

# Six

Only one of their old friends who were still on the island turned out to be unavailable, and her absence was understandable. She'd just given birth to her first child and wouldn't be making it to Jenny's wedding either. The others were due to arrive in half an hour. Dan was expected to bring Jenny a half hour after that, at seven o'clock.

Ariel fussed over the hors d'ouevres that Mrs. Thompson had helped her prepare for the gathering.

"Everything looks fine," Gran said, polishing a tiny spot at the edge of a silver tray.

"Do you think so?" Ariel asked. She couldn't remember the last time she'd felt this nervous. What if no one showed up? What if Jenny didn't appreciate her gesture? What if the evening turned out to be a bust, and she became more of a social misfit with the women than ever?

Besides, being in New York, it had been impossible to be a maid of honor to Jenny. Jenny, Gran and Mrs. Thompson had planned everything without a drop of input from her. She wanted to do something nice to give Jenny the proper send-off. That meant the evening had to be perfect.

Gran patted Ariel's shoulder. "You're going to

worry yourself into a coma," Gran said, her humor barely hidden. "These girls are your friends."

"I know." Ariel gave everything one last look. She had wine and soft drinks chilling on ice. Napkins, utensils and glasses had already been laid out in the sitting room. All that was left was to transport the food into the other room. "I just want everything to be all right."

Ariel's gaze lifted to her grandmother's face and beyond, to where Jarad stood in the open doorway. Suddenly, she remembered the last time she'd been this nervous. It had been this very morning in this very kitchen when Jarad asked her if he were free to do whatever he wanted.

She felt the same deluge of warmth suffuse her as she'd felt then, the same tingling awareness of all the feminine areas of her body. Her eyes wandered over him, noticing the snug fit of his short-sleeved shirt, the way his black jeans rode low on his hips. Her gaze returned to his face, to his dark, intense eyes. For a long moment, they simply stared at each other.

The spell was broken when Gran said, "It lives!" She clasped her hands together as if she'd just been granted a great favor. "I didn't think we were going to see you for the rest of the night."

"I'm made of sterner stuff than that, Gran." He went to the older woman and put his arm around her shoulders.

Gran tilted her head, looking up at him. "You're made of something, all right."

Ariel laughed, watching the two of them. Gran obviously liked Jarad a great deal.

"Now, young man," Gran said, continuing on her scold. "Would you please tell my granddaughter that she looks beautiful and the food is fine?

Maybe she'll listen to you." Gran moved out of Jarad's embrace, heading toward the entranceway.

"Gran, aren't you going to stay?" Ariel asked.

"And listen to all that nonsense you young women talk about?" Gran gave a mock shudder. "I've got better things to do. You girls enjoy yourselves."

Ariel watched her grandmother leave, until Jarad's movement in the periphery of her vision caught her attention. His hand was poised over one of the canapés she'd artfully arranged on a tray.

"Don't you dare," she said. She picked up the tray in both hands. "These are for the ladies." She circled around him, heading for the door. "Why don't you make yourself useful and bring the other tray?" she called over her shoulder.

Once in the sitting room, she placed the tray on the mahogany coffee table and looked around. The dark room looked unusually festive with the few white streamers and white bells Ariel had taped up. Napkins and a small tablecloth in shades of rose, blue and cream complemented the stark white china and gleaming silverware she'd set out.

"Your grandmother is right. Everything looks lovely."

"Thank you." Ariel took the tray from Jarad's hands, carried it over to one of the end tables and set it down. She didn't realize he'd followed her until his arms closed around her from behind.

"And you are the loveliest thing in the room."

She felt his warm breath on her cheek as he bent and placed a soft kiss on her ear. "Jarad," she protested. "You have to leave now."

"Why?"

"The guests will be arriving any minute." She pried his hands away from her waist and walked

over to the bar. She tested with her palm the coldness of one of the bottles chilling there.

"Afraid to be seen with my ugly mug?"

His "mug" was so far from being ugly that she
laughed. "No, but this is a party for women. Unless
you're willing to shave your legs and put on a
dress, you'll have to go."

He sighed, affectedly. "If I must, I must."

"Jarad," she warned, turning to him. She wasn't
in the mood for his humor.

"Relax, sweetheart," he told her, coming up beside her. "You are worrying over nothing." He
started to uncork one of the wine bottles. "Jenny
will love the surprise, your friends will have a good
time, and if anybody starts to look bored, you can
tell them how you tricked me into going fishing
with you this morning."

"I did no such thing." When she looked up into
Jarad's handsome, smiling face, he winked at her.
She supposed she was being ridiculous. At least as
far as worrying about the success of her party was
concerned. It was the women's reaction to finding
Jarad there with her that really bothered her.

If he stayed, she'd have to answer questions
about who he was to her, and what could she honestly say? I'm having a fling with this famous film
director over here? The term "fling" itself was mis-
leading. Didn't having a fling imply the flinger was
having sex with the flingee? She hadn't, and probably never would. She wasn't about to tell anyone
that Jenny had dared her into the whole thing in
the first place.

Truthfully, it wouldn't matter what she said about
him. Her opinionated friends would make up their
own minds, anyway. That was the bothersome part.
She'd never been on the receiving end of their

teasing. She wasn't sure she wanted to be. Her only recourse was to get rid of him—now.

Jarad extended a half-full glass of merlot toward her. She accepted it with a quiet "thank you." The rich wine slid down her throat and hit her empty stomach with a splash. Immediately, a curling warmth spread through her.

"Better?" Jarad asked.

"Much." But to be on the safe side, she put her wineglass down on the bar. She would never hear the end of it from him if she got soused on one glass of wine. "Now about your leaving . . ." She grasped his forearm in both her hands, hoping to lead him toward the door. He wasn't cooperating, however, refusing to budge from where he stood.

"Why are you so anxious to get rid of me?"

"Why are you so determined to stay?"

"I'm curious, that's all. I was wondering about what sort of girls you grew up with."

"You'll meet them at the wedding."

"How about I stay until Dan gets here?"

"He's dropping Jenny off. He's not coming inside." She gave another tug on his arm. "Now be a good boy and make yourself scarce."

"All right," Jarad conceded. "I know when I'm not wanted." He extracted his arm from her grasp and put it around her waist, pulling her to his side. "Walk me to the door?"

"Of course." She fell into step beside him, suddenly feeling bad for kicking him out. She hadn't meant for him to leave the house necessarily. She'd only thought as far as getting him out of the room. "What are you going to do tonight?" she asked.

He grinned at her. "I spoke to Dan earlier. We decided to meet at Charlie's."

Her eyes narrowed as she regarded him. That

rat! He'd had plans to leave all along. Out of sheer spite, she said, "Are you sure you can find the place by yourself? Or should I draw you a map?"

They reached the front door. Leaning his back against the sturdy oaken structure, Jarad pulled Ariel close to him with his hands on her hips. "Just like a woman," he said, shaking his head. "You learn a man's faults and never let him forget them."

"It's not hard, when you seem to have so many of them."

"I'm going to make you pay for that later," he warned, touching a finger to the tip of her nose. "For now, kiss me good night so I can get out of here."

She didn't argue with him. Going up on tiptoe, she wrapped her arms around his neck and pressed her lips to his. His arms closed around her, his hands sliding down her back to cup her derriere. That brought her in intimate contact with his arousal, just as his tongue slid between her lips to find her own.

Unable to help herself, she moved against him restlessly. She knew she should protest his embrace, right there in the open where anyone could see them. But she'd never felt him so intimately before, so close to the source of her own passion. She felt dizzy, out of control. With a soft moan, she pressed closer to him, until her breasts were crushed against his chest and his growing erection was cradled by her hips. Jarad groaned, and she felt the reverberation of it travel through her body like an inner caress.

Her eyes flew open as Jarad abruptly set her away from him. Breathing heavily, he said, "I'd better go."

All she could manage was a brief nod. Her heart thundered like a jackhammer, her breathing labored as if she'd run a five-mile race. Yes, it was best he left now, before she really did something to embarrass herself. Like throw him down on the floor and have her way with him. Her girlfriends would really have something to talk about then!

Cool night air rushed in when Jarad opened the door. It felt heavenly against Ariel's heated skin. Jarad took her hand, leading her under the archway.

"Have a good time, sweetheart." He kissed the back of her hand. "But don't do anything I wouldn't do."

Hearing him echo her words from the night before and remembering his response, she smiled saucily. "Then that means I can do a-ny-thing." She drew out each syllable for emphasis.

"As long as it's with me." With his hand at her nape, he pulled her closer until her lips met his. It was a brief kiss, but wholly stirring nonetheless. When he released her, she swayed on her feet. He winked at her, and she wanted to swipe his smug, self-satisfied grin from his face. Whistling, Jarad turned and sauntered down the stairs.

It was only then Ariel noticed the woman emerging from a car that must have recently pulled into the driveway. She was staring in the direction of the garage where Jarad had gone. Her hand lifted in a small wave, then flitted over her hair, as if checking to see that everything was in place.

Ariel groaned. Why did Vicky have to be the first one to show up. Boisterous, flirtatious Vicky, who hadn't a clue how to keep her mouth shut. To Vicky, tact was a four-letter word. Vicky moved to-

ward the steps, stopping to watch as Jarad's car
pulled out into the driveway and onto the street.

Vicky turned, and Ariel felt the other woman's
intense gaze on her. "Ariel Windsor," Vicky said.
"You've got some serious explaining to do."

"Really?" Ariel said, feigning ignorance.

Vicky stood at the base of the steps, hands on
hips. "Who was that gorgeous man, and what was
he doing kissing you?"

Dressed in her own fuchsia bathing suit, Ariel
headed down to the beach to claim a little stretch
of sand close to the water. Lying down on her
stomach, she noticed the towel next to hers, emblazoned with the name of a hotel on Paradise Island where she'd once stayed. She had an exact
replica of it stashed somewhere in Gran's house.

She laid her head down on her arms and closed
her tired eyes. Not only were the last-minute prepa-
rations for the wedding tomorrow keeping her
busy, she was having trouble sleeping, a fact which
delighted Jenny to no end. She'd come to the
beach mainly because lying in the sun made her
drowsy. With any luck, she'd be sleepy enough to
get a quick nap before dinner.

She had almost fallen asleep when she felt something wet dripping on her back. Startled, she
turned over quickly to find Jarad standing above
her. He was using the Bahamian towel—her
towel—to dry his hair. Her eyes roamed over the
bare expanse of his muscular chest, to a flat stomach that disappeared into black swim trunks. His
legs were long and lean.

He must have looked exactly the same the other
morning when he'd grabbed her in the kitchen,

but somehow the effect was more profound this time. Perhaps it was because they were away from the others now. Maybe it was because in a strange way she missed him. She hadn't seen him since he'd walked out the door on the way to Charlie's last night.

But he stood there in front of her, using her towel as if everything were normal. Involuntarily, her eyes traveled back to the scanty black material plastered to his masculine form. Startled by her own prurient thoughts, she forced her eyes to return to his face.

"Long time, no see, stranger," Jarad said, sitting on the edge of her towel. He leaned forward, resting his forearms on his knees, breathing heavily from the exertion of his swim. Touching the towel to several damp spots on his face, he turned to look back at her over his shoulder. "How did your soiree for the ladies go last night?"

"Why do you ask? Afraid we got a little wild and woolly at our primitive female bonding ritual?"

"Did you?"

"I'm sworn to secrecy," she teased. "But I will tell you that Jenny was very pleased and surprised by the party. You were right about that."

That's all she intended to say about the previous evening. He didn't need to know she'd opened her own big mouth and told all and sundry about her relationship with Jarad. It wasn't her fault. If Vicky hadn't implied that she, staid, sensible Ariel Windsor, couldn't possibly have attracted a man like Jarad Naughton, she knew she never would have said anything. Vicky's words were a kind of dare Ariel had felt powerless to resist.

Jarad raised a questioning eyebrow, but for once she was not going to respond to a challenge from him. She turned over on her stomach, scrunching over to make room for his large body as he stretched out beside her. The sun felt wonderfully warm on her skin. A few minutes later, she felt a more heated caress along her spine.

"What are you doing?" she asked as his fingers traveled from the small of her back to the edge of the bandeau top she wore. She raised her head to look at him.

"Getting your attention."

He had that, but his fingers kept weaving tantalizing patterns on her skin. "Yes?"

"I liked your other bathing suit better," he said, smiling and looking to her for a reaction.

"You mean because this one fits?" Though she knew it was almost as revealing as the other.

He nodded. "Although I do like this color better. What is it, pink?"

"Actually it's fuchsia, if you want to be precise about it."

"The only thing I want to be precise about is that I want your lips precisely here." He pointed to his own.

"Jarad, there are still people on the beach."

"And none of them are looking at us." He pointed again, but when she didn't move, he added, "You didn't have any objection to kissing me the other day in Edgartown, on a city street and everything." He spoke the last words as if they revealed a shocking secret.

"You make it sound as if I'm afraid to kiss you."

"Well . . ." He was taunting her with that smile of his.

"Well, I'm not. It's that growing up in a small town where everyone knows who you are and what you're doing, you learn to value your privacy. Besides, we were *inside* the car."

"You're not going to kiss me, are you?"

She smiled wickedly. "No."

"Then let's go for a swim."

"You just had one."

"I know, but you weren't there."

"I really don't feel like it." He was up to something, she was sure.

"I insist."

She didn't offer any resistance as Jarad took her hand and pulled her to her feet. The water was only a short distance away, and the sand was becoming noticeably cooler as they walked. "It must be freezing."

He tugged on her fingers when she stopped at the water's edge, waiting to test the temperature of the next incoming wave. "That's the chicken's way of getting in the water."

For once she was not going to respond to that word. "I am not a chicken," she declared. "I'm deciding whether I want to go in or not."

"You're going in," Jarad said determinedly. He picked her up easily, carrying her out until the water was up to his mid-thighs. Her toes bobbed in and out of the rising surf, testifying that the ocean was indeed very cold.

Ariel looked around in dismay. A small group of children was watching them intently. She didn't like being part of this spectacle. "Take me back to the beach," she said under her breath. "You're making a scene."

"I'm a director. I'm supposed to make a scene." Jarad seemed to crouch down lower in the water. "Are you ready?"

"For what? Don't you dare let go of me."

"Don't worry if you're not a strong swimmer. I won't let you drown."

"I can swim rings around you any day," she boasted.

"Go ahead and try."

Ariel's eyes flew open, realizing he'd tossed her into the water like a fish too small to keep. The chill of the ocean went clear down to her bones. She came up, sputtering and mad enough to fight.

She looked around for Jarad, but he was gone. A few feet out, she could see a dark head above the foam. That had to be him. With short, even strokes, she made her way toward him. They were far away from any other swimmers when she finally caught up with him.

"You are a good swimmer," he said, wiping the salt water from his eyes.

"I asked you not to do that," she screamed at him. Why had she bothered to go after him at all? If she had headed in the opposite direction, she'd be on the nice warm beach by now. He had incensed her so that she hadn't thought of it. She splashed water at him with the heel of her hand. "That wasn't a very nice thing to do."

"No it wasn't. I'm sorry." He didn't look contrite. He seemed ready to burst out laughing at any second. He held out his hands to her. "Come here, sweetheart. I really am sorry." He moved closer to her, and she realized that he was still standing. She was treading water and he was standing.

"Boy, you're short," Jarad teased, slipping his arms around her waist, pulling her up against him. "Is this private enough for you?"

She simply stared at him, wondering how he'd gotten so sneaky in only thirty-four years of life.

Then he kissed her, and her fingers went to his

nape and she trembled and sighed just as she was supposed to. He tasted salty and sweet. The hands on her back that slid lower to cup her bottom elicited a throaty moan from her lips.

Jarad's breathing was ragged when they finally separated. "I think we probably evaporated half the ocean."

She glanced over his shoulder. "No. It's still here. Want to give it another try?"

"I should have known." Jarad shook his head gravely.

"You should have known what?"

"What an animal you are. The ones that look the quietest at first usually are. The way you attacked me on the beach the other night should have tipped me off."

Ariel looked at him incredulously. "In the first place, I did not attack you on the beach. You kissed me."

"That's not how I remember it."

"Then you remember wrong. And I am not an animal, whatever that means. I'm a normal woman with normal . . . appetites."

"And what are you in the mood for?"

*You*, was the first thought that popped into her mind. Instead she said, "Dinner. Swimming makes me hungry."

"Me too." The feral look in his eyes made her doubt he was talking about food. "Let's head back."

She released her hold on Jarad's shoulder, falling back in the water when he released her. Using her arms to pull away, she brought her feet out in front of her. "Race you back," she taunted.

"You've got to be kidding."

"We'll see how funny it is when I'm back at the

house and you're still in the water." She splashed him with her feet as she started to backstroke toward the beach. She'd swum a few feet when she noticed Jarad had started to swim after her. Turning onto her stomach, she swam in earnest. She was in the shallow water when he caught up with her. She tried to run past him when he scooped her up and carried her back to the beach.

They were both laughing when he laid her down on the large towel. He lay down beside her, as they both waited for their breathing to normalize. This time the beach was empty except for the two of them. "What were you trying to do? Kill me?" Jarad asked.

"Is the competition too much for you, old man?"

"Never. It was the head start I gave you."

"I didn't ask for that." She sat up, wringing the moisture from her hair. "We'd better get going. It's getting late."

"Come back here." Jarad pulled her back down. She was pinned between his arms, as his upper body rolled on top of her. "I don't think I'm ready to let you go inside yet." He kissed her slowly, thoroughly, until her arms wound around his back, pressing him closer. The tiny curling hairs on his chest tickled her skin, making her wriggle beneath him.

"Don't do that, honey." He placed a calming hand on her hip. "You don't know what you're doing to me."

If it was anything like what he was doing to her, it was torture—exquisite torture. "I can't help it. You were tickling me." She ran a hand over his muscled chest. "Who told you to be so hairy?"

"Didn't anyone ever tell you you talk too much? Now shut up and kiss me."

She tried to, but each time she raised herself close to him, he pulled away, just out of reach. "Cut that out," she cried, seeing the devilish grin turning the corners of his lips. Her hands went to his shoulder blades, forcing him back down to her. Their lips met, and Ariel felt herself melting from the heat of their embrace.

Opening her eyes, she saw a flash of light in the sky. It must be about to rain, she realized. The beach was the worst place to be during a thunderstorm. No matter how intoxicating Jarad's kisses were, she didn't want either of them fried to crispy memoriam by a bolt of lightning.

"We'd better head back," she said. "I just saw lightning."

"I did too." They quickly stuffed rather than re-packed Ariel's little bag. With an arm around her waist, he led her back to the house.

Jarad paused at the glass patio doors, looking back toward the beach and the jetty that stood only a few feet from where they'd been. The solitary figure he'd noticed there a moment ago was gone. That fact didn't relieve him any. It only made him more certain that the man who'd been sitting there was the same man they'd met in town the other day.

How long had he been skulking there without either of them noticing? And why? All the possibilities that sprang into his mind unsettled him. He'd probably hoped to catch her there alone, away from the house where he was not welcome and away from Jarad's protection. That seemed like a logical conclusion, seeing that once it became apparent that he and Ariel were leaving together, the other man left, too.

Maybe he was being paranoid. Maybe the man on the jetty had been a complete stranger who wanted to get in out of the coming storm, just as they had. Something in his gut told him he wasn't mistaken. Well, that idiot could hang around all he wanted to. He would never get to her, not if Jarad had any say in it.

"Close the door. You're letting in all the bugs," Ariel teased, drawing his attention to her. "What's so fascinating out there, anyway?" Ariel peeked around him to look outside.

"Absolutely nothing." With his hands on her shoulders, he gently pushed her back inside. He followed her in, closing and locking the door behind him.

# Seven

Hours later Ariel checked the clock for the fourth time. Two-fifteen. How infuriating! The wedding was tomorrow afternoon, and she couldn't sleep. Jenny had kept her up half the night gossiping. This was their last night together as single women, Jenny had rationalized. They couldn't let that go to waste. She'd been almost too sleepy to keep her eyes open. Where was that drowsiness now?

She kicked off her covers and put on her lavender silk robe. Going out on her balcony, she looked up at the sky. The stars overhead twinkled brightly as they always did on the Vineyard. This was the first time, however, that they reminded her of the way a certain man's eyes sparkled. She'd only known him five days, yet he stirred something inside her no other man had been able to touch.

Despite what she told her family, love was important to her. She just didn't seem to be any good at it, not the man-woman kind. Look at the men she'd chosen to be with. First there was Peter. He'd been a graduate student going for his masters in English literature when she met him the summer of her sophomore year in college. She'd thought herself falling in love with him, until the night he tried to bed her. She'd been so scared and he'd been so impatient with her that she couldn't go through with it. He'd called her some very unpleasant names that she couldn't repeat even in her own head.

Then there was Sadler, her human sexuality professor. She thought she'd be safe with him. He was well-liked by his students, and who else would be more qualified to teach her about sex. After Peter, she hadn't wanted to trust her emotions again. She'd dated, but she always broke things off before they became serious enough for sex to become a consideration. The decision to sleep with Sadler she'd made with her head. She didn't love him, but she liked and respected him. He praised her budding psychological abilities as no one else had.

She would have expected him to be a passionate lover, considering his ardent but secret pursuit of her and his obvious fervor for his subject. In truth, he was as warm as a cadaver and just as considerate. He'd hurt her and humiliated her, patting her behind when it was over, telling her, "You really must loosen up, Ariel." Then he went to take a shower, leaving her to dress and depart in solitude. A week later, a classmate warned her about him. His true specialty, the girl told her, was deflowering the virgins in his classes.

After that, she hadn't dated much at all. She no longer trusted her own judgment where men where concerned.

Would Jarad be a tender lover? He'd been nothing but gentle with her so far. But then, neither Peter nor Sadler had shown their true colors until it was too late.

She wondered what he would do if she truly offered herself to him. What would he say when he found out she'd only been with a man once? He'd laugh, probably. Even she had to admit her love life was pretty pathetic.

Ariel rested her elbows on the railing. "Jarad, Jarad, Jarad," she sighed. "What am I going to do with you?"

"What do you want to do with me, Ariel?"

Ariel spun around at the sound of his voice. Jarad was standing a few feet away from her on his side of the balcony, separated from her by a thick railing.

"How long have you been standing there?" she asked, feeling self-conscious.

"A few minutes. I just wanted to watch you. You looked so pretty in the moonlight."

There was something about the way he said that that made her look at him more closely. He wore only a pair of black pajama bottoms. He looked tired, tense. She'd never seen him like this before. "Jarad, what's the matter?" she asked.

"Nothing." He was looking straight ahead, his eyes hidden from her by the dim moonlight and the sweep of his lashes.

She longed to hold him and soothe away whatever was bothering him. She sensed something terrible must have happened. "Would you please tell me what's wrong?"

"No."

"Why not? Because men aren't supposed to show their feelings. I know you don't believe that."

"No, I don't."

"Then why not?"

"Ariel, go to sleep. I'll see you in the morning." She didn't budge. After a moment, he turned and started to walk back into his room.

"Jarad Naughton, you come back here." When

he didn't immediately return, she considered going to his door and knocking, but discarded that idea immediately. Not only would she risk having someone discover her there in the hallway outside his door at this ungodly hour of the night, there was no guarantee that he'd let her in.

She huffed out a breath, resigning herself to taking the best course of action available to her. She climbed over the chest-high railing, hopping down into a crouched position on his side of the balcony. When she straightened, Jarad was standing directly in front of her, framed in the open doorway to his room. The chilling look on his face was enough to freeze her in place.

"Are you completely crazy?" Jarad said. "You could have hurt yourself."

"I'm sorry, but I'm concerned about you. Why won't you tell me what's the matter?"

He sighed heavily. "It's nothing, really. Go to bed. Use the door this time."

"No. I don't trust you." His sense of humor might have returned, but that could be an act for her sake.

"Believe me, I'm fine."

"Then come back into the moonlight and talk to me."

"I think we can find something better to do than talk."

"Never mind, you." She took his hand and led him onto the balcony. "Now talk. I'm not leaving until you tell me why you're upset."

Jarad leaned against the balcony, pulling her alongside him. He took both of her hands in his and kissed the palm of each. "You are a very unusual woman, Ariel Windsor, and the most ador-

# An important message from the ARABESQUE Editor

Dear Arabesque Reader,

Because you've chosen to read one of our Arabesque romance novels, we'd like to say "thank you"! And, as a special way to thank you, we've selected four more of the books you love so well to send you for only $1.99.

Please enjoy them with our compliments, and thank you for continuing to enjoy Arabesque...the soul of romance.

*Karen R. Thomas*

Karen Thomas
Senior Editor,
Arabesque Romance Novels

# 3 QUICK STEPS
## TO RECEIVE YOUR "THANK YOU" GIFT
## FROM THE EDITOR

Send back this card and you'll receive 4 Arabesque novels!
These books have a combined cover price of $20.00 or more,
but they are yours to keep for a mere $1.99.

There's no catch. You're under no obligation to buy anything.
We charge only $1.99 for the books (plus $1.50 for shipping
and handling). And you don't have to make a minimum
number of purchases—not even one!

We hope that after receiving your books you'll want to
remain an Arabesque subscriber. But the choice is yours to
continue or cancel, anytime at all! So why not take us up on
our invitation to receive 4 Arabesque Romance Novels, with
no risk of any kind. You'll be glad you did!

Call us
TOLL-FREE
at 1-888-345-BOOK

Check out our website at www.arabesquebooks.com

## BOOK CERTIFICATE

**Yes!** Please send me 4 Arabesque books for $1.99 (+ $1.50 for shipping & handling). I understand I am under no obligation to purchase any books, as explained on the back of this card.

Name _____

Address _____ Apt. _____

City _____ State _____ Zip _____

Telephone ( ) _____

Signature _____

*Thank you!*

AN129A

Accepting the four introductory books for $1.99 (+ $1.50 for shipping & handling) places you under no obligation to buy anything. You may keep the books and return the shipping statement marked "cancel". If you do not cancel, about a month later we will send 4 additional Arabesque novels, and bill you a preferred subscriber's price of just $4.00 per title (plus a small shipping and handling fee). That's $16.00 for all 4 books for a savings of 25% off the publisher's price. You may cancel at any time, but if you choose to continue, every month we'll send you 4 more books, which you may either purchase at the preferred discount price. . . or return to us and cancel your subscription.

THE ARABESQUE ROMANCE CLUB: HERE'S HOW IT WORKS

**THE ARABESQUE ROMANCE CLUB**
**c/o ZEBRA HOME SUBSCRIPTION SERVICE, INC.**
**120 BRIGHTON ROAD**
**P.O. BOX 5214**
**CLIFTON, NEW JERSEY 07015-5214**

AFFIX
STAMP
HERE

able kook I've ever met. Considering I know the rest of your family, that's a high compliment."

"Thanks, I think." Her voice was uncertain.

"Even your name is weird. Isn't Ariel the spirit that helped Prospero in Shakespeare's *Tempest?*"

"Yes," she nodded. "It's also the name of the mermaid they made a cartoon movie about a few years ago." She slipped from his grasp and went to stand at the railing beside him.

"What's the matter, honey?"

She smiled. "Nothing." She spoke in the same tone he'd used earlier. He nudged her with his shoulder and she continued. "It's strange you should mention that, that's all. I've been thinking about my grandfather. Grandy is the one who came up with that name for me. I gave him his name, too, because I couldn't say Granddad. It's funny, but after all these years, I still miss him."

"Of course you do. It's natural to miss people you love when they're gone—no matter how long ago it was."

"It's not just that. Grandy was very special to me. I loved my parents, but for the first ten years of my life I thought he was the person in the world that knew me and loved me best. Then one day he was gone. I didn't know it at the time, but Grandy had been battling cancer for years."

Ariel paused, breathing deeply. "The one and only time I ran away from home was because of Grandy. I was lucky it was in the summer, because it wasn't until nightfall that one of the older kids who was staying here found me. If it weren't for him I probably never would have gone home that night."

Jarad stroked her hair away from her face. "You

were hiding in the weeds in the Old Sailor's Graveyard, mad as hell that somebody had found you."

She looked up at him, amazed. "That was you?"
No wonder she hadn't remembered him. He'd
seemed so much older than she at the time. And
he'd spent most of his time there chasing after a
pair of eighteen-year-old twins whose family had
rented a house down the street. She'd been too
busy instigating trouble among the younger kids to
pay too much attention to him. "Why didn't you
tell me?"

"I thought you might try to emasculate me
again."

She laughed. "That was an accident. You were
trying to drag me home."

"Where you belonged."

She laughed. "We would have gotten home
much sooner if you hadn't gotten us lost. And just
like a man, you wouldn't listen to a mere woman
tell you anything."

She leaned into his embrace, as, chuckling, he
wrapped his arms around her. She laughed too,
remembering how indignant she'd been to be led
around by someone who clearly had no idea
where he was going. She'd had enough when he'd
stopped in front of the cemetery with the giant
statue and remarked that they'd been that way before.

"Of course we have," she'd shouted at him.
"How many huge glow-in-the-dark Jesuses do you
think we have around this place?" After that he'd
allowed her to show him the way home. They were
there less than five minutes later.

"You never did tell me why you ran away," he
said more soberly.

Ariel swallowed, remembering the emotions that

had driven her from her home. "It was Grandy's birthday. Every other year we had a big party and everybody came and Grandy would read his poetry. He'd always write something special for the occasion that would make us laugh. But that year there was nothing. It seemed like everybody had forgotten about him. I couldn't bear it."

She looked up at the stars, feeling the same emotions wash through her, only they were dulled now by the passage of time. She could feel Jarad stroking her hair back from her face, feel the warm fan of his breath on her face. She breathed deeply, inhaling the musky aroma that was his natural scent combined with the remnants of his cologne.

"Do you remember what you told me that night?" Jarad asked her. She shook her head. "You said you were never going to love anybody else if they were going to die on you like that."

His voice was a soft whisper in her ear. She rested the back of her head against his chest. She hadn't remembered that either. But in an odd way, it made sense. People's adult lives were often shaped by childhood events they no longer recalled, terrors that in retrospect seemed trivial.

It saddened her to realize she'd kept that long ago promise to herself. Looking at her life now, she realized she'd withdrawn from the people she loved. Not all at once, but slowly as the years went by. She hid herself down in New York, away from the binding closeness of her family. She sniffled, fighting back the tears that threatened to overtake her.

She felt Jarad turning her in his arms until her face was pressed against his chest. "It's okay, sweetheart," he crooned against her ear. "Let it out."

She pushed against his shoulders, stepping back

out of his embrace. "I don't want to cry," she said, quickly wiping at her eyes as she turned her back to him. "I'm fine." She took a deep breath, trying to gain control over her emotions. When she looked back at Jarad, he was regarding her through narrowed eyes. "I'd better go," she said.

She was shutting him out, and he had no idea what to say to convince her to let him in. It was galling to him, as a man who spent his working life coaxing emotion out of people for the sake of their performance. But this wasn't a movie set. There were no cameras waiting, no lights, and he couldn't yell "cut" if he didn't like how things turned out.

She moved to walk past him, toward the door. He grabbed her arm and swung her around to face him. "Why not, Ariel?" She seemed to think tears were a particular failing in herself, both now and as a young girl. "Everybody needs to let loose once in a while."

"I don't," she challenged, her eyes glistening with tears, belying her words. "I can't afford to. What good would I be to anyone if they came to me in tears and I sobbed right along with them. People need someone to comfort and support them, not fall apart with them."

Jarad wondered briefly if there were anyone to comfort and support her if she cried, but he knew she'd never allow anyone to see her in what she would consider a moment of weakness.

He tilted her head upward, with a finger under her chin. "There're only the two of us here now," he said softly. "You don't have to be strong for me. I can handle a few tears. In fact, I'd welcome them."

Backlit from the lamp in his room, his eyes seemed incredibly fluid. That could be a visual trick, she noted, as she felt the salty sting of her own tears.

She couldn't fight it anymore. She couldn't fight him anymore. Wrapping her arms around his waist, she wept with the intensity of a child. All the tears she'd stored inside slid relentlessly, endlessly down her cheeks. Jarad held her to him, his hands moving in soothing motions over her back. Her sobs tore at his heart, but he didn't dare try to get her to stop after all he'd done to bring it on. Jarad kissed her eyelids, the sides of her face, smoothing away the salty drops with his lips, until her sobbing became more sniffling than tears.

"I'm sorry," she said, lifting her head to look at him. She almost started in again. There were tears in his eyes, too.

"And you called me a softy," she teased.

"Guilty as charged." He raised a hand as if being sworn in. He brought it down to cup her chin, tilting her face up to his. "Are you okay?"

She nodded. She felt more than okay. It was as if she'd been carrying around a heavy burden and she finally had the sense to put it down. "Thank you."

"For what?"

He didn't understand what he'd done for her. It was rare to find someone who would simply hold you if you cried, without also trying to silence. Rather than try to explain it, she went up on tiptoe and pressed her lips to his.

She intended the kiss to be a sweet expression of her thanks, but it turned into so much more. She clung to his shoulders for balance. With one arm around her waist, his other hand was free to explore. It slid down her back to cup her bottom, then traveled back over her waist, her rib cage, one sensitive, malleable breast. Then his head bent to sample what his roving hand had found. Pushing aside the thin lavender material, he made a pleased sound, realizing she wore nothing at all underneath her robe.

She gasped and arched her back as his tongue danced over her tender flesh. He concentrated on one eager peak then the other, until she moaned and clutched his back.

Then he kissed her senseless. At least more senseless than she'd been before. Lifting his head, intense brown eyes bored into hers. "Is it time to say yes, Ari?"

God, she wanted to. She practically ached with wanting him. But she had to consider where they were. "I . . . w-we can't. Not here." She laid her face against his chest, trembling a little.

"I know." He stroked her hair, letting his hand settle on her back. "Is that the only reason?"

Could he possibly doubt she wanted him? "I, unlike you, um, I haven't had much practice." She buried her face in his chest.

He burst out laughing and she was mortified, refusing to look at him, though he tried to coax her to.

"Oh, honey," he said finally. "You should know I'm more talk than action by now." He brushed back her hair and kissed her forehead. "Go on back to bed, sweetheart. We'll talk about it tomorrow."

The next day dawned a glorious day. The sun was warm, with a gentle sea breeze from the east. Only a few puffy white clouds spoiled the perfect

blue sky overhead. There couldn't be a better setting for a wedding.

Ariel showered and dressed quickly in a sleeveless
beige jumpsuit and white sneakers. She didn't
bother to put on any makeup or fuss with her hair.
Jenny's hairstylist would be coming by later to take
care of that. She wrapped an elastic band around
the ponytail she created, then headed out the door.

She was halfway down the stairs when the doorbell rang. "I'll get it," she called to anyone listening.

Diana Windsor strutted past her daughter, pausing just briefly enough to kiss her on the cheek.
She wore the summer-weight cape Ariel had given
her for her last birthday. Underneath she wore a
beige raw silk shirt and matching pants. "Mother,"
she called, stepping into the expansive foyer and
looking around. "We're here!"

Ariel was about to suggest she try the dining
room, but her mother was already headed in that
direction. Falling in step behind her was her husband. "Hi, Daddy," Ariel said as he entered the
foyer. He wore a pair of casual pants and a blue
short-sleeved shirt. As always, the two of them were
a study in contrasts.

"Hi, muffin. Did you see which way the tornado
went?" He ruffled her hair as he passed by. She
smiled back warmly. No amount of coaxing had
persuaded Steve Windsor that his nearly twenty-
eight-year-old daughter was past the age when pet
names like muffin or sweetie or the one she hated
most, little witch, were usually appreciated.

"Dining room."

Ariel followed him, intending to get a cup of coffee and relax in the sitting room. The mere sight
of people eating that early in the morning was

enough to turn her stomach. Her mother was performing her usual ritual of kissing everyone in sight on the cheek; first Gran, then a bedraggled-looking Jenny, then Charlie and finally Mrs. Thompson, who brought in fresh coffee. "Isn't it a glorious day for a wedding?" she announced.

"Yes, Diana," Steve said dryly. "Now sit down and have some breakfast." Looking around the table he said, "She's been saying that all morning."

"I have every right to be excited. It's not every day my only niece gets married."

"Be excited after breakfast, would you. It's too early in the morning to be so exuberant."

"Ariel, sit down and have something to eat."

"Mother, you know very well I haven't had a meal before noon in my entire life. Coffee will do me just fine." She added milk to her cup.

"By the way, Mother," Diana said, helping herself to two strips of bacon. "Didn't you tell me that Bob Naughton's son was here? I've been looking forward to seeing him again. He was such a nice boy."

Ariel looked up from the task of stirring her coffee to find three pairs of eyes staring at her: Jenny's, Gran's and Mrs. Thompson's. "I don't know where he is," she said defensively. She saw her mother's eyebrows raise questioningly. She would have to wonder awhile longer, Ariel decided. She tucked a copy of the newspaper under one arm. She picked up her coffee cup in the other hand. "If anyone wants me, I'll be in the sitting room."

The trip there was a precarious one. She'd filled the cup to the rim, and it teetered in its saucer as she walked. Opening the door was a strange balancing act, which might have been successful if she hadn't found Jarad seated on the sofa. He was reading a copy of the *Vineyard Gazette*, a pair of glasses perched on his nose. She stopped short, spilling her coffee. She dropped her paper as the hot liquid splattered her hand.

"Darn it," she gasped, switching the saucer to the other hand.

Jarad was on his feet immediately, coming to her side. "Are you all right?"

"Sure. I just love burning the daylights out of myself." She was laughing, but it really did hurt a lot.

He took the cup from her and led her over to the sofa. "Sit down. I'll get some ice." He set her cup down on the table next to his. He discarded his glasses before going to the small refrigerator in the bar which had already been restocked with fresh ice.

Ariel plopped down on the sofa, feeling petulant. He was treating her like she was three years old. "You're being ridiculous. In the first place, you're not supposed to put ice on a burn. It's too much of a shock to the skin." She picked up his glasses, holding up the lenses so she could look through them.

"Stop arguing with me, woman." He sat close to her on the sofa. He took the glasses from her, placing them on the table. "Give me your hand."

His tone was light, but she didn't think he'd take no for an answer. She held out her hand, which he inspected. He placed the ice wrapped in a cloth napkin on her seared skin. She had to admit that it did feel better. She rested the offended hand on her lap, using the other hand to hold the ice.

"That's a good girl."

She gave him a venomous look. "Woman. Contrary to macho opinion, any female over the age of eighteen is a woman."

"Not if they're under five feet tall. Isn't there a height requirement?"

"No there's not. And I am over five feet tall. I'm five feet two inches."

"Short."

"I prefer to think of it as petite. And I thought I already expressed my feelings about tall people picking on shorter ones."

"You're guilty of the same thing, you know. You called me 'big' twice." He draped his arm behind her on the sofa.

"I thought men liked to be considered big," she said saucily.

"Not when words like oaf and idiot are attached to it. And I'm not that tall, barely six feet."

"Really?" How odd, when he seemed to fill up whatever room he was in. Even standing alongside Charlie and Dan, who were two self-confessed tall men, her eyes went naturally to him.

The ice on her hand was beginning to melt, soaking the leg of her jumpsuit. She placed the dripping bundle on top of her coffee cup. "That's better," she said, sitting back.

"Speaking of feeling better." He rubbed the arm of her scalded hand. "How are you doing today?"

"I'm fine." She smiled demurely. "I hope I didn't wrinkle your shoulder permanently, crying all over it like that."

He shook his head. "I've got this other dry one over here, too." He pointed to it. "Just in case."

"I don't think I'll be needing it." She snuggled closer to him. "It occurs to me you never did tell me what was bothering you last night."

"Nothing important. It must have been the full moon."

He wasn't going to tell her, and she didn't want to press him. At least, whatever it was didn't seem to be upsetting him anymore. She supposed she could live with that for now. "Are you ready for the wedding?" she asked.

"Looking forward to it. I hope everything goes well for Jenny. She's a great girl." He smiled devilishly.

"Woman," she corrected.

"Yes, woman. In fact, I think your whole family is pretty terrific."

"That reminds me. My mother got here this morning. She was looking for you."

"I remember her. Tall, thin, red hair." Ariel nodded. "I think I had a crush on her."

"On my mother?"

"She's a *woman*, isn't she? And you said she was looking for me."

"My father is here, too."

Jarad let out a heavy sigh. "Another boyhood fantasy shot to hell."

She laughed, looking up at him. "You are a crazy person, do you know that?"

"I'm crazy about you." He smiled seductively, and his eyes on her were intense. "Why do you have to be so cute?"

Ariel swallowed hard. How was it that they could sit there so long, as companionably as old friends, then a glance and a few words could cause such a reaction in her. "I-I'm not."

"I forgot. Short people are never cute. How about gorgeous? Sexy? Beautiful? You take your pick."

That wasn't what she meant, but she had no time

to tell him that. His lips met hers in a kiss made brief by the sound of coughing behind them.

"I hate to interrupt." Diana Windsor stood in the doorway, one hand resting on the frame. "There's a phone call for Jarad in the kitchen."

"Hello, Mrs. Windsor. It's good to see you again." Jarad rose to kiss her on the cheek.

"You certainly are a handsome thing, aren't you? Go answer your phone call. I'll talk to you again later. And call me Diana. Mrs. Windsor sounds so old."

"Hate to interrupt, Mother? You? I thought that was one of your favorite pastimes." Jarad had gone, and Diana had taken his place on the sofa.

"There's no need to be snide with your mother. I must say I'm surprised to see that what Gran and Jenny told me was true. I thought you'd given up on men."

"I never said that. I said they were fine as long as they stayed in their proper place. There is a bit of difference between those two sentiments."

"Not really." Diana shifted to face her daughter. "Any man worth having isn't going to stand for your sort of nonsense. You couldn't respect a man who would let you walk all over him. That's why you're not getting married too, you know. You're depriving me of planning your wedding."

"Mother! Aren't you the one who raised me to take care of myself, to never have to lean on anyone else for anything?"

"Yes. And I may have done my job too well. No woman should need a man in her life to make it complete, but every woman should be able to have a man—to share your life with, to see you through the good times as well as the bad. That's what husbands are for."

Ariel studied her mother's concerned face. "Why didn't you ever tell me this before?"

"You would have accused me of meddling in your life as you always have."

"That's what children are for."

Diana straightened the edge of her daughter's collar. "At the risk of pressing my luck, I have to ask, are things between you and Jarad getting serious?"

"I've known him precisely six days. What of consequence could happen in that time?"

Her mother gave her a look that suggested she knew precisely what could have happened. Leave it to her mother to boil things down to the most elemental level.

Ariel got up and took their cups to the bar. "Jarad and I are attracted to each other. Physically, I mean."

"That's a start."

"But that's all there is to it."

Ariel herself didn't believe that anymore. She liked him as a person, too. It was strange to admit she liked being able to turn to him, to trust him with what she was feeling. But there was no use getting her mother's hopes up. It was only an experiment. One that was due to end in a little over two weeks. It would do her good to remember that herself.

"How can you possibly know that?"

She turned around, resting her hands on the bar behind her. "He lives in California. I live in New York."

"So do lots of filmmakers. It's like a second Hollywood."

"How do you know that?"

"Your grandmother is a wealth of information. What other excuses are you going to give me?"

"Excuses for what? Why I haven't run off with him to Acapulco yet?"

"No, why nothing could ever come of your relationship. I know that's what you're thinking."

"I'm not sure what our relationship is. Half the time we spend fighting. The other half we're . . ."

"Making up?"

"Yes."

"Oh, Ariel," Diana said, putting her arm around her daughter's shoulders. "How can you be a psychologist and know so little about men and women?"

Ariel put her arm around her mother's waist. "Maybe that's the problem," Ariel said thoughtfully. "When I see people they're at their worst. I see so much of what's wrong, how do you ever know when something is right?"

"You have to trust your heart," Diana said, giving her daughter a squeeze. "You have to have faith."

That sounded so simple. But she knew many women who had done just that, who had allowed their feelings to dominate their common sense. They were swept away by love, and when the ride was over, they found themselves married to men who were abusive or cheated or were wrong for them in some other way. She didn't want things to turn out that way for her or Jarad.

"You'd better go help Jenny get ready for the wedding," Ariel's mother said, walking her to the door. "But remember what I said."

Ariel nodded. "I will."

Diana Windsor watched her daughter walk out of the room. "Please, let me have done the right thing," she begged, looking heavenward. After a moment she smiled. It would be all right. Some mother's intuition told her so.

"There you are," she heard Steve say from behind her. "Are you ready to help supervise the festivities."

"Strangely enough, yes." She walked over and put her arms around him. "I love you," she said, kissing him briefly on the mouth.

Not a stupid man, he kissed her back with equal passion. "What was that for?"

Diana shrugged. "Nothing." *For teaching me how to love. Now it's time someone taught our daughter the same thing.*

# Eight

"Where have you been all day?" Jenny asked when she saw Ariel enter her room through the connecting bathroom. Jenny left her place at the window to claim one of the wicker chairs. Ariel sat down in the other.

"If I didn't know better, I'd think it was the Twilight Zone."

"I'm not even going to ask." Jenny's eyes focused on the package in Ariel's hands. "What's in the box?"

Ariel presented the medium-sized square box. "It's goodies for you."

"Oh? This couldn't have anything to do with my wedding today, could it?"

"Stop talking and open the box."

Jenny did as she was told. "What is all this stuff?"

"You're doing it all wrong. Let me do this." She leaned over Jenny, searching for a gray velvet box. She held the box against her chest. "You already have something old—your mother's dress. Now you need something new." She handed the box to Jenny. Opening the lid, Jenny revealed a bracelet made of three perfect strands of pearls. The clasp was an ornate gold design. "I had my dad make that up for you."

"You didn't." Jenny laid the bracelet against one palm. "It's gorgeous."

"He's a jeweler. What else was I going to have him do. Then something borrowed." A pair of matching earrings and a necklace were in a larger box.

"I can't borrow these. They were your eighteenth birthday present."

"If you don't wear them you won't have anything borrowed. You can't get married without something borrowed."

"Thank you, Ari." Jenny leaned over and hugged her. "I wondered why you told me not to pick out any jewelry. I didn't expect this."

"The operative word here is borrowed. Remember that. Except for the bracelet, of course."

"Maybe I'll get to lend it to you one of these days."

"Yeah, right." It wasn't as dim a possibility as it once was, but that discussion would have to wait for another time.

"Finally, something blue." Ariel produced the lacy blue garter she'd gotten in Edgartown and swung it around on her finger. "You thought I forgot about that tradition, didn't you?"

"No way," Jenny said, waving her hand dismissingly. "I refuse to have a room full of people gawking at my legs. The most I'll do is throw the bouquet."

"Make sure not to throw it in my direction, okay. If I catch it, my mother will take it as an omen and start baking the wedding cake."

Jenny sighed, and Ariel dreaded what she knew was coming. Jenny was going to ask her about Jarad, and Ariel had no idea what to tell her.

"Before I get married," Jenny began, "there's

one question I have to ask you. And you have to
answer truthfully. You've been smiling and sighing
these last couple of days, and you picked over your
dinner last night. Are you falling in love with
Jarad?"

She'd been asking herself that same question for
the last hour. She'd known she was attracted to
him. That she could gauge. Falling in love was
strange territory, despite any supposed "signs of
love" she might be exhibiting. What to call what
she was feeling was a mystery. "Honestly, I don't
know."

"All right! There's hope for you yet."

" 'I don't know' is cause for celebration?"

"A week ago you would have told me I'd lost my
mind just for asking the question." Jenny sat back
in her chair, putting her hands on the back of her
head. "I am to be congratulated on this."

"You? What did you do?"

"I thought up the experiment," Jenny said, as if
she'd discovered the cure for the common cold.
"It isn't merely a test anymore, is it?"

"I don't know," Ariel said, helplessly.

"Listen, you," Jenny said, getting up. "You'd better not do anything to mess this up. Don't look at
me like that. I know how you are. I think Jarad's
a terrific guy. I wouldn't mind having him for a
cousin-in-law."

"Aren't you getting a little ahead of things?"

"Maybe. But you'll be gone by the time I get
back. This is probably the last opportunity I'll have
to advise you."

"That's an interesting choice of words. 'Advise
me.' Lecture me is more like it. You'll have to finish while we get ready, or you'll be late to your
own wedding. Are you nervous?"

"I'm petrified." Jenny touched her hand to her forehead. "I almost forgot. I have something for you, too." She went to her closet and pulled down a flat, rectangular box. "Wear it in good health."

Wrapped in lavender tissue paper was a pale pink bustier, garter belt and matching panties made completely of lace. A pair of sheer stockings in the same color lay beneath them.

"We are getting quite risqué in our old age." Ariel stood in front of the full-length mirror behind Jenny's door and held the bustier up in front of her. "It's beautiful, but what made you think of getting this for me?"

"Oh, I don't know. I was hoping Jarad would see you in it. It would drive him wild."

"Jenny!"

"I'm incorrigible. I know." Jenny got up and sat on the bed, closer to where Ariel stood. "But seriously, if it should come to that," Jenny opened the drawer to her nightstand and pulled out a package wrapped in plastic, "you might need these."

Jenny tossed the box to her, and Ariel caught it in one hand. Ariel smiled, looking down at the box of three each of three different kinds of condoms. "You think of everything, don't you?"

With a voice full of mock solemnity, she said, "I try, I try."

The ceremony went off perfectly. The string quartet Gran hired to play the wedding march sounded melodious and nostalgic as Ariel walked down the aisle. She nearly stumbled when she saw Jarad sitting in the first row between her mother and Gran. He looked so darkly handsome in the black tuxedo and white shirt he wore. His eyes were on her, not Jenny, as the music swelled declaring the entrance of the bride.

He stood, and his heated look was like a daring caress on her skin. His gaze traveled from her eyes to her throat, to the décolletage of her gown and back again. It was a wonder she didn't drop the nosegay she carried.

After the ceremony, she congratulated Jenny and Dan, who both practically illuminated the room with glowing smiles. There was a throng of well-wishers waiting to congratulate the bride and groom, so Ariel made her way toward the ballroom. That's where the new Mr. and Mrs. Edwards were scheduled to end up.

A bar was set up at one corner of the large room. She asked for a mimosa, a delicious blend of champagne and orange juice. After all the excitement, the drink was cool and calming. The band was playing an easy ballad. That helped, too.

"You look good enough to eat." Jarad's voice was a sensual growl in her ear. His hands were at her shoulders, turning her to face him.

"Sorry, I'm not on the menu." She looked up at him, smiling playfully.

"You will be." His hand slid down her bare back, drawing her closer.

"Jarad, cut it out," she protested. "My parents are standing no more than ten feet away from us."

"And you are a very private person."

Ariel wondered what made him say that. "Yes."

"I think the newlyweds have come in." The music switched smoothly to a waltz meter. Dan was leading Jenny to the center of the floor for the first dance. They moved beautifully together, she thought.

Once the guests were invited to join in, Jarad extended his arm gallantly. "Shall we?"

Since the wedding party was so small, Jenny decided to forgo the traditional dictates of who dances with whom, leaving her free to dance with Jarad. "Yes, we shall," she said, taking his arm and following him to the dance floor.

He was a wonderful dancer, she thought as they glided over the floor. His smoother, surer steps made up for her clumsier ones. She had thought Jenny was wasting her money taking waltzing lessons. Now she wished she'd done the same thing.

Looking around the room, Ariel felt contentment wash over her. There were so many people there to wish Dan and Jenny well—all the friends they'd known all their lives as well as some of the more famous residents of the island. Everyone looked so happy and festive.

Jenny and Dan were still at the center of the floor. Jenny's long train was draped over her left arm. The chapel-length veil and mantilla were replaced by a large white bow at the nape of her neck. She looked just like the woman in the old photo album wearing that same dress with the plunging back and full skirt. Jenny wore the dress as a tribute to the mother she'd never really known and no longer missed.

She saw her own mother and father dancing animatedly. Her mother's hair was pulled back in a sleek chignon, exposing the elaborately sequined shoulders of her form-fitting mauve gown. Gran wore a similar dress, though less clingy, in pastel pink.

It was wonderful to have them all together again. She couldn't remember the last time all of them were in one place. Too bad her parents had to leave that night to catch up with their cruise.

"It's a good thing you're so little," Jarad said when she'd stepped on his foot for the fourth time. "If you were any heavier it might actually hurt."

"Oh?" She stepped on his foot on purpose this time.

"See what I mean?"

He spun her around, leaving her breathless. She held onto him tightly to steady herself. "Where did you learn to avoid stepping on women's toes?"

"My mother believes there are three things every man should be able to do: take out the trash, kill bugs and be able to dance well enough not to embarrass his wife on the dance floor."

He dipped her as the music ended. "Show-off," she told him, nudging him with her elbow when he released her so they could applaud. The musicians quickly resumed, playing another slow number. Jarad started leading her around the floor before she had time to say anything.

"I'm the maid of honor. I'm supposed to mingle."

"The waiters are handing out champagne for the toast. After that you can mingle." He drew her closer into the circle of his arms. His voice was low and sensuous when he asked, "Any more protests?"

"Not a one." She rested her head against his chest, savoring the feeling of being in his arms. His cheek rested against her temple, as his hand made slow circular movements on her back. What was he thinking, she wondered as he held her so tightly against him. These past few days, she'd been so concerned about her own feelings, she hadn't really considered his. He'd been an experiment to her, but what was she to him? Was he rocked by the same powerful emotions he aroused in her, or was she merely a summer fling he'd forget about as soon as their time together was over?

The song ended, and the best man wished the couple happiness and prosperity. Ariel sipped deeply from her glass, watching Jarad over the rim. He took her free hand in his, raising it to his lips to kiss her palm. "Go do your mingling," he told her. "But save all the slow dances for me."

"We'll see," Ariel said. Then she disappeared into the crowd.

An hour later, Jarad stood by the bar nursing a Scotch. He was tired of talking with people he didn't know just to be polite. Or answering tactless questions about his relationship with Ariel. He supposed it was the nature of small-town people to be inquisitive about their own, but enough was enough.

"How are you doing there, son?" Steve Windsor punched him playfully on the arm. "You look like I feel."

"How's that?" Jarad smiled. He liked Steve. He was an easygoing, affable man. Besides, any man that could stay married to Diana Windsor was okay by him.

"Like you've just been marooned. You haven't seen my wife in the last half hour, have you?"

Jarad shook his head. "Sorry."

"They're in their element now. We don't stand a chance." Steve leaned closer to him, as if to tell him a secret. "The curse of the Ludlow women."

Jarad sighed. "Not you, too, Steve. I've already been given the treatment."

"Take a look at the group of people over there. Do you notice anything strange?" Steve nodded in the direction of some men standing a few feet away. They ranged in age from middle thirties to late forties. As one of the men shifted position, Jarad got a glimpse of something pink at the center. It was Ariel. She was holding a glass of what looked like wine, her head tilted back in laughter. As if knowing he watched her, she turned to look at him. She shrugged her shoulders and waved, then went back to the conversation.

"Wipe that scowl off your face, young man. She's not doing it on purpose. She's being polite. Ludlow women don't flirt, and they don't like it if you flirt with them either. On top of that, they're bright, witty—get them in a room full of people and watch the men disappear."

Jarad had never thought of himself as a jealous man, but that disturbed him. He fought down the urge to go over and break up her little encounter group. He knew what her reaction to that would be. He'd be lucky if she'd speak to him for the rest of the night. She valued her independence, and he had to respect that. But did she have to make him insane in the bargain? "What do you do when this happens?"

"Nothing. I go find some other poor soul to commiserate with." Steve poked him in the ribs with his elbow, and they both laughed.

"You boys haven't seen Isabel, have you?" Charlie came over and clapped Steve on the back. "I thought it was just going to be you and me again, old boy. I see we have a new member."

"One of us really should have warned him. Why didn't you say something, Charlie?"

"I did. He didn't believe me. None of you did. It serves you right. Now you're stuck with them for the rest of your lives. Jarad's got the worst of 'em."

"Isn't that the truth." Steve gave a mock shudder. "She's my daughter and I love her, but I wouldn't want to be the man to fall in love with her. That one'll drive you nuts."

Jarad laughed. There had been times in the past few days when be could have gladly throttled her. Like now. "Any advice for the new kid on the block?"

"Run. It's your sixth day, isn't it?"

He had thought of that. Last night. If he hadn't seen her, he might have been able to do it. No, that wasn't true. He couldn't have left her without being haunted by those green eyes the rest of his life.

"Be serious, Charlie," Steve admonished. "If you love her or think you might, go after her. She isn't going to come to you. If you have anything less serious in mind, leave her alone. She doesn't need that kind of heartache. And if you hurt her, you're going to have to answer to me."

"Thanks, Steve," Jarad said, handing him his glass. He saw Ariel walking toward him. The band had struck up an old ballad, one of his favorites. They'd already missed three of their slow dances together. He didn't want to miss another.

"Why didn't you come and rescue me?" Ariel asked once they were on the dance floor. "I know you saw me over there."

"You looked like you were having a good time."

"I was nearly snoring in my drink. I've known most of those men since I was a child." She wondered what had happened to make him so testy with her. He couldn't be jealous, could he? How amazing! She couldn't keep from smiling as she added, "I was just being polite."

He kissed that smile right off her face. "Jarad!" she exclaimed, her chest heaving. "Don't you have any manners?"

"Of course I do. But in California we kiss our

women whenever and wherever we want to. We're not quite so stuffy as Vineyarders."

"Our women? I didn't know there had been a cattle roundup."

"You know what I mean." His gaze wandered over her face, the golden expanse of her bare shoulders, then back to her face. "You'd better stop giving me orders before I really show my lack of good taste." The hand on her back traveled lower, to the tiny row of buttons holding her dress together. She reached around a hand to stop him before he reached her derriere.

"Okay, okay," she conceded. "I'll keep my small-town mores to myself. Now can we stop fighting and start dancing?"

"I've been dancing all along. What have you been doing?"

"An endurance marathon." To soften her words she touched her fingertips to the side of his face. He turned his head and kissed the pad of her thumb. Ariel inhaled deeply, as a wave of heat rushed through her at his simple touch. "Do me a favor?"

"Anything, sweetheart."

"Shut up and kiss me."

Laughing, Jarad did as he was told.


Hours later, Ariel stood in the bathroom on the first floor surveying her reflection. Her makeup was holding up, but her hair needed some adjustment. That was partially due to Jenny's aim in throwing the bouquet. Ariel hadn't exactly caught it; it had stuck in her hair. She'd had no choice but to accept it. Jenny had hugged her after that, whispering in her ear, "Tell your mother to make it chocolate."

Then Jenny and Dan had driven off, showered in rice. That was half an hour ago. Most of the guests had left since then. The few stragglers were still dancing in the ballroom or saying their goodbyes in the foyer.

Finally satisfied with her appearance, Ariel stored her little purse under the sink cabinet. Jarad was waiting for her at the bar, and she'd already taken more than the fifteen minutes she'd said she'd be.

Exiting the bathroom, she felt a hand on her arm. She turned to see who was trying to get her attention, her eyes widening in surprise to find Peter standing in front of her. He was dressed appropriately in a dark suit, but his tie was askew, and, if she wasn't mistaken, he'd had more than his share to drink.

"What are you doing here, Peter?"

He shrugged. "I crashed. I wanted to see you."

"Well, you've seen me. I think you'd better leave."

His grip on her arm tightened. "There's something I want to talk to you about."

She shrugged out of his grasp. "Couldn't we do this some other time?" She spoke as diplomatically as she could. There was no point in antagonizing a drunk man. "I have to get back."

"I know. He's waiting for you."

Peter's voice was getting louder and his features became more belligerent. This would never do, she realized. Departing guests still crowded the foyer and a few of them had turned to look at them. "Let's go out on the patio," she suggested. "We can talk out there." And maybe the fresh air would sober him up a little.

She led the way down the hall and onto the tiled floor. He followed her sullenly, slamming the glass doors shut behind him.

"Peter, if you don't tell me what this is about, I'm going to go back inside and leave you here. It's too cold for this nonsense."

"Take a look at this."

He reached inside his jacket, pulling out a folded newspaper. He flung it on the patio table. She walked over to it and picked it up. She could barely make out the masthead in the moonlight. "When did you start reading this rag?" That's what Jared called them, wasn't it?

"I didn't have to read it. Just look at the picture."

Ariel let out a sigh, feeling nearly exasperated. What was the point of all this? "Turn on the light, please. It's on the left-hand side of the door."

He did so, and the cover, dominated by a single photograph, was illuminated. It pictured a man carrying a woman out of the ocean onto the beach. It took her several moments to recognize them. It was her and Jarad. She read the caption three times to make sure. "Naughton's Newest Playmate."

"Oh my God," she gasped. Someone must have been following them around and they hadn't known. No wonder Jarad hated these papers. The reporter hadn't even had the courage to ask for an interview. She knew Jarad would have said no, but he wouldn't have punched the guy out as seemed to be fashionable these days. Well, she didn't think he would. Right now, she was mad enough to take on the photographer herself.

Sinking down into the chair behind her, she nearly tore the first page off in a rage. A full page was devoted to the story, an extensive amount of copy punctuated with graphic photographs. The two of them on the beach, by the basketball courts, their kiss on the ferry.

She put her face in her hands, feeling mortified. A nation full of strangers would be staring at her picture.

She felt a hand on her shoulder. "I thought you should see that."

She'd forgotten Peter was standing there. "Thank you." She looked up at him. He looked at her so compassionately. Maybe she had been wrong about him. "I've been so busy, I haven't had time to go by a newsstand, let alone read a paper."

"I figured as much."

She turned back to the paper. "I can't believe this. It says here that I'm going to star in Jarad's next picture. Can you imagine? Don't these people bother to check their so-called facts?"

"Probably not. These sort of papers aren't known for their accuracy."

"I suppose not." She stood up, grabbing the paper. "I need to tell Jarad about this."

"Not yet." Peter's hands were on her shoulders. "You need to calm down first. Come take a walk with me. You'll only upset him if he sees you like this."

She started to protest, then changed her mind. She wouldn't tell Jarad about this tonight. They'd had such a lovely time. There was no point in ruining their evening over some nonsense printed in the paper. After the initial shock, she wasn't really angry about it anymore for herself. It was how he would react to it that troubled her. What she needed was a few moments to collect herself. She'd do that a lot better without Peter around.

"Why don't I walk you to your car?" she suggested.

"Didn't bring it. Well, only part of the way. I parked down by the Steamship Authority. Walk me down to the beach?"

*How convenient.* That way, no one could recognize his car and question his being there. She narrowed her eyes, watching him. Maybe she was being paranoid, but she sensed there was more to his guileless request than he let on. She shrugged. At least this way, she'd be sure he left. He extended a hand to her, which she ignored. "Let's go."

She walked with him to the end of the yard, stopping when they reached the sand. Ariel crossed her arms in front of her. "I guess this is good night."

"It doesn't have to be."

Ariel tensed as his hands grasped her arms, just above her elbows. He couldn't possibly believe she was interested in reviving her relationship with him. "We've been through this before, haven't we? What was it, six years ago?"

"Seven, but I never stopped thinking about you." His hands roved up her arms, trying to draw her closer, but her hands at his shoulders prevented it. "Have you forgotten what we had together?"

What they'd had was precisely nothing. She couldn't tell him that. She could smell the liquor on his breath, and he was beginning to scare her. Sober, she doubted he would do anything to hurt her physically. In his present condition, she wasn't so sure.

Whatever he intended, she was certain he'd had it planned when he'd lured her down to the beach. She'd been stupid enough to oblige him. "Peter," she said, trying to sound calm. "That was a very long time ago."

"Not so long that I don't remember what it's like to hold you in my arms." His hands slid around her back. She assumed he was trying to be seductive, but all he inspired in her was revulsion. "I just thought . . ."

She was beginning to get the picture now. "You just thought I'd be so grateful you showed me that newspaper, I'd fall into your arms. Well, that isn't going to happen. Now let go of me, or I'm going to scream."

"Go ahead. Scream your head off. Who'll hear you?"

It had been a bluff, and he'd called her on it. Who would hear her over the music up at the house and the lapping of the waves on the shore. "Someone will notice I'm gone." *Please let Jarad notice I'm gone,* she prayed silently.

"Tonight maybe," he said, so low she barely heard him. "He'll tire of you just like he has all the others."

"All what others?"

"You should read the article. It gives a lot of insight into the sort of man you've chosen to have an affair with."

"We are not having an affair. Jarad and I are friends."

"Yeah, right," Peter drawled sarcastically. He gave a short bitter laugh. "Did you know I saw the two of you together? That day you were on the beach. You used to tell me you wanted to be my friend. You never kissed me the way I saw you kissing him." He moved to kiss her, but she turned her face quickly. His lips landed clumsily on her ear.

How long had he been watching them? she wondered. And from where? He hadn't been close enough for her to see him, so how had he seen them? The whole thing struck her as being incredibly warped.

"What does it take for me to get to you?" Peter demanded, shaking her. "After some of the things I said to you, any other woman would have cried or at the very least slapped my face. Not you. You just stared at me with those cold eyes of yours and walked out."

She had cried, later when she was alone. She had no intention of allowing him to make her that upset again. She pushed against his chest with both hands, breaking his hold on her.

"Go home, Peter, and I will try to forget I saw you here tonight." Gathering her skirt, she started walking back toward the house.

She let out a heavy sigh, grateful nothing more serious had happened. Then she felt his hand on her arm, spinning her around. He pulled her so close to him that their faces were only inches apart.

"It would take the human torch to melt you, wouldn't it, baby?" He pulled her closer, making her stumble. He hauled her up, giving her a shake so hard her head snapped back on her shoulders. "Tell me, ice princess, does *he* have what it takes or does he wear his thermal underwear when he gets in bed with you?"

"Stop it," she cried, but her throat was tight with emotion. "What is the matter with you?"

He continued as if she hadn't spoken. "Maybe I should tell your boyfriend what a cold-hearted bitch you really are."

"Maybe you should get your hands off her if you want to live through the next five minutes."

Ariel froze, hearing Jarad's voice. He sounded so calm, but there was a deadly undercurrent to his words that made the hair on the back of her neck bristle. Peter let go of her and she turned to see Jarad standing a few feet away from her. She saw his blatantly hostile stance, saw his hands fisted at his sides. Before she could say anything, Peter grabbed her waist, pushing her behind him.

Ariel shrieked, feeling Peter's hands on her. She hadn't imagined Peter capable of moving that fast in his drunken state. "Back off man," Peter yelled. "The lady and I were just having a conversation."

"Which is now over."

Ariel closed her eyes a moment, silently praying for strength. The two of them were faced off like a couple of rams at a rutting contest. Jarad was coming toward them. Lord only knew what would happen if the two of them got within striking distance of each other. Of the two, Jarad was surely the taller, the stronger, the more sober—and the angrier.

She had to get Peter out of there. No matter what he'd done, she didn't want to see Peter hurt. Whatever his problem was, he wasn't himself. That much she was sure of. The Peter she'd known wasn't the cruel, hard man who'd been holding her. Before Peter could respond, she stepped in front of him.

"Peter," she said, trying to sound as solicitous as possible. She grabbed his sleeve to get his attention. "Peter, please go back to the house. Please. I'll come inside in a minute."

He looked down at her contemptuously, then shrugged her hands from his arm. "I guess I have my answer, then." To Jarad he said, "Congratulations on thawing the iceberg." Then he turned and staggered back toward the house.

Ariel stood watching him a moment, closing her eyes when she felt Jarad's arms close around her from behind. A tear slipped down her cheek and she wiped it away. "I'm sorry, baby," he said against her ear. "I should have been here. I knew that guy was trouble. You shouldn't have been alone."

She shook her head. It wasn't his fault. She'd been the one stupid enough to come out here with Peter in the first place. It was her psychologist's ego—thinking she had more control over other people's behavior than she actually did. She shuddered, thinking of all the things that could have happened if Jarad hadn't found her.

"You're trembling," Jarad said. "Did he hurt you?" His voice was harsh, and she ran her fingers over his arms to soothe him. She shook her head, still unable to find her voice. Peter hadn't really done anything to her physically. She would never forget the words he'd said to her. They'd chilled every nerve, every sinew, every synapse of her body. She knew he'd been angry when she'd ended their relationship. Yet she'd never known how bitterly he felt toward her.

She wondered how much of his tirade Jarad had heard—certainly that last bit of venom Peter had spewed at her. She shivered, thinking about it. Did he believe what Peter had said about her? Did he think less of her because of it? He turned her in his arms so that she was facing him, but she couldn't look at him. She buried her face against his chest, feeling mortified for the second time that evening. She wished he'd never come out here to witness her humiliation, even though his presence had ended it.

"I'm sorry you had to hear all that," she said.

His hands stroked over her bare back, the nape of her neck, her shoulders. "It's over, sweetheart," he said comfortingly. "It's over."

She knew Peter was gone, but she couldn't stop trembling. She didn't think she'd ever feel warm again. Jarad shrugged out of his jacket, draping it around her shoulders. It held his scent, and she inhaled deeply. "Come on," he said. "I'd better get you back to the house."

Diana Windsor was pacing the foyer when they came inside, arm in arm. She'd changed into one of her many pantsuits in preparation for leaving on their trip. Steve was putting their suitcases back into the car. She was glad he wasn't here to see his daughter's disheveled appearance.

Diana stepped between her daughter and Jarad, putting her arm around Ariel's shoulders. Diana knew something had happened to her daughter, and she was determined to find out what it was.

"What is going on?" Diana asked, leading Ariel toward the kitchen. "First you disappear for half an hour. Now there's a young man passed out in the sitting room. Who is he?"

"You remember Peter, Mother. We dated my sophomore year in college."

Ariel's voice sounded flat, without emotion. That only worried Diana more. She led Ariel to one of the kitchen chairs and practically pushed her into it. "What's he doing here?"

"It's a long story." Jarad came into the kitchen then, carrying a snifter of brandy. He pressed it into her hand. She took a sip without having to be prompted. It burned its way down her throat, warming her.

"I've got plenty of time."

Ariel knew there was no way she was going to get out of giving some sort of explanation to her mother. "Peter was here at the reception tonight. I went outside with him because he said he wanted to talk to me." She shrugged. "It turns out talking wasn't exactly what he had in mind. Luckily, Jarad came along before anything happened."

Diana looked from her daughter to Jarad and back again. There was more to this story than Ariel was telling, but she knew her daughter well enough to know she wouldn't get another word out of her.

"Your father and I are about to leave for the airport. If there's something the matter, we'll stay."

Ariel patted her mother's hand, trying to smile. "No, you'd better go. I'm fine. Enjoy the rest of your cruise."

"I'll take care of her," she heard Jarad say.

"You'd better."

Ariel smiled, genuinely this time. The fiercest lioness had nothing on her mother when it came to protecting her young.

"I suppose I should go," Diana said. "Her father would have a fit if he saw her like this." Ariel leaned forward to accept her mother's kiss. "Good-bye, dear."

Jarad walked her mother out. Sitting there alone, Ariel began to replay Peter's words in her mind. He couldn't be right about her. She wasn't made of ice. How could she be when she knew, looking up at Jarad as he re-entered the kitchen, that she wanted this man more than she'd wanted anything else in her life. His tie was undone, his shirt was opened a button or two, revealing more bronze skin and a hint of dark curly hair. He was a strong, sexy, vital man. She wanted him to make her feel like a woman.

She didn't protest as he took her hand, pulling her to her feet. "It's time we got you into bed," he said. She was surprised to feel a little light-headed when she stood. Then she remembered she hadn't eaten much all day and she wasn't used to drinking brandy. After she stumbled on the stairs the third time, he picked her up and carried her the rest of the way.

Once inside her room, he turned on the light, set her on her feet and hugged her. She hugged him back, running her fingers over his muscled back. "Thank you," she whispered up at him.

He pulled back from her, his eyes searching her face. "For what?"

"Rescuing me." She stood on tiptoe and kissed him on the mouth. His arms came back around her, but he ended the kiss almost immediately.

He set her away from him. "You're welcome. But if you really want to thank me, you'll turn around."

She did so. "Why?"

"So I can get you out of this dress and into your bed." Ariel felt a little thrill run through her as he set to work on the tiny buttons. It only took him a few seconds to undo the buttons it had taken fifteen minutes to close. When he was through she turned around to face him, holding onto the front of the dress. She noticed Jarad's gaze travel from her face to the décolletage of her gown, which was now lower than it had been before.

"Are you going to be all right?" he asked.

"Sure," she said, confused.

"Good night, Ariel," he said, kissing her on the

forehead. "Sleep well." He turned and exited the room.

She stood there a moment, dazed. They were the only people in the house and he was leaving her there alone? Undoubtedly, Gran and Charlie would be back in the morning, and there would go their only chance to be together. Didn't this man have any sense at all?

"Jarad," she called. He appeared at her door almost immediately, looking worried. His shirt was off and his pants were zipped but not buttoned. Ariel sucked in her breath at the sight of him.

"Are you okay?" he asked.

She was still standing where he'd left her, holding the dress up in front of her. Only now, she'd let the dress slip down to reveal the top of the bustier's lacy cups. She smiled at him demurely. "I couldn't unbuckle my sandals." She hadn't tried, but it seemed like a safe thing to say. She sat down on the bed, put one foot on the cover and, with one hand, lifted her gown to her knees, revealing the offending shoe. "Help."

He groaned, sat down on the bed, and took her foot in his lap. His large fingers fumbled with the tiny clasp. In seconds, he slid the sandal from her foot. "Next," he said. When he finished the other shoe, he looked up at her. She was leaning back on her arms. The top of her gown was down about her waist.

"Don't do this to me, Ariel," he said through clenched teeth, his gaze averted from her.

"Do what to you?"

"Tempt me."

She smiled alluringly. "Why not?"

He pushed her feet to the floor and stood. He walked to the door before turning to face her. "It's late, it's been a long, trying day and that brandy went right to your pretty little head. I think it's time you went to bed."

He turned to leave. "Jarad," she said.

"What?" he said, exasperated. He didn't bother to turn around.

Her little bit of confidence fled her. "Could I? Tempt you, I mean."

Then he did turn to face her. She was kneeling amid the taffeta folds of her gown. Her head was down, tilted away from him. "Look at me," he commanded. She did. It broke his heart to see tears in her eyes. "Oh, sweetheart," he said, sitting on the bed next to her. He brushed her tears away with the pads of his thumbs as he cupped her face in his hands. "If you think the rantings of some drunken fool are going to change the way I feel about you, you're going to be disappointed."

"What if it's true?" she whispered.

"How could it be? From the first time I saw you, I wanted you. Why do you think I kissed you on the ferry? I couldn't help myself. I've spent the last few days struggling to keep my hands off you. Do you know how hard it was for me to let you go back to your room last night, after I'd seen and touched and tasted so much of your beautiful skin?" His hands wandered from her face down the side of her throat, to her bare shoulders.

Ariel moaned and her head lolled back on her shoulders. "You don't hold anything back from me, do you sweetheart? No woman made of ice could be as passionate as you are." His words and his breath fanning her heated skin excited her. His lips on her shoulder as he pulled her against him excited her more.

"Then why . . ."

He pulled back to look at her. "I don't want you to go mistaking me for someone else who's made love to you."

She got up from the bed, taking the dress with her. Her back was to him. The dress was at waist level, and she had trouble both holding on to it and walking the few steps away from him she took. She looked at him with fresh tears in her eyes. "Peter never . . . I mean, I—" She couldn't seem to form the words she wanted to say. "There hasn't been anyone else who's made love to me, not really." The dress slid to the floor. "Show me the difference."

He felt about to boil over as his gaze slid over her, dressed only in stockings and several bits of lace. He stood, reached for her, lifted her over the confining circle of the dress and into his arms. If it wasn't every man's fantasy to see his woman dressed in an outfit like that at least once, he didn't know what was. Did she think of herself as his woman? He kissed her as if to brand her so.

He held onto her with one hand and pulled the covers across the bed with the other. He laid her down on the bed gingerly. She looked so soft and vulnerable lying there among the oversized pillows. Was he taking advantage of that vulnerability? If he made love to her now, would she look at him in the morning with regret?

"Are you sure this is what you want?" he asked, praying her answer was anything but "no."

Oh, she was a witch, all right. She had to be to do this to him. In six short, glorious days, she'd made him fall in love with her. The minute he'd taken her in his arms down on the beach, he'd known it. She'd trembled against him so fiercely, he'd wanted to murder that jackass for scaring her like that. Charlie was right. His troubles were only beginning.

In answer, she withdrew the package Jenny had given her from the drawer of her nightstand and placed it on top. She smiled up at him. The look on her face could only be described as shy. "We've got one whole night, Jarad. Let's not waste it."

# Nine

Ariel watched with fascinated eyes as Jarad stood to divest himself of the rest of his clothing. In a few seconds he stood before her, gloriously, unabashedly nude. He was magnificent, she thought, lean yet well-muscled in the way of men used to leading active lives as opposed to working out.

He was watching her, and his gaze caused a heated response in her body. She felt naked, exposed, but in more than a physical way. Jarad was obviously comfortable having a woman's assessing eyes on his body, but she was not. She wasn't beautiful or famous or glamorous as she imagined the women he'd been with to be. From the aroused state of his body, she knew he wanted her. But she was herself only, and she wondered if she would disappoint him.

Then he joined her on the bed, kissing her with more urgency than she'd ever felt in him before. All she could think about was answering his passion with an equal measure of her own.

"Come here," he said, rolling onto his back, pulling her on top of him. One of his hands rested on her back, the other tangled in her elaborate, ruined coiffure. She felt him pulling out pins until the entire mass of her hair spilled down around her shoulders.

She lay on top of him, her breasts flattened against his chest, her legs tangled with his. She moved restlessly as his hands smoothed over her back, and lower to cup her derriere, bringing her hard against him. Her hands roved over his shoulders, the sides of his face, then around his nape, bringing him closer. Brazenly, she kissed him, sliding her tongue over his lower lip, then inside to mate wildly with his own. It was thrilling to hear his groan, feel his arms wind more tightly around her.

He laid her on her back, stroking her hair from her face. He rested alongside her, his head propped up on his elbow. "There's my little temptress," he said, his voice a sultry whisper. His fingers traced the line of lace the bustier created along her breasts. "Who would have thought this was hiding under that dainty pink dress of yours."

She moaned as his fingers dipped lower, grazing her nipples. Then he shifted, sitting up to undo the row of hooks and eyes that held the garment together. She closed her eyes as his head bent to kiss each inch of flesh he uncovered. Self-consciously, she crossed her hands over her breasts when he pushed the material away from her.

"Don't tell me the woman who spent half an hour luring me to her bed is turning modest on me." As he spoke, he gently took both her hands in one of his, which he held over her head. He stroked his other hand over her breasts, her belly, her hips. "You are so lovely."

She blushed, averting her gaze to his chest. "You don't have to say that," she told him.

"I know I don't." He cupped her chin with one hand, forcing her to look at him. "I want to. You are very special to me."

Then he kissed her, and at once the tenor of their lovemaking intensified. His mouth moved over hers hungrily, as his hand cupped a breast, rousing its dark tip to a sensitive, hardened peak. Then his lips followed, suckling at each tender nipple. She moaned, arching against him.

"That's it, baby," he said, his voice harsh, his breathing ragged. He inhaled deeply, fighting for a measure of control. He wanted to take it slow, take his time, please her as she deserved to be pleased. He wanted to prove to her that he wasn't like those other men who'd mistreated her. But she looked so damn feminine and sexy lying there all in lace and silk. He felt his restraint slipping.

He slid her panties over her hips and down her legs until she was free of them. When he was finished, both of her feet were in his lap. He ran his hands along her stockinged legs. He groaned as her toes wiggled provocatively against him.

He rolled down each stocking, allowing his lips and tongue and teeth to savor every inch of her he uncovered. His hands slid under her hips, trying to unfasten her one remaining article of clothing. The clasp wouldn't give, but with one tug she was free. He spread her legs and knelt between them, resting his arms on either side of her. She writhed seductively beneath him as he bent to kiss her.

His hands on her bare skin excited her. His mouth was sweet torment. He nipped and kneaded and tasted every inch of her—except the one spot that cried out for it most. He was teasing her now, as he did in all things. But this time, he'd taken her to a place beyond sanity, apart from reason. She could only focus on the need he'd created in

her and its ultimate fulfillment. "Jarad." It was
more of an exhalation than a word.

"Yes, baby," he said. His hands were at her waist,
and his head bent to trace a circle around her
navel with his tongue. "What do you want me to
do?" She shrugged helplessly, having no words for
what she wanted. His mouth dipped lower, and
lower still, until he found what he sought. Ariel's
back arched off the bed and her hips rocked con-
vulsively in response.

She called to him again, and he came to her,
covering her with his big, powerful body. She was
hot and moist, and she shivered as her body
yielded to him. It was the most exquisite feeling,
having him bonded so intimately with her. She
clasped him to her, letting her hands roam over
his back, his shoulders, his face. She sighed. He
was trembling too.

She kissed him and wrapped her legs around
him as they moved in a rhythm as primal as Adam
and Eve. She breathed in gasps and sighs against
his neck, feeling as if every cell, every nerve ending, was riveted to that most sensitive core of her.
It was like a tide of sensation that ebbed and re-
ceded, spreading further and further each time.

"Jarad," she cried as a wave so powerful washed
over her, that she went completely still, clutching
his shoulders. A moment later she heard Jarad's
throaty groan, and his body shuddered beneath
her fingertips.

Still breathing heavily, Jarad raised himself on his
elbows to gaze down at her. There was such a look
of wonder on her face that he smiled. He laughed
outright when she put her hand to her forehead
and whispered, "Wow."

"That about covers it," he agreed. He, too, felt

awed by their lovemaking. He'd had his share of
lovers, though he wasn't the satyr the papers made
him out to be. Never once had he felt so moved
by a woman. She'd bewitched him, taking him to
the highest highs, wringing every drop of strength
and emotion out of him.

Yet, she left him feeling complete in ways that
were more than just physical. She was in love with
him, too, if only a little bit. She wouldn't have
given herself to him so freely otherwise. Did she
know the depths of her own feelings, he wondered,
or was she fighting what she felt for him as val-
iantly as she tried to keep her other emotions at
bay?

He leaned to one side, stroking his hand over
her body. Her breast heaved in his palm from the
exertion of her breathing. "Are you okay?" he
asked.

"I'm wonderful." She caught his hand in hers.
"You were wonderful." She brought his fingers to
her lips, surprised to find his knuckles bruised.
"When did that happen?" she asked between kisses
to each of his injured fingers.

"It's nothing," he said. He laced his fingers with
hers, bringing her hand to his lips. "It's you who's
wrecked me, sweet Ariel."

She smiled, feeling his words like a curl of
warmth inside her. Cupping his face in her hands,
she kissed him sweetly.

"What was that for?" he asked when she relaxed
back on the pillows.

She shrugged, not knowing what to say. "It
seemed like the thing to do."

He rose from the bed, holding out his hand to
her. "The thing to do is wiggle that delicious little
derriere of yours into the shower." She smiled,

hearing the compliment in his words. She took his hand and followed him into the bathroom.

Under the spray of warm water, Jarad soaped his hands and scrubbed them along her lax, tired body. That got them so excited they made love again, his hands braced against the shower wall, her legs around his waist. When they finally returned to her bed, Jarad was so exhausted he could barely pull the covers up over them. She snuggled against him, breathing softly against his chest.

"I love you, Ari," he said, but she was already asleep.

Ariel woke slowly the next morning. She stretched, feeling strangely sore in several places. Then she smiled, remembering all the wicked, wicked things Jarad had done to her the night before. She felt heat rise within her just thinking about it.

She looked over her shoulder to see if Jarad was still beside her. He was gone, but there was a note on the pillow where his head had lain.

*Good morning,* it read in bold expansive script. *Had to see to the cleanup downstairs. Come down when you're ready. Jarad. P.S. you snore.*

"I do not," she told it. There was no mention of the time on the note. He could have left it five minutes or an hour ago. She looked at the clock on the bed stand. It was almost noon. She couldn't remember the last time she had slept this late.

She threw off her covers and headed for the shower. Fifteen minutes later she was dressed in a pair of tight jeans and a slouchy purple sweater that continually dropped off one shoulder. She didn't wear a bra underneath, feeling daring and feminine and much too happy for her own good.

She found Jarad in the kitchen, drinking a cup of coffee and reading the morning paper. He was sitting at one of the high counter stools that ran along the far side of the center island. Seeing him, all her aches and pains vanished. He looked so handsome and serious, his dark head bent slightly toward the paper.

"Good morning," Ariel said cheerily. "Or is it afternoon?" She walked over to him and turned her face up for his kiss.

"Morning," he confirmed, before giving her a kiss that was much too brief to suit her. She also noticed him place his newspaper under a copy of the *Vineyard Gazette*. Funny, that's what she'd thought he'd been reading.

He ran a hand along her arm. "Are you hungry? I could make you some breakfast."

"No, thanks." She went over to the counter and poured herself a cup of coffee. "This is about all the breakfast I can handle at the moment." She took the stool next to him. "Anything interesting in the paper today?" She reached for it.

"Not a thing." He leaned his arm on it so she couldn't budge it.

"I can decide that for myself."

"Drink your coffee."

Ariel sighed. This was not how she expected the morning after their night of love to be shaping up. She wanted him to hold her, to kiss her and tell her she'd pleased him. At the very least, he could speak to her in a civil tone of voice. "You should think about changing your title from director to dictator," she told him. "I'm sure there's some totalitarian regime somewhere in need of a new leader."

"Damn it, Ariel. You know very well what's in the paper."

"So you found the paper Peter left here. I'd forgotten about that."

"You'd forgotten about it?" He sounded as if he didn't believe her.

She shrugged. "You have to admit finding out about the newspaper article wasn't the most memorable part of the evening."

"No, it wasn't." He pulled her against him, kissing her just like she wanted him to. "I'm sorry, sweetheart," he said against her ear. "I had no idea any of this was going on."

"I know you didn't." She stroked her hand down his chest. "I was more surprised than anything. That picture of us on the beach was taken only two days ago. They must have stopped the presses to get that one in."

*She doesn't know,* he thought, taking one of her hands in his. It wasn't a real newspaper that bastard had handed her, but a mock-up of one. The pictures were grainy and there were obvious cut lines where graphics and type had been laid in. In the dim light on the patio, she must not have noticed. Peter had probably counted on her not noticing anything other than the pictures. As for the rest of the "paper," it was a doctored up copy of the *Vineyard Gazette.*

Jarad didn't doubt the real thing would hit the newsstands any day now, but as yet it hadn't. Only someone involved with producing it would be able to get their hands on something like that. He wouldn't be surprised if that guy had taken the pictures himself.

"You aren't upset?"

Ariel shook her head. "That someone had been following us around? Not really. Totally embarrassed that people who don't know me are going to be gawking at my picture, yes. And I'm furious at Peter for doing what he did. Whatever happened to him anyway?"

"I couldn't give a flying—"

"Jarad!"

"—*fig* what happened to him."

Frankly, she couldn't care less, either. She'd be content if she never had to see him again. She changed the subject. "So what happened to Gran and Charlie? Shouldn't they be back already?"

"Gran called this morning. No baby yet. They decided to stay another day. Your mother called, too."

"What did she want? Didn't they make it back to the ship on time?"

"They did." He stroked the side of her face with the backs of his fingers. "She was worried about you."

"Why? I swear, she still treats me like I'm twelve and in need of mothering."

"Sweetheart, no mother wants to leave her daughter alone in a house with a man she doesn't know very well, no matter how old that daughter may be."

Ariel supposed not. "What did you tell her?"

"That you were fine, but you were sleeping." Jarad reached out and tucked a strand of hair behind her ear. "I'm not sure she believed me."

"Why didn't you wake me?" Surely her mother would have preferred to hear that from the source.

"You looked so beautiful lying there, I couldn't."

Why did he have to keep saying things like that. "Would you cut it out. You're embarrassing me."

"You'd better get used to it, 'cause I'm not going to stop saying it just because you don't like it. I've never had so much trouble convincing a woman I thought she was pretty in my life."

She laughed at his exasperation. It wasn't that she didn't think she was pretty, she'd never felt comfortable with men commenting on her looks. She supposed she would simply have to get used to his compliments, for in truth, she enjoyed them.

"So what do you feel like doing today?" he asked her.

She smiled suggestively, moving closer to show him exactly what she had in mind. The phone and the doorbell sounded almost simultaneously. Ariel pulled back, sighing. "You get the phone. I'll get the door," she said.

The doorbell sounded again before she could get there. She pulled the door open, wondering who could be so anxious to get in. She was shocked to see Peter standing in the doorway. His back was to her, but she recognized him. He seemed to be scanning the road outside. "What are you doing here, Peter?"

He turned around and she gasped. Peter had an enormous black eye and the corner of his lip was cut. "Oh, my God," she said. "What happened to you?"

"I had a little trouble finding my car last night."

Ariel covered her open mouth with her hand. Words escaped her. She remembered Jarad's bruised knuckles and knew exactly what trouble Peter had encountered the night before. Jarad must have shown him the door while Ariel was in the kitchen talking to her mother. He hadn't left her any other time. What amazed her was that Peter looked like that, and Jarad hadn't even looked winded.

"He isn't here, is he?" Peter asked. "I mean, I don't see his car."

She stepped forward letting the door close behind her, until it was open only a crack. "Yes, he's here." She knew she should be angry with him, but he looked so dejected standing there that her inquisitiveness won out over her animosity. Besides, she could always call Jarad if he got out of hand. "What do you want?"

He ran a hand over his face, as if composing himself. "I wanted to apologize for what I did last night. I really don't know what got into me."

"A few too many Scotch and sodas?" she ventured, remembering his drink of choice.

"Yeah, that, too." He smiled sheepishly. "Look, I just wanted you to know that I'm sorry. I know that it doesn't change things, but I've been through some tough times lately."

"Poor baby."

"I know. I deserve that." He stuffed his hands in the pockets of his black pants. "But everything in my life seems to be falling apart. My career's a mess. My wife, well, she left me about a month ago. I came back here to get some perspective, you know. Then I saw the two of you together. It made me go a little crazy."

"Why?"

He laughed self-deprecatingly. "You can't really be that blind," he said. "Because I'm in love with you. I was in love with you seven years ago when you walked out on me. I'm in love with you now. Seeing you look so happy with another man nearly drove me insane."

She looked at him as if seeing him for the first time. She never would have believed he imagined himself in love with her. She'd thought he was merely tired of waiting for her to go to bed with him. It was curiosity, not love, that had led her to his bed that night. Any thought he might have truly cared for her at all was squashed by his harsh words when they'd parted.

"I'm sorry, Peter," she said quietly. "I didn't know." That didn't excuse what he had done, but at least she understood why he had done it. "I'm sorry I was such a disappointment to you, too."

"That's just it," Peter said, shaking his head. "You weren't. You were so young and sweet and shy, and I acted like a complete ass. Maybe if I hadn't come at you like an octopus with an extra set of tentacles, things would have turned out differently.

"You know, that's what I came here to tell you— to apologize and tell you you weren't to blame for what happened between us. I know I led you to believe it was all your fault, but it wasn't true. I was angry with myself and I took it out on you. I told myself if you'd just talk to me, I'd never make that mistake twice. I blew it all over again, didn't I? But I never would have hurt you. You have to believe that."

Oddly, she did believe him. "Good-bye, Peter," she said. He nodded and walked back to his car. She watched him drive away as she closed the door in front of her. She rested her forehead against the door frame a moment, wondering at the pain human beings caused one another due to miscommunication, lack of insight and plain old stupidity.

"How very touching."

Ariel spun around, green eyes blazing, hearing

the sarcasm in Jarad's voice. "You were spying on me," she accused.

"Yup. Some people around here need looking after."

His arms were folded across his chest. She mimicked his posture. "I need looking after? What about you? You're the one going around beating people up."

"I didn't beat anyone up. My fist just said hello to his face a couple of times." He took a step toward her. "And I wouldn't have put a hand on him if he hadn't swung at me first."

"Stay away from me," she said, backing up. She felt the doorknob at the small of her back. She moved to one side, pressing her back to the door. "And I'm supposed to take your word for that after you lied to me about your hand? You told me it was nothing."

"It *was* nothing." His eyes narrowed on her as he took another step toward her. "And I can't believe you are defending him to me. Maybe you have forgotten what he tried to do to you last night, but I have not."

She couldn't believe she was defending him either. Nor was she angry at Jarad for what he'd done. She hadn't meant to start a fight with him, but once she started on that course she couldn't seem to get off it. "Peter wouldn't have hurt me. He thinks he's in love with me."

"Whoopee," Jarad said sarcastically. "That makes two clubs I've joined this week."

"What?"

"Never mind."

She put her hands in her hair, feeling frazzled. She didn't want to argue with him anymore, especially not about Peter. She decided to change the subject. "Who was on the phone?" she asked.

"Sam, a friend of mine. Samantha."

"Samantha, huh? And you gave her *my* phone number?"

Jarad let out a heavy sigh. "Sam and I have been friends forever. Just friends. She's got this actor fiancé who thinks he's a stuntman. She was hoping I could talk him out of doing some fool thing or other."

She was looking up at him as he was standing right in front of her. He rested his hands on the door on either side of her head. "Honey, you're going to have to tell me what this is all about, 'cause I sure as hell don't know."

"Nothing," she said, shaking her head. She stepped closer to him, wrapping her arms around his neck. His arms came around her, holding her tightly. "Everything." How could she explain it to him when she wasn't sure herself what she was feeling. She was overwhelmed by all that had happened in the last twenty-four hours. First Jenny's wedding, then Peter's appearance, then making love to Jarad. Her emotions had gone on one crazy ride, and that was before Peter showed up on her doorstep this morning. It was too much.

"Can we get out of here, go do something? Anything?" She pulled back to look at him. "Please?"

"If that's what you want." He stroked her cheek with the tips of his fingers. "Where do you want to go?"

She considered it a moment. "Let's go to Gay Head."

"Gay Head?" he laughed. "I don't know if I like the sound of that."

"It's an Indian reservation on the other side of

the island, and the greatest place in the world. I can't believe you've never been there."

"I might have. Who remembers?"

"You'd remember if you'd been there. I think there's some sort of festival going on there now."

A few moments later they set out in Jarad's car. They spent the eighteen miles of their journey talking and laughing as they always did, and Ariel began to relax. The small dirt road they traveled on was bordered by the lush greenery of the countryside. A light fog hung over the ocean to the left, giving an ethereal quality to the scenery.

"I have been here," Jarad said, exiting the car. They walked toward the little row of shops that lined the entranceway. "Where's the old Indian?" Jarad asked as they passed the ornate totem pole.

Ariel smiled, remembering the tall, stoic man that had stood like a sentinel next to the large wooden carving. In all the years, all the times she had been there, she couldn't recall him saying a word. Somehow, his presence had always been comforting, as if he had protected the visitors from the outside world from the spirits of his own.

"He died a few years ago. It doesn't feel the same without him, does it?"

"No."

They peeked in a number of the open-air shops, marveling at the lovely jewelry, carvings, scrimshaw and other items handcrafted by the Indians. Ariel admired one ring in particular. The silver setting was exquisite and the large turquoise stone embedded in it was lovely, but she balked when Jarad wanted to buy it for her. It was much too expensive and much too personal. She insisted on buying

him a chief's headdress which he refused to wear.
She put it on her own head.

They ate lunch at one of the little picnic tables outside the concession stand. He excused
himself, saying he was going to the men's room.
Then he went right back to the shop and
bought the ring for her. He didn't know when
he would give it to her, but definitely when they
were away from there so she couldn't try to
make him take it back.

She was supposed to be waiting for him at the
table. On his way back, though, he saw her standing alone at the edge of the cliffs by the light-
house. She looked like some ancient protectress
standing guard over the island, save for the too-
loose sweater and the too-tight jeans.

"What are you doing over here?" he asked her,
coming up behind her. He put his arms around
her, gathering her back to him. She'd been too
close to the edge to suit him.

"I was just watching the water," she said. "You
know, this is where I climbed up the mountain and
nearly scared poor Gran to death. I think I was
about nine at the time."

Jarad looked down to the white sand way, way
below. He felt himself get a little dizzy thinking
about it. She could easily have killed herself.

"Only then, the cliffs were covered with all different color clay. I was wearing red pants that day.
By the time I got to the top, I looked like an es-
capee from a Play-Doh factory." She leaned forward, pointing. "Do you see that purple line along
the coast?"

"Um-hmm," he said, not really looking. He held
onto her tighter. There was something about her
mood that worried him. He'd been concerned

about her since she'd woken up that morning.
She'd been through a lot in the past couple of
days. He'd expected some repercussions from that.
It bothered him anyway to see her upset.

"That used to be a great big piece of clay in the
shape of a smiling face. That's where the reservation got its name. Years ago it slipped off the
mountain into the water. That's what happened to
all the clay. Time and the salt water and the wind
eroded it all away."

"That's what you got me up here for? A lesson
on Wampanoag history?"

She giggled as he tickled her. "No." It was her
own personal history that she'd been thinking
about. She'd been wondering how she'd gone from
being a daring little girl to such a restricted woman.
It might have started with her grandfather's death,
but it went way beyond that.

She blamed her psychological training for some
of that. Clinicians were supposed to be able to
observe, to treat, while remaining detached themselves. That was fine when applied to therapy, but
she'd made it a way of life. Funny, but Jenny had
been right about her all these years.

She looked out at the landscape, running her
fingers over Jarad's arms as he held her. She felt
his warmth surround her, not only that of his body
but of his affection as well. She didn't want to be
that person anymore. She wasn't that person.
Knowing Jarad had changed her in some undefin-
able way. She knew she was falling in love with him,
and it scared her right down to her bones. But she
didn't want to run. She wanted to hold him to her
until that inevitable day when they'd have to say
good-bye.

She turned in his arms, putting her arms around

his neck. "I'm sorry about this morning," she told him.

"Want to tell me about it?"

She shook her head. "No."

Jarad sighed. "Here we go again."

"What is that supposed to mean?"

"Have you noticed that every time I ask you a personal question, you either change the subject or flatly refuse to say anything?"

"I don't do that."

"Yes, you do."

"I don't mean to."

"I never said you did." He stroked his hand over her shoulder. "Now, do you want to tell me about this morning?"

"No, I'd rather do something about it, instead." She took his hand, pulling him along with her in the direction of the car. "Let's go home."


It was early evening when they walked through the front door. Ariel went to the kitchen in search of something to eat. The night was cool, so Ariel asked Jarad to start a fire in the sitting room fireplace. That would be cozier than eating in the dining room, which would seem all the more forbidding since no one else was there.

Looking through the refrigerator, Ariel found all sorts of tidbits to eat. She knew the food from the buffet had been given to charity, but there were a ton of hors d'oeuvres left: shrimp rolls and crab puffs and a whole tray of little quiche lorraines. There was an assortment of cheeses, fresh fruit and vegetables, and a hunk of rare roast beef from the carving board. She nuked the hot dishes in the microwave, then loaded it all on one of Gran's large serving platters, along with some freshly whipped cream for the strawberries.

She stopped when she walked into the sitting room, tray in hand. Jarad had gotten one of her old sleeping bags from the hall closet and covered it with a comfy blanket. It made a lovely picnic area right before the fire. Sultry saxophone music emanated from the stereo speakers. Ariel flushed as she imagined herself and Jarad eating before the fire, then making love snuggled under the blanket.

He'd propped the throw pillows from the sofa against its side. He lay back among them, his legs stretched out in front of him, crossed at the ankle. He looked like a sultan waiting to be pampered. Kneeling beside him, she sat back on her heels, willing to oblige him.

"What's all this?" Jarad asked as she set down the tray to her right. He handed her a glass of wine from the bottle he'd opened. Ariel sipped hers deeply, hoping for courage. She set her glass on the tray.

"What I cook best. Leftovers." She picked up one of the little quiches and held it before his mouth. "What do you think?" she asked. He nibbled it from her fingers, his tongue snaking out to lick her fingers. His gaze on her was so hot, she felt scorched by it.

"Delicious." He returned the favor, offering her a shrimp roll dipped in cocktail sauce. She took a dainty nibble. A drop of sauce lingered on her lips. Jarad leaned over to kiss it away.

"You taste better," he said. He kissed her in earnest. She sighed deeply, running her hands over the strong muscles of his arms and shoulders.

Jarad's touch was more intoxicating than the wine she'd just consumed.

She pushed him back against the pillows, placing his arms behind him atop the pillows. His smile was amused, but sexually charged as he waited, indulging her in her ministrations. He accepted another morsel, watching her as he chewed slowly. He caught her hand as she was about to bring a piece of cheese to his lips. "What are you doing?" he asked.

She felt heat rise in her cheeks, but she looked him right in the eye. "I'm seducing you."

"Honey, you don't have to do anything special for that." He slid one hand around her waist, drawing her across his upper body. This brought her throat right to his lips. His other hand cupped the bare shoulder the slack neckline of her sweater revealed.

She braced her hand on his thigh, running her fingers upward until she could feel his arousal through the heavy material of his jeans. She squeezed gently, feeling Jarad's answering groan resonate deep in his chest.

Hearing it, Ariel felt a surge of feminine power. She loved knowing she could make Jarad just as wild as he made her. Last night he'd nearly driven her crazy with her need for him. She wanted to do the same thing to him.

She sat back on her heels, kissing him with all the passion she felt for him. Her hands roved over his back, then down to the waistband of his pants, pulling his shirt free. She broke the kiss only to lift the shirt over his head. She sank back against him, smoothing her fingers over his chest.

But Jarad was not about to relinquish control that easily. He pressed her onto her back, running his hands over her breasts over the cover of the fuzzy sweater. Then his hand slid under the sweater, pulling it up to her chin. "What's this? Miss Ariel Windsor not wearing a bra? What is the world coming to?" She laughed with him, until his tongue touched the sensitive peak of her breast. She sucked in her breath as it tenderly circled her nipple. "Mmm," she sighed as he repeated the process with the other.

But she had to stop him, she thought as he slid the sweater over her head. If she wanted to go through with her plan, that is. She sat up, rising to her knees. His arms came around her hips, but she pushed them away. "Oh, no, you don't," she said. "Tonight is my turn." She raised an eyebrow provocatively. "Think you can handle it?"

He lay back against the pillows, arms spread wide as if someone had just told him he was the latest Lotto winner. "Do your damnedest," he said.

And she did. Her fingers played over his shoulders, his chest, his back. Her caresses were tentative at first, growing more emboldened with his lustful response to her. She teased and sampled and suckled, much as he had done the night before. They had one big anatomical difference, which she explored with her hands and lips and tongue, until he grabbed her hips and issued a one word edict: "Now."

Straddling him, she smoothed a condom down the length of him, caressing him, inflaming him even more. Then she let him sink into her sweet, fluid warmth. Her sweat-dampened body clung to his as her hips rocked against him, a powerful momentum building.

"Oh, baby," he groaned, grasping her bottom and holding her closer to him. He rolled over, taking her with him. He rose up on his elbows, looking down at her. "My sweet Ariel," he said between kisses to her mouth. "I've waited such a long time for you."

Then he sank into her, obliterating the curious demon in her that wondered what he meant. She wrapped her legs around his waist and bit her lip as he reprised the rhythm she'd started. She heard his rumbling, satisfied groan, and that was the catalyst for her own release. It came in several electric bursts deep in her body, that brought the sting of tears to her eyes.

"Baby, what's the matter?" Jarad asked, kissing away the salty droplets. She could only shake her head. The sheer power of their lovemaking had overwhelmed her. She tried to force a smile to her lips, but in the firelight, she knew it must look like a grimace.

"Don't cry." He gathered her to his chest, holding her. She slid her arms around his neck, her head slipping back a little. He kissed the column of her throat, and she squirmed beneath him. "Better?" he asked.

"Mmm," she purred. "Much."

And they fed each other the fruit from their tray, dipping it in the whipped cream she'd set out for the strawberries. He put a dollop of cream on each of her breasts, and licked it off her sensuously. Then he dropped little white dots all over her body. He took his time on the last little dot at the junction of her thighs. He joined with her then, and this time it was he who called her name.

Ariel smiled against his shoulder. Turnabout was fair play, after all.

* * *

Ariel awoke slowly the next day. Usually, her room was cool early in the morning. Today there was something big and warm beside her. Sighing, she burrowed closer to it.

"It's about time you woke up," she heard him say.

Her eyes flew open to see Jarad looking down at her. She touched a hand to his cheek to make sure he was really there, that she wasn't imagining him being with her. "Why are you looking at me like that?" she asked sleepily.

"How am I looking at you?" He turned his face and kissed the palm of her hand.

"As if you're a cat and I'm a saucer of milk you're about to lap up."

"That's not a bad idea." He lowered his head, swiping his tongue over one bare nipple, then the other.

"Jarad," she moaned, feeling herself blush from the roots of her hair downward.

"Can't handle a little foreplay so early in the morning?"

*No*, she almost told him. She was barely handling him being there at all. Ludlow women did not wake up with men who were not their husbands in their beds. At least not under the Ludlow roof they didn't.

"How about if I whisper sweet nothings in your ear instead?"

Ariel tensed as he lowered his head until his breath fanned her ear. "Sweet nothing, sweet nothing, sweet nothing," he whispered.

Laughing, she smacked him on the shoulder. His arms closed more tightly around her. He rolled onto his back, pulling her on top of him. His hands smoothed up and down her back, before he hugged her to him with one hand at her nape, the other at the small of her back.

His touch wasn't impersonal, but neither was it the urgent caress of a man bent on making love. She rested her cheek against his shoulder, enjoying merely being held by him. If this was what it was like to wake up with Jarad, she could get used to it.

*No I couldn't,* she reminded herself. There probably wouldn't even be one more morning when she could lie in his arms as she did now. Gran and Charlie were sure to be home before the day was through. That would be the end of their temporary idyll. Unconsciously, her arms wound tighter around his neck as she strove to get closer to him.

"What's the matter?" Jarad asked, stroking her hair back from her face.

She shook her head against his shoulder, not wanting him to know the direction of her thoughts.

Cupping her face in his palm, he lifted her chin until their noses were only inches apart. "Are you ever going to trust me enough to simply tell me what you're feeling?"

She heard the resignation in his voice, and wondered about it. Didn't he know she did trust him? She'd given him her body and her heart, knowing there was no promise of tomorrow to cling to. If that wasn't trust, she didn't know what was.

If he wanted to know what she was feeling, she'd tell him. "I need you, Jarad," she admitted shamelessly. *I need to know that you care for me, if only a little,* she thought as his lips covered hers.

He pulled back a moment later, appearing to study her face. She thought he was about to say something, until his head lowered and his mouth closed over hers once again.

Ariel moaned and clutched him to her more tightly. Since no words of love were forthcoming, she'd have to settle for his passion instead.

# Ten

Much, much later, they lay together stroking each other's sated bodies in a lazy fashion. "What's that?" Jarad asked.

"That's my hip," Ariel replied, placing a restraining hand over Jarad's roving one.

"No. I meant the noise. Don't you hear it?"

It took her a moment to recognize the sound of the doorbell being rung repeatedly. Who could be bothering them now? Probably some friend of Gran's coming by to gossip about the wedding. She didn't want anything to disturb the delicious feeling of afterglow that pervaded her. "Go away," she yelled, knowing that whoever it was couldn't possibly hear her.

Laughing, Jarad asked, "You want me to see who it is?"

"No. I'd better go." Reluctantly, she rose from the bed, quickly pulling on an oversized T-shirt and a pair of shorts. Barefoot, she hurried down the steps and flung open the front door. In front of her stood a man dressed all in white, save for the bright yellow blazer he wore. A pair of sunglasses was perched on top of his head. He seemed to recognize her, but she hadn't a clue who he was.

"Can I help you?" she asked.

"Jarad Naughton's staying here, right?"

"Are you a friend of his?"

"That remains to be seen."

Ariel turned, hearing Jarad's voice. She hadn't heard him come up behind her. He was still tugging on a T-shirt as he extended a hand to the man who stood on the doorstep.

"What brings you out to this stretch of the woods?" Jarad asked.

The man shook Jarad's hand, moving past Ariel into the foyer. Ariel closed the door behind him, turning to watch the interaction between the two men.

"It's a long story," the man said. "I'll tell you for the price of a cup of coffee. And an introduction to this lovely lady."

Jarad grasped Ariel's hand, pulling her to his side. "Tom, this is Ariel Windsor. Ariel, this pain in the butt is Tom Merrit. We've worked on a few projects together."

"And I've been carrying him all the way."

Smiling, Ariel extended her hand to him. He took it in both of his, kissing her wrist. "You have my sympathies if you're mixed up with this guy." He nodded in Jarad's direction.

"Why is that?" Ariel glanced up at Jarad, who seemed to enjoy the good-natured teasing.

"You could have had me."

Ariel laughed, her gaze swinging from one man to the other. She had to admit Jarad's friend was attractive, with deep brown skin, light brown eyes and a lean build. But to her, there was no contest as to which man was more compelling.

"If I'd only known," she teased back, looking up at Jarad. He pulled her closer, until their sides touched.

"Why don't you go get dressed," he whispered against her hair. "I'll entertain our guest."

She nodded, excused herself and headed for the stairs.

Jarad set up the coffeemaker as Tom took a seat at one of the kitchen chairs. Jarad glanced at Tom, wondering what brought him out to the edge of nowhere to find him. He obviously wanted something from him, but what? Whatever it was had to be big for him to seek him out in person. "What's this long story you want to tell me about?" Jarad asked.

"It's not that long, really. I didn't want to say anything in front of your lady friend. A certain story hit the newsstands this morning. Have you seen it?"

"Yeah."

"She's not really in the business is she?"

Jarad shook his head. "How'd you know?" Jarad handed him a mug of steaming black coffee.

"Doesn't have the look." Tom took a sip from the mug. "That's a shame. She is one fine—"

"You didn't come all the way out here to discuss my love life, did you?" Jarad placed his mug on the counter, trying to control his temper. He wasn't interested in Tom's appraisal of Ariel. No doubt, Tom would think whatever he said was flattering, but Jarad knew from experience it would probably make him want to deck him. The day they gave out Neanderthal, Tom must have hogged the line.

"No. I wanted to talk to you about a proposition. I've got a new project in the works I thought you might be interested in."

"Really?" Jarad sipped his coffee, watching Tom closely. Behind Tom's guileless brown eyes lurked a shrewd mind with a keen sense of self-preservation. He'd backed out of their partnership when he'd thought Jarad couldn't cut it. Now that Jarad was hot, Tom wanted back in. Tom wasn't the only person offering him work but he was the only one brazen enough to show up on someone else's doorstep to do so.

"I've got the rights to the new Neil Thurston book," Tom continued.

He had to be kidding. Thurston's kind of shoot 'em up, crash-and-burn stories were definitely not his style. "What made you think I'd be interested? The only thing I know about blowing things up is when to duck."

Tom shrugged. "What's to know? That's what special effects guys are for." Tom put up both his hand as if in surrender. "And you know me. I'd stay out of your hair as far as the creative stuff is concerned. So long as you don't blow the budget, I couldn't care less what you do."

Jarad shook his head. He wasn't interested in committing himself to anything else right now. He was set to do some promotion for his latest film in another couple of weeks. That would take him away from Ariel long enough. After that he was free, and he wanted to stay that way.

"Don't give me an answer now," Tom said as Jarad opened his mouth to decline. "Think about it for a while and let me know."

Jarad sighed. His answer wouldn't change, but it wasn't worth arguing over. "What do you have planned for today?"

"Not a thing. I was hoping to impose on you."

Jarad laughed. "I figured as much." He put his coffee cup on the counter. "In that case, I'd better go get dressed."

***

Freshly shaved and showered, Jarad knocked on Ariel's door.

"Come in," she called.

He opened the door to see her standing by her bed, which was littered with her clothes. She wore only the lavender robe she'd worn the night she climbed over his balcony. Thinking of that night, he instantly grew harder than a stone. He'd spent the entire morning making love to her, and now he couldn't wait to be with her again. Would he ever get enough of her?

Jarad pushed aside the clothes at the head of the bed and sat down. "I invited Tom to spend the day with us."

"I thought you might."

Seeing the worried expression on her face, he asked, "That's all right, isn't it?"

"Of course. I couldn't decide what to wear."

She was worried about what to wear. It charmed him that she would worry about embarrassing him in front of his friend. Of course, it wouldn't matter to Tom if she wore nothing at all. But then Jarad would have to kill him. "Whatever you wear will be fine," he said, hoping to reassure her.

She gave him a sour look. "You are such a man sometimes."

"Thank you," he said, not really knowing what that comment was supposed to mean.

"That was not a compliment."

Jarad chuckled. "Okay, wear the red dress. The one you had on the first night at dinner."

She pulled it from the pile of clothes and laid it on top. "You really think so?"

"Oh, yes." He loved the way the dress clung to every curve.

She turned to him, then nodded toward the door. "You have to leave now."

"Why?"

"I have to get dressed."

"And you can't do that with me here?"

"No."

He pulled her toward him by the knot in the sash of her robe until she stood between his legs. He wrapped his arms around her hips. Resting his chin on her stomach, he looked up at her. "I have seen and touched and tasted every inch of your beautiful body, and you still can't get dressed in front of me?"

"No."

"How about I dress you instead." He pulled on the sash with his teeth until the knot gave and the robe slid open. He'd known she wore nothing beneath that robe, but seeing her nude body inflamed him beyond reason. He placed a soft kiss on her belly, feeling her muscles contract at his touch. He had to get out of there before he threw her down on the bed and made love to her, clothes and all.

"I have to go." He rose from the bed, moving around her toward the door. His hand shook as he reached for the door knob.

"I thought you were going to dress me," she teased.

"Some other time."


When Ariel came down the stairs fifteen minutes later, both men were waiting for her in the foyer. She immediately went to Jarad, taking the hand he extended to her.

"It's about time," Jarad joked, lacing his fingers with hers.

"Aren't I worth the wait?" she whispered up at him.

"Definitely." He traced a path along her cheek with his index finger.

"Cut that out, you two. My chariot awaits, but my stomach won't. You're going to have to feed me."

Tom's chariot turned out to be a sleek, black stretch limousine, equipped with every conceivable amenity. Ariel wondered how she could have possibly missed noticing the enormous car, but Tom confessed he had the driver park out on the street in case Jarad didn't want to see him. Then it would've seemed he had no visible means of getting back to town.

Ariel slid into her seat, testing the plushness of the leather against her fingertips. Jarad sat next to her, holding her close with an arm around her shoulders.

They ate lunch at a posh restaurant in East Chop that, like many other restaurants on the Vineyard, specialized in freshly caught fish. The food was delicious, but Ariel could only pick at the scallops on her plate. She felt restless, bored to tears by the men's conversation about the comings and goings of the people on "the coast," as they called it. Jarad tried to include her, but she really couldn't care less. In her heart, she knew this was the last day she and Jarad would have alone together, and she didn't want to share it with a man that seemed to have all the depth of a rain puddle. If everyone in Hollywood was this fascinating, she could see why they called it La La Land. She didn't want to be inhospitable, but she wanted to go home.

* * *

As the day wore on, Jarad noticed Ariel's withdrawal. "Had enough?" he asked her as they exited the car at her favorite art gallery. They'd been to the historical museum and back out to Gay Head, places she thought Tom would like.

Ariel nodded. "I want to see if there are any new figurines in the collection. I'll be right back."

"It's finally happened," Tom said, clapping him on the back.

"What are you talking about?" Jarad asked, his eyes still on Ariel.

"You're in love with her," he said, nodding toward Ariel.

"Is it that obvious?" Jarad asked.

Tom snorted. "Are you kidding? You're going to make a lot of ladies mighty unhappy."

Jarad shrugged. His only interest was making one lady *very* happy. "I hope you don't mind cutting the tour short," Jarad said.

"Not at all. I'll drop you guys off at the house and be on my way." Tom shoved his hands into his pants pockets. "Look buddy," Tom said. "I know I blew it not going in with you on the last one. I hope you won't hold that against me."

Jarad shook his head. "It's nothing personal. I'm taking a break, that's all."

"I hope she's worth it."

Jarad smiled. "She is."

Twenty minutes later, they pulled up in front of the house. Ariel's spirits plummeted seeing the brown Mercedes parked in the driveway. That could mean only one thing.

Gran and Charlie were back.

***

The next morning, Ariel awoke to the sound of laughter. Her room was as cold and empty as it had always been every morning except the day before. Throwing off the covers, she showered quickly and dressed in a black V-neck top and matching shorts.

She was about halfway down the stairs when she saw a young child run in from the garden in pursuit of Dudley's ball. It was one of the little girls that had come looking for Dudley the other day. The girl squealed as the dog caught up with her, licking her face several times before heading back to the yard. It appeared Dudley had his girlfriends back.

"Good morning everyone," Ariel said, stepping onto the patio.

"Good morning, dear," Gran said as Ariel kissed her on the cheek. "How did you sleep?"

"Very well." She cast a silencing look at Jarad. There was no telling what that man might say. The wink he sent her way was suggestive enough. Ariel helped herself to coffee from the urn on the wrought iron table.

"Good morning," Jarad said when she sat in the seat next to him. "As you can see, Dudley stole his girlfriends back."

"We're baby-sitting today," Gran added. "Their mother has a touch of the summer flu, and she didn't want the girls to catch it." Gran took a sip from her cup. "Today might be a good day to head out to Katama. What do you think?"

Katama by any other name was South Beach, one of the best places on the island for romping in the waves and tanning a dark, delicious brown.

"Put me down for a yes," Ariel said cheerfully.

She was about to suggest they take along some of Mrs. Thompson's delicious cranberry cookies when she remembered the housekeeper was probably still in Connecticut with her daughter. "I almost forgot to ask. Was it a boy or a girl?"

"A lovely seven-pound girl. The cutest thing you ever saw."

Ariel listened as Gran rhapsodized about the new baby, surprised to feel a wave of envy wash over her. She'd never heard a peep from her biological clock until that moment. She glanced over at Jarad, who watched her with an expression she didn't understand. What would it be like, she wondered, to. . . . No, she refused to indulge in any fantasies of things that could never be. She gazed down at her lap, which at the moment seemed the safest place to look.

Having finished her monologue on babies, Gran tapped her hands on the tabletop. "So do we head out to Katama?"

The others seconded and thirded the motion, and soon all of them rose to get ready to go. She and Gran took charge of the two little ones, whose names were Kesha and Kendall, while Jarad brought in the disobedient setter.

Fifteen minutes later, the six of them were in Gran's Jeep, heading out of Oak Bluffs. Gran preferred the drive along State Beach, Ariel knew, since the ocean was in view for much of the way. By the time they got to their destination, all of them would be ready to leap from the car and head directly for the water.

The trip was peaceful, save for the bickering of the two girls, who could rarely agree on what toy belonged to whom. It was just about noon when Jarad pulled the car onto the sandy area used for parking. Gathering all their paraphernalia from the trunk was an undertaking in itself. Gran had insisted on bringing a lounge chair and umbrella, along with every newspaper on the island. Jarad insisted on bringing that blasted Frisbee. The girls had mini-surfboards. Ariel felt almost naked with only a towel and a small bottle of suntan lotion.

Ariel was surprised by how many people were already frolicking in the foamy waters before her. Few people had known about this beach when she was a child. There certainly wasn't a lifeguard on duty at the time. "Swim at Your Own Risk," a sign in the middle of the beach had declared. The splendor of the ocean had not changed though. As far as she could see, mountain-like waves rolled toward the shore, crashing loudly on the cool beige sand.

They set their blanket near the water's edge, barely taking time to discard their clothes before she, Jarad and the kids headed for the water. Gran stayed behind as she always did, claiming the water would shrivel her old bones.

The waves lapping over Ariel's feet were bitingly cold. She retreated instantly, watching as the others dove right into the water, disregarding the icy temperature. Ariel shivered just thinking about it.

Returning to the water's edge, Ariel stuck a toe in the foamy water. "Brr," she said, wrapping her arms around herself. She was going to have to warm herself gradually, or she would never get in.

"Didn't I tell you that's the chicken's way of getting in the water?" She looked up to find Jarad walking toward her. "Come on in. It'll get warmer once you're wet."

"No way," she said, but not loud enough for him to hear.

"I guess I'll have to convince you the same way I did last time."

"I'll go. I'll go." She walked gingerly into the water to meet him.

"Too late." He scooped her up in his arms and carried her out. "I enjoy having you in my arms too much to miss this opportunity."

"Put me down, Jarad," she insisted. Both children were staring at them wide-eyed.

"Whatever Ariel wants . . ." He released her and she tumbled into an oncoming wave.

"Why do you keep doing this to me?" she screamed at him, surfacing. She threw several handfuls of water at him.

"Because it's fun." He splashed her back playfully. Soon the kids caught onto the game of "wet Ariel." Resigning herself to the chilly temperature, she dove under a massive wave.

Coming up a few feet away, she stuck her tongue out at Jarad, daring him to follow her. He did so in a few easy strokes. He came up beside her, grasping her tightly around the waist. "I told you the water would get warmer," he said huskily.

"You said once I got wet," she reminded him. The ocean did feel wonderfully warm, about to reach boiling point any second.

"You're wet." Ariel watched his eyes travel over the long expanse of her golden brown skin to where her bathing suit was plastered against her breasts, and below, to the point where her waist disappeared into the water. He held her tightly as a wave rushed up behind them, pulling them under before they surfaced a few seconds later at its crest. Underwater, his fingers had traced a slow, tantalizing path where his eyes had roamed.

"Jarad . . ." Ariel warned. This was not the time

or place for such activities. The kids were only a
few feet away, and Gran was sitting contentedly on
the shore.

"I missed you last night."

"I missed you, too." Ariel had gone to bed with
a headache almost immediately after returning
home. Her bed had seemed so cold and lonely
without Jarad beside her. After only two nights,
she'd gotten used to sharing it with him. But more
than that, she'd missed him, his company, his way
of making her feel warm and cared for and special.
Looking up into his handsome, smiling face, she
wondered if she made him feel the same way.

As if to answer her question, he cupped her face
in his palms and kissed her, a sweet caress of his
lips on hers. Ariel let her eyes drift closed, giving
herself up to Jarad's tender embrace.

She pulled away a second later, feeling a pair of
small hands on her leg. "Ooh, they're kissing," she
heard Kesha say. She surfaced to their right. Kendall was behind her.

Jarad scooped them up, one per hip. "What do
you two munchkins want?" He tossed one child
then the other into the water. They came up begging for him to do it again. They stayed in another
half hour, jumping the waves in a chain.

Lunch was a variety of sandwiches, cheese, fruit
and, for dessert, Mrs. Thompson's delicious cookies. Somehow a few of the sweet, chewy confections
had managed to remain uneaten in the cookie jar.
Ariel ate ravenously, the salt air exaggerating her
appetite.

"Better than the Black Dog Bakery," Gran announced. "Only don't tell Emma I said that. She'd
be baking morning, noon and night."

Ariel laughed, knowing Emma Thompson would

do just about anything for Isabel Ludlow. The pair were more like two old friends than employer and employee.

"Who's ready to go back in the water?" Jarad called.

"We are," two little voices intoned. Jarad and his two small charges sprinted back toward the water.

"No swimming for half an hour," Gran called, but Ariel doubted any of them would listen to her.

"Jarad told me what happened with the newspaper and all," Gran said after a few minutes had passed.

"I wish he would forget about that." She made a face, wondering what "all that" consisted of.

"He cares for you a great deal."

"I know, Gran. I care about him, too." She more than cared. She grew more in love with that crazy man the more time she spent with him.

"What's this all about, Gran?"

Gran looked out at the horizon. "In my experience I've found that life doesn't offer you endless chances for happiness. You have to seize your opportunities when you find them."

Ariel studied her grandmother. The older woman was worrying the hem of her short-sleeved shirt. "Are you talking about Jarad and me or you and Charlie?"

Gran turned to Ariel, a surprised look on her face. "You always were a perceptive child, if someone could get you to listen," Gran said.

Ariel put her hand on Gran's knee. "I'm listening, now. I've always wondered why you wouldn't marry Charlie."

"Partly because I didn't want to upset you girls' memory of your grandfather."

Ariel patted Gran's hand. "Charlie could never

do that. We've all always loved Charlie in his own right."

"I realize that. Another part of it was that I'm so used to being alone. Charlie's at the house a lot, but it's still my home and my time to do with as I please. We're alike in that way, Ariel."

She nodded, watching her grandmother. "But that's not all of it."

"No," Gran answered. She put her newspaper aside, turning in her chair to face Ariel more fully. "Did you know that your grandfather and I were distant cousins?"

"No." Ariel's ears pricked up. Finally, a story she hadn't heard before.

Gran nodded. "My maiden name was Ludlow, too. That's why I'm always telling you about Ludlow women. I came into it honestly." Gran paused a moment, seeming to collect her thoughts.

"I met your grandfather when I was fifteen. My branch of the family had fallen on hard times, and my mother sent me to stay with my father's second cousin. Your grandfather was her son.

"We hit it off right away, even though he was a lot older than I was. You see, he believed as I did that blacks needed to be educated to survive in the world, especially in those days. We'd spend hours together reading, debating, quoting our favorite passages to each other.

"I went back home, but in a few years when my parents thought it was time to marry me off, they remembered how friendly I had been with your grandfather, and the next thing I knew the two of us were engaged."

Ariel's eyes widened and she leaned closer to her grandmother. "You had an arranged marriage, Gran?"

"No, not really. I could have said no, but I didn't think to. There was no one else, and I wanted a home and children. Also, your grandfather's side of the family had been so kind to me, I felt I owed them something. Your grandfather wouldn't have kept his nose out of a book long enough to find a woman if it hadn't been for me."

Ariel's mouth dropped open. "You weren't in love with Grandy, were you?"

Gran shook her head. "No, but I liked him. I respected him. We didn't ring each other's bells, so to speak, but he, like I, had to marry someone. Then I met Charlie."

Gran laughed, bringing her hand to her chest. "Charlie was such a funny man, not a clown, but very witty. He could say things that would make you laugh until you cried and stare at you like he couldn't understand what you were carrying on about. And when he looked at me . . ." Gran lifted her shoulders and sighed.

Ariel knew the feeling that Gran described. She felt it herself every time Jarad looked at her. She could imagine her grandmother as a young woman. She thought of one old sepia-toned picture housed in one of the family albums. It showed Gran in an evening dress, her hair straightened and waved in an elaborate style. In the picture Gran's medium brown skin bore none of the lines and creases it did today. If Ariel weren't mistaken, she'd actually been wearing makeup. Isabel Ludlow had been a beautiful young woman. She had a real problem imagining Charlie as a handsome young Romeo, however.

"So, why didn't you marry Charlie instead?"

"I'd given my word. I didn't meet Charlie until a month before I was supposed to be married. I don't think either your grandfather's family or mine would have understood me calling off the wedding at that point. I had no way of knowing if our attraction would have turned into something more permanent, and I was afraid to take the chance. Charlie begged me to change my mind, but I refused. He didn't speak to me for years after that."

Ariel was stunned. She'd always thought of her grandmother as being perfect, as never having been mistaken about anything. She realized she was still seeing her through a child's eyes, not a woman's. "When did you realize you loved Charlie?"

"I think I've always known. When your grandfather died, I turned to Charlie. But by then, he'd gotten married himself. She was a sweet girl, and I would never have expected him to leave her. When she passed, Charlie wanted me to marry him, but I felt so guilty, I couldn't. You see, we'd wasted so much time, and it was all my fault. If I hadn't been such a coward, we could have spent all those years together instead of apart."

"How can you blame yourself for that, Gran? You did what you thought you had to do." Ariel took Gran's hand in both of hers. "Isn't it time you stopped punishing yourself for something that wasn't your fault?"

"Maybe you're right, Ariel," Gran said, finally smiling. "You know, Charlie asked me again the night of Jenny's wedding. I told him I'd have to think about it. I think you've given me my answer."

Ariel whooped. "Oh, Gran!" She embraced the older woman, who seemed genuinely surprised by the outburst. "I'm so happy for you two."

"It only goes to show you should never give up

hope," Gran said, giving Ariel a squeeze to emphasize her point.


That night Ariel and Jarad took the girls to the Flying Horses, as Gran decided to take Charlie out to dinner to break the news to him. The carousel was housed in a red wooden building off Circuit Avenue. Once inside, Jarad bought a large enough supply of the little red ride tickets to last a family of ten for two weeks.

When the ride stopped, Kesha and Kendall scrambled to claim two horses on the outside. Ariel strapped in one child and Jarad the other. As the music started, the room was silent, save for the sounds coming from the arcade in the other room.

Ariel's eyes strayed over the brightly colored wooden horses, whose paint had been redone so many times the smiles on the animals' mouths looked grotesque. The girls stayed on for so many rides, Ariel was sure they would both have motion sickness.

In the periphery of her vision, Ariel could see Jarad standing next to her munching on some of the freshly made popcorn sold at the little concession counter. She wondered what he was thinking as he watched the children going round and round, giggling as they tried to grasp the rings that were still beyond their reach.

For a moment, she imagined they were her children, hers and Jarad's. With a certainty that was absolute, Ariel knew she wanted such a future with him. Jarad had told her he cared for her, that she was special to him, but he had never spoken to her about love or commitment or anything else that might lead her to believe his feelings were the same as hers. He'd made love to her beautifully, but she wasn't naive enough to confuse sex with love. Her feelings for him went way deeper than that.

She wondered what he would say if he knew what she was thinking. He'd probably tell her she'd lost her mind. This was a summer fling they were having, and she should know well enough to obey the rules. Yet, some part of her felt compelled to tell him about her love for him, no matter what the consequences might be.

"What's the matter?" Jarad asked.

She turned to look at him, seeing concern in his eyes. "I was just thinking."

"Oh, no!" he said in mock horror. "No more thinking."

No, she decided. Not if she knew what was good for her.

"Come on," Jarad said, leading her toward the ride. "Let's show these kids how it's done."

"This is silly." She followed him anyway.

He lifted her onto the floorboard of the already slowing carousel and leapt on himself. "I bet I can catch more rings than you." It was a challenge issued from one first grader to another.

"Bet you can't." Ariel made a face at him.

The ride started up again. Ariel gave her ticket to the teenager collecting them, anticipating the moment when the rings would be loaded into the chute attached high on the far wall. Then the fun would really begin.

One by one, the rings would appear through the opening, and the trick was to catch as many as possible at every turn. From experience she knew the best way to catch a lot of rings was to fill up each finger separately rather than grab with your whole hand.

Ariel straddled the yellow and brown horse, standing in the stirrups for balance. She was still only a few inches taller than Jarad, who remained on the floorboard. She heard the clanging of the rings as they were released into the chute. She leaned far forward, ready to start grabbing for the little metal circles as soon as possible.

After the first pass, Ariel counted six rings. Not bad, and she was only warming up. Jarad had a mere two. She looked at him with pretend disdain when he hung them on the prong shooting up from the top of the horse's head.

"Looks painful," he said testing the sharpness of the metal against his fingertip. Ariel laughed, flinging her rings into one of the receptacles that lined the sides of the building.

They went for another pass, then another. Soon Jarad was imitating her strategy, catching as many rings as she did or more. Ariel saw the girl load the brass ring into the arm. She knew that, not this time, but the next, someone would win the free ride. If she couldn't beat Jarad at catching the most rings, the least she could do was catch *the* ring.

As they came around for the final pass, Ariel saw the ring gleaming in front of her. The little boy in front of her missed it. Confidently, she plucked it from the arm. She turned to Jarad, ready to gloat about her victory, only to realize they shared the ring like two holders of a wishbone.

For a moment, their eyes locked, and it seemed prophetic that they should be there together, sharing that symbol of promise.

"Does this mean we both get the free ride?" Jarad asked, breaking the spell.

"No," Ariel said haughtily. "I defer to you. Age before beauty."

"Then I should go first on both counts." She gave him a playful smack on the top of the head, as he helped her down from her horse.

Later that night after the girls had gone home, they laughed about their juvenile competition. Jarad had refused the extra ticket in light of the stream he already had.

They were sitting in one of the wicker chairs in her room. Actually, Jarad was in the chair. He'd insisted Ariel sit on his lap. She nestled closer against his chest as their laughter subsided. His hands were gentle as they moved over her back, pulling her closer.

There was something about the way he held her that concerned her. "Is something the matter?" she asked.

"I've got to leave in the morning."

There were the words she had dreaded hearing most. Especially now that she'd admitted to herself that she loved him. "I see," was all she managed to say.

"Something's come up. I *have* to go." Did that mean he wanted to stay with her? she wondered, until he added, "I'm not sure where I'll be. I'll call you."

If that wasn't the quintessential New York exit line. She didn't object to Jarad's intensely bittersweet kisses. They were sweet because they were his, bitter because they were the last she would receive.

"There's so much I want to tell you," Jarad said.

She silenced him with a fierce kiss of her own. She didn't want to hear any platitudes about how much their time together meant to him. She wanted them to end their relationship as honestly as they had begun it. And she wanted him. She needed one last time in his arms and then she could release him. Each of them had their own lives, and he was obviously ready to get back to his.

"Come to bed," she told him, rising and taking his hand. "Be with me one more time before you have to go."

Jarad went to her, making love to her tenderly, slowly, hoping to convey with his body what he feared to tell her with words. His love for her had come upon him so fast, he himself had a hard time believing he could feel so strongly in such a short time. She was a much more reserved person than he. He didn't want to risk scaring her away when he knew she was coming to care for him, too.

As she slept, he stroked his hands over her slack body, wishing he had some way to bind her to him, to make her see that he wanted her, not only for today but for always. For now, he'd have to settle for holding her. It wasn't until the first streams of daylight sifted into the room that he left her passion-filled bedroom for his own.

When she awoke the next morning, she knew he was gone. On her hand was the beautiful ring she'd admired at Gay Head. He'd bought it for her, even though she told him he shouldn't. But what message was he sending her by slipping it on her finger in the dead of night? Was it a promise of things to come or a final gift to say good-bye?

She showered and dressed and went down to the kitchen to get a cup of coffee. There was a note from Gran saying that she was out dropping Jarad at the airport. "Great!" she said aloud. She was completely alone, except for Dudley, who wasn't any comfort at all.

Unable to keep still, she wandered around the big house, but everywhere she went reminded her of Jarad. The sitting room, the patio, even her own room held the memory of him. Would she ever be able to sleep in that bed again without thinking of him?

Gran smiled at her so kindly when she told her of her predicament. "You're the only one around here who didn't know you were in love with Jarad. Except maybe him. Did you tell him?"

"No." She looked down at her lap, shaking her head.

"Why not? The man had a right to know before he went gallivanting off to California."

"Because I was afraid of making an idiot of myself." She rested her head on her grandmother's lap. "I couldn't beg him to stay."

"No, but you could have asked nicely."

Ariel laughed for the first time. "Oh, Gran," she said. "What am I going to do?"

"You have to have faith, sweetie. You told me yourself you didn't know why he left. For all you know, he just needed time to think. You have to admit, this all happened pretty fast."

Have faith. That was what her mother had said. But in the days that passed, following either woman's advice was terribly difficult, since there was not a word, not a call, not a note from Jarad. She would have gone home had Gran not hidden her car keys.

On Friday, she was helping Gran in the garden when the doorbell rang. She scrambled to get it, hoping it would be Jarad. On the other side of the door was a delivery man holding a vase of the most exquisite white roses Ariel had ever seen. She was disappointed it wasn't Jarad, but the flowers might be from him.

She accepted the crystal vase wrapped in clear plastic, slipping the card out of the tiny envelope with unsteady fingers. "See you soon, my little witch," it read. "I love you."

Somehow Gran must have gotten a message to Ariel's father and he'd sent these flowers to cheer her up. How like him. But "little witch"—he hadn't called her that in ages. She left the flowers unopened on the table by the door.

Three days later, she set out for town in Gran's Jeep. Since Mrs. Thompson was still in Connecticut with her daughter, she'd volunteered to do the shopping. She had nothing else to do, and she wanted to keep busy.

She was standing in the checkout line when she saw it. The latest copies of the tabloids caught her attention. There was Jarad in living color, kissing the cheek of a redheaded woman. Her hand was on his shoulder. The diamond she wore was so large it could only be described as a rock.

"Tearful Reunion For . . ." She couldn't read any more. It wasn't some*thing* that had come up. It was some*one*. And what a someone it was. She was exactly the type of woman she believed Jarad would be attracted to. She imagined they'd probably had a fight before he'd come to the island. That red-haired woman read their story in the paper, realized what a fool she was for letting him go, and begged him to come back. She thought of the phone call the other morning from a woman that was supposedly his friend, and she realized they'd probably used her own grandmother's telephone to reconcile.

She had no idea if the story she envisioned was true, but it hurt to think she'd been nothing more than a diversion for him while the woman he loved came to her senses. That was the trouble with being a psychologist: you could always invent scenarios and motivations for any situation you came across.

Somehow she managed to put her items on the little conveyor belt, pay for her groceries, and even get the right change. She loaded her bags into the back of the Jeep and drove home as if on autopilot. She parked in the driveway, not trusting herself to make it into the garage safely.

Gran and Charlie came out to help her, but she barely noticed them. She went straight to her room and closed the door behind her. Leaning her back against the wooden surface, she scanned her room through eyes blurry with unshed tears.

"Damn you, Jarad," she railed. "How could you do this to me?" She slid down the door until she was sitting with her arms wrapped around her knees. "Damn you," she repeated.

And then her tears came.


Over the next two days, Ariel kept mostly to herself. She couldn't stand seeing the sympathetic look in Gran's eyes whenever the two of them were together. Broken hearts were painful, not fatal. She'd get over it, eventually. If she lived to be 200, maybe.

At least half of Jenny's hypothesis proved true: Ariel Windsor was quite capable of loving if she left herself open to it. That's what she should have done, reminded herself that it was only an experiment. Then she might have realized what the outcome was going to be. An essential phase of every experiment was being able to predict the results.

For now, she'd worry about getting through one day at a time. She couldn't eat, couldn't sleep, couldn't think. It was funny, the signs of heartbreak were surprisingly similar to the signs of love. She would have to tell that to Jenny the next time she saw her.

Ariel let out a tired sigh. Gran and Charlie had left early that morning to pick up Mrs. Thompson, who was finally ready to come home. Ariel sat in the sitting room wearing one of Jarad's shirts she'd found in the wash that morning, over a tank top and a pair of cut-off shorts. It was silly, really. Having his shirt on didn't make him any closer, didn't change the fact that he preferred another woman to her. But somehow it was comforting to her. Ariel picked at the salad she'd made for lunch. Another meal gone to waste.

She flicked on the TV searching for something to watch—something mindless and funny and entertaining. She stopped on a channel featuring the "Three Stooges." You couldn't get more mindless than that. Moe was upbraiding Curly for some infraction or other and ended up hitting Larry instead. Ariel laughed as all three of them ended up in a brawl.

The doorbell rang, and she wondered who could be bothering her now, when she'd finally managed to be in a good mood.

She flung open the door, hoping to get rid of whoever it was quickly. She wasn't in the mood for company, especially not Peter, who stood on the steps before her dressed in casual clothes. An expensive-looking camera hung from his neck on a multicolored strap.

She started to close the door on him. She was home alone and didn't want to have to worry about fending him off by herself. No matter what she'd told Jarad, she no longer felt comfortable around him. Besides, she knew she looked half-undressed with Jarad's shirt hanging to her mid-thigh, completely covering the shorts underneath. She didn't want to give him any ideas.

He was quicker than she thought, wedging one foot in the door before she could close it. "I only want to talk to you," she heard him say through the door.

"So talk."

Peter was silent for a moment, then said, "I came to say good-bye."

She opened the door slightly, looking at him. "Good-bye?"

"Yeah. I've caused enough trouble around here. I spoke to my wife last night. She's just mad enough at me to take me back and make me miserable for the rest of my life."

She smiled at him, leaning against the door. "I hope it works out for you." She meant that sincerely. Somebody should come out the better from all this.

Peter cupped her chin in the palm of his hand. "I saw the picture in the newspaper," he said quietly. "I hope I didn't have anything to do with that."

She shook her head, dislodging his hand. "No."

His hand rested on top of hers on the doorknob. "Look, Ari, there's something I have to tell you."

She wondered what it was, since he wouldn't

look her in the eye. She didn't want to hear anything that was going to make her feel worse than she already did. She wasn't sure she could feel worse. "Please, don't." She closed her eyes a moment. "Not now."

"You're really hung up on him, aren't you?"

She nodded, letting out a sigh. "That obvious, is it?"

"Hey," Peter said. "I wouldn't have taken the guy for such a chump, either. I would've sworn he really cared for you."

Ariel swallowed over the lump in her throat. She would have sworn the same thing herself, until she saw the picture of him with her own eyes.

"Take care of yourself," he said, stepping forward to kiss her on the mouth. It was a brief embrace which she didn't respond to in any way. "One of these days we're going to have to have a talk." He smiled at her, chucked her under the chin sympathetically, then started down the stairs.

It was only then that Ariel noticed the taxi parked out on the road. As Peter drove off, the back passenger door of the cab opened. Jarad stepped out, wearing a khaki-colored loose-knit sweater over a pair of black dress pants. He pulled a garment bag out from the seat beside him. He looked so handsome as he walked toward her that her breath caught in her throat and her heart pulsed to a staccato beat.

She almost ran to him, forgetting her pride, forgetting his betrayal of her. The chilling look in his eyes froze her where she stood. He fastened a look so contemptuous on her that she felt physically stunned by it. He stopped at the bottom step, dropping the garment bag to the ground at his feet.

He spread his arms wide in a mockery of someone expecting to be embraced.

"Hi, honey," he said. "I'm home."

# Eleven

Ariel merely stared at him, her thoughts in chaos. What could he want from her now? And why was he angry with her? For what? Standing in her own grandmother's doorway talking to a man? He had no right to be angry with her, considering his own defection. Sure, Peter had kissed her. It was no more serious than the way many people greeted each other every day.

And was he actually planning to stay here? she wondered, remembering the bag lying at his feet. Why? Had the red-haired woman thrown him out again and he'd decided to give Ariel another try?

Well, she was pretty angry herself, now. Her eyes narrowed on him. "What are you doing here, Jarad?" she asked.

"That's the same question I've been asking myself the past few minutes. What did you decide to do—give him what he's been pining for all these years?"

His voice dripped sarcasm, leaving no doubt what he was talking about. "What are you implying?" she asked anyway. If he was going to accuse her of something, she wanted him to say it.

"I'm not implying anything." He raised his hand, palm up, gesturing in her direction. "Look at yourself," he said. His hand moved as if to encompass all of her. "Your hair's all tumbled, your feet bare, a man's shirt on. If that isn't the classic picture, I don't know what is."

Ariel put her hand to her hair. Of course it looked a mess. She hadn't bothered to comb it. She'd just run her fingers through it to smooth it down when she got up that morning. She hadn't cared how she looked. Even if she had slept with Peter, who was he to judge her? He'd made his choice. She was free to do whatever she wanted.

She felt tears brewing behind her eyes, and she'd be damned before she cried in front of him. She did the only thing she knew how, she attacked. "What did you expect me to do?" she asked. "Spend my days weeping over you like some love-sick puppy?"

"Not crying, no. But I hoped you would miss me. Obviously, you didn't do much of that." He laughed bitterly. "Just do me a favor—don't get up from the bed you share with your lover and put on my clothes."

She'd forgotten what she was wearing. She gathered the shirt at the hem. "Want it back?"

"Not on your life," he said through clenched teeth. Ariel watched him as he covered his face with his hand, remaining absolutely still for a moment. Abruptly, he turned away from her, walking in the direction of the garage.

"And what about you?" she called after him. She ran down the two front steps but didn't dare step into the driveway. Her bare feet would never survive the gravel. "Did you think I wouldn't see that picture of you?"

He stopped mid-stride and turned to face her. "I would think that you of all people would know better than to believe everything she sees in the paper."

He turned from her, and soon she could hear the garage door opening and the revving of an engine. A moment later, Jarad pulled his car out of the garage, stopping in front of her with a screech.

Ariel's mouth dropped open seeing him drive up in front of her. His car had been here the whole time? She remembered Gran's note telling Ariel she was dropping Jarad at the airport. He hadn't taken his car. He would have had to come back for it some time. Her mind whirred considering this new information. Jarad's car was here. He'd intended to come back all along.

He got out of the car, walking around the hood toward her. She felt a second of hope before she realized he was only picking up his bag. "See you around, sweetheart," he said, giving her a salute. He opened the passenger door and tossed the bag in. He slammed the door shut. Without looking at her, he started toward the driver's side of the car.

"Why did you leave, Jarad?" Her voice was so faint she feared he hadn't heard her. But he paused, not saying anything for a moment.

With his back toward her, he said, "You know everything. You tell me."

Right then, she didn't think she knew anything. She didn't know what to believe. But if there was a chance of saving what she and Jarad had, she wanted to take it. "I don't know. Tell me. Please."

"All right." He sat on the car hood, bracing one foot on the bumper. "I'll tell you. My friend Sam's fiancé—I told you about him. Well, he got himself in a little accident. He decided those guys in NAS-CAR were having too much fun without him. He got on the track, hit a pylon and they had to scrape him up off the concrete. Naturally, she was a little upset about this. Forgive me for thinking she needed me more than you did."

"Oh, my God," she said, her hand on her chest. "Is he all right? Why didn't you tell me?"

"He's fine, aside from a few broken bones. And as I remember it, I did try to tell you the last night I was here. You didn't seem to be in the mood to listen."

He sounded so cold to her, and his gaze on her was as frigid as the deep blue sea. "No, I do not forgive you," she told him. "So what if I didn't want to listen just then. You could have called me and told me. You could have let me know whether you were alive or dead instead of letting me worry about you. Then when I do 'see' you, it's on the cover of a newspaper with some redhead draped all over you."

Jarad opened his mouth to speak, but Ariel silenced him with a wave of her hand. "Now you show up here, accusing me of the most awful things. If that's what you want to believe, go ahead. But I'll tell you one thing, I am not going to spend another minute defending myself to anyone, not even you."

Turning, Ariel marched up the stairs and into the foyer, slamming the door behind her. Feeling more angry than she ever had in her life, she pulled Jarad's shirt over her head, rolled it into a ball and threw it on the floor. Wishing it were its owner, she stomped on it a few times, then kicked it across the floor.

She exhaled deeply, not feeling any better after her explosion of temper. She needed to think, not vent her spleen like a two-year-old. As her anger

began to recede, she tried to look at her situation
with her normal rational approach, but it was difficult. All her assumptions from the last few days
were turned upside down by Jarad's appearance on
her doorstep.

What was she going to do now? In truth, she'd
half expected Jarad to follow her inside. It wasn't
like him to back down or walk away from an argument. She went to the door and peered out the
narrow windows that ran along either side of the
door frame. Jarad was still out there, standing by
the driver's side door. His arms were folded over
the top of the car and his head was down.

Ariel straightened, letting the curtain fall back in
place. He seemed as affected by their argument as
she was. She put her hand on the doorknob, about
to turn the latch. Then she heard the sound of a
car's engine turning over, the revving of an engine
and the crunch of gravel as Jarad quickly drove
away.

Jarad watched through the windshield of his car
as the second ferry in an hour pulled out of the
slip on its way to Woods Hole. That's how long
he'd been waiting on the stand-by line outside the
Steamship Authority building in Oak Bluffs. He'd
bought a return ticket for later that evening, and
if the line didn't start moving, he wasn't going to
have an opportunity to use it.

He ground his teeth together in frustration. He'd
expected Ariel to be with him on the return trip.
He'd hoped he would be able to convince her to
come back with him for a few days. The engagement ring he'd planned to use as the convincer
lay in its case in his front pants pocket. It dug into

his thigh like a bitter reminder. She'd never even seen it.

He cursed himself for being the fool that he was. But when he'd pulled up in the taxi and seen Ariel standing on her grandmother's doorstep, he'd lost it. She'd been smiling and mussed and provocative, and that son of a bitch had his hands all over her. He'd held himself rooted inside the car, because he didn't trust what he might do if he got his hands on the other man. When he did get out, he'd seen the smile fade from her lovely features.

She hadn't been happy to see him. That was the thing that bothered him most. Even before he'd opened his big mouth and all that nonsense poured out.

It was his own fault. He'd been so busy thinking about the future he was planning for them, he'd forgotten about the present. He hadn't called her as he'd promised, afraid he'd blurt out the surprise he planned for her.

No, it was worse than that. It occurred to him that he'd behaved more like he was arranging a movie deal than a marriage: keep your mouth shut until everything's in place, then wow them with what you've got. Understandably, Ariel hadn't been terribly impressed.

He should have known what her reaction would be to seeing his and Sam's picture in the paper. She wasn't used to the tenacity of the press, the way they could squeeze a story out of the driest kernel of truth. Then again, he hadn't expected Sam to cry all over him at the airport either, drawing attention to them both.

He'd sent her the flowers then, as a sort of apology. Obviously she'd never gotten them, and in the absence of any word from him, she'd thought he no longer cared for her. He couldn't really blame her for that. He'd jumped to much worse conclusions on evidence that was just as scanty.

If he'd thought about it, he would never have accused her of sleeping with Peter. He of all people should have known that wasn't the kind of woman she was. After seeing the two of them together, some primitive male part of his brain had taken over. Rationality had been the farthest thing from his mind. He'd driven off, realizing he was a second away from storming into her house and shaking some sense into her. That would have made him no better than that other fool.

Jarad heard a car honk behind him, jolting him back to the present. The long line waiting to embark upon the ferry had started to move. What were all these people doing leaving the island now? he wondered. It was the middle of the week.

Why was he here? He should go back to her and ask her to forgive him for his stupidity. He waited until the car in front of him pulled up a little, then steered his way out of the line, enduring the honks and calls from other drivers waiting to advance.

When he got to Gran's house, he didn't see Ariel's car in the driveway as it had been when he left. Knocking on the door yielded no answer. As usual, it was unlocked. He went inside, searching first the lower floor, then the upper. Ariel's room was as bare as if she'd never been there. Her clothes were gone from the closet. Her personal items were missing from the dresser.

Jarad sank down on the bed, facing a truth that was inescapable. Ariel was gone.

* * *

He found her right where he expected her to be: sitting in the weeds to the right of the State Lobster Hatchery. She'd changed into a pair of jeans and one of her own T-shirts. Her back was against one of the wooden headstones which was so old the inscription on the stone had been worn away.

She looked so dejected that Jarad's heart twisted seeing her there. As he got closer to her, she lifted her head and watched him approach, her eyes narrowing and her chin lifting defiantly. "What are you doing here?" she asked him when he squatted down beside her.

He didn't answer her, taking another tack instead. "Why don't you come out of there," he suggested, "before some tick bites you and you come down with Lyme disease."

She shook her head, looking down at her lap. "That isn't going to work," she told him. "You can't joke your way out of this one."

"I know, sweetheart," he said, cupping the side of her face in the palm of his hand. "I'm sorry I said those things to you. I wasn't thinking. I—"

"Well, I have been thinking," she interrupted. She looked up at him, her eyes limpid with unshed tears. "I can't be with a man that doesn't trust me, who thinks the worst of me at every possible opportunity. You didn't even ask me if anything happened between Peter and me. You just assumed it had."

"Isn't that what you did when you saw the picture of Sam and me in the paper?" he asked softly.

She turned her gaze away from him. "I tried not to. But what was I supposed to think when I didn't hear from you? Only a fool goes on hoping when all is hopeless, and I am tired of being a fool."

Jarad ran his hand over his face. "What are you saying, Ariel?"

"I'm saying that you shouldn't have wasted your time in coming back. That you had the right idea when you left in the first place. There isn't any future for us, Jarad. Maybe you should just go home."

Jarad knelt beside her, taking both her hands in his. She was tearing his heart out and she wouldn't even look at him. "Please don't do this, Ariel," he begged her. "I can understand your being angry. I acted like a horse's ass and I'm sorry. But don't tell me we have no future. I love you, Ariel."

She did look at him then. "You know, that's the same excuse Peter gave for doing what he did." She pulled her hands away from his, drawing attention to the ring she still wore on her left hand, for she hadn't really given up hope before. She slid it from her finger, placing it in the center of his palm and closing his fingers around it. "I don't want it anymore," she told him. "Go home, Jarad."

She turned away from him, drawing her knees up and wrapping her arms around them. He felt like he was crumbling, that in a strong wind he would scatter and blow away. He touched his hand to her shoulder. "Ariel," he began, not knowing what to say to her.

"Please, Jarad," she whispered. "Please go away."

Sighing, he withdrew his hand. He didn't know how to reach her, what words to say to make her change her mind. She refused to look back at him, though he called her name again. Instead, she laid her cheek on her knees, facing away from him. After a while, he gave up, went back to his car and drove away.

* * *

It was after eleven that night when Ariel pulled up outside the house. She was tired and cold and wet, since it had begun to rain a half hour before. The house was dark, except for the flickering of the TV in the sitting room, which was visible to her as she dragged her duffel bag from the trunk of her car.

When Jarad left the first time, she'd thrown everything she had with her into her bag, intending to get away from the island that now reminded her so much of him. On the way to the ferry it had occurred to her that she would probably end up on the same ship as Jarad if she left right away as she had planned. She'd gone to the cemetery to wait when he'd found her there.

She left the duffel bag propped up against the wall in the foyer, then went to find Gran. She was sound asleep on the sitting room sofa, a fire still burning in the grate, the television playing on unnoticed.

Ariel got a blanket from the hall closet. There was no point in waking Gran, who seemed comfortable where she was. Besides, Ariel was in no mood to explain to the older woman all that had transpired that day. Ariel felt like she could sleep for a hundred years and still wake up exhausted.

She tucked the blanket around Gran, starting with her shoulders and ending with her feet. When she bent to place a kiss on Gran's forehead, she was startled to see Gran's piercing green eyes staring back at her.

"Gran," Ariel cried. "I didn't know you were awake."

"Neither did I," Gran replied. "But I'm glad I am." Gran sat up, bringing the blanket with her.

She used the remote to click off the TV. "Sit down, Ariel," Gran said. "I want to talk to you."

"I'm really tired," Ariel began. "Can't we talk in the morning?"

"Sit," Gran ordered, and Ariel obeyed. She had never heard her grandmother use that tone of voice before, at least not as an adult. "What I have to say to you will only take a few minutes."

"Okay, Gran," Ariel said, dreading what was to come. "I'm listening."

"What on earth is wrong with you, child?" Gran asked. "I thought both my granddaughters had at least one lick of common sense. What happened to yours?"

Ariel blinked, staring at her grandmother. "What do you mean?"

"I mean, how can a woman spend days pining over a man, and then when he shows up she tells him to go back where he came from?"

"How did you know Jarad was here?"

"I found him sitting on my doorstep when Charlie, Emma and I got home. It was the most pathetic sight I'd seen in a long time," Gran said drolly. "He told me he'd ruined things between you and begged me to talk with you on his behalf."

"And that's what this is about—you talking to me on his behalf?" Ariel asked, feeling completely abandoned by everyone. "Are you on his side then?"

"No, child." Gran took hold of her hand. "I like Jarad a great deal, but I am your grandmother, and you are the one I am concerned about. Tell me what happened."

"Oh, Gran," Ariel said, going into the older woman's waiting arms. She told Gran everything that had happened since Jarad first showed up until he left the second time. Then she sat back, looking at Gran for a reaction.

Her jaw tight, Gran said, "You have really screwed things up this time, Ariel."

"Gran," Ariel cried, surprised both by her grandmother's assessment of the situation and her language. She'd never heard Gran say a word harsher than "darn."

"Ariel, let me ask you a question. What would you have thought if the situation were reversed, if you saw Jarad kissing some woman from his past? And I mean not on some newspaper cover, but right there in front of you. What would you do?"

"I don't know," Ariel said, not wanting to be drawn into Gran's line of questioning.

"I know what I'd do if I caught Charlie kissing some gray-haired hussy. I'd scratch both her eyes out and then I'd kill Charlie. And I don't think I'd wait for any explanations, either."

Ariel giggled, envisioning Gran doing just that. "What's your point?" Ariel asked when her laughter subsided.

"What did Jarad do while you were saying goodbye to Peter?"

"Nothing. He didn't get out of the cab until Peter left."

"An amazing display of restraint, if you ask me. Too bad. That boy has a good beating coming to him."

"Gran!" Ariel said, surprised by the venom in her grandmother's words. Gran had never said anything one way or another about Peter.

"Well, he does," Gran averred, nodding her head for emphasis. "And don't you see, child, Jarad was asking you to tell him what happened, in his own way."

"And he couldn't just speak to me like a normal person?"

"Couldn't you have given him a straight answer instead of telling him to think whatever he wanted?"

Ariel looked down at her lap. "So you are saying it's my fault?"

"No, but I am saying you aren't blameless, either. He came back to make things right with you, and you sent him away. It seems to me you were testing him, testing his love for you, and he failed. If he stayed with you, he'd have to face you ignoring him. If he left, you'd fault him for that too." Gran stroked her hand over Ariel's hair. "What's the matter, child? Don't you love him?"

Ariel didn't have to think about her answer. "Of course I love him, Gran."

"Then what is it? Why would you do this?"

Ariel laid her head in her grandmother's lap. "I'm afraid, Gran. I'm afraid of making the biggest mistake of my life. We both know I haven't had the best luck with men. What if Jarad turns out to be no better than Peter?"

"I think we both know Jarad is nothing like Peter," Gran said. She grasped Ariel's shoulders, pulling her into a sitting position. "Now you listen to me, Ariel Windsor. Haven't you learned anything from your old grandmother? If you love him, as you say, are you willing to take the chance of losing him because you're afraid? Do you want to have to wait fifty years to be happy, like I did, when your body betrays your intentions and your mind is weighted with your own regrets?"

Gran took a deep breath, exhaling slowly. "Don't do that to yourself, Ariel. Believe me, it isn't a pleasant way to live your life."

Gran patted Ariel's shoulder, disentangled herself from the blanket and stood. "It's time I got these old bones into bed. You think about what I said," Gran said, pausing at the door. "Good night, sweetie."

"Good night, Gran," Ariel echoed, watching her grandmother retreat from the room. She knew Gran was right. She missed Jarad already. She missed his handsome face and his sense of humor and the way her body blossomed whenever he touched her. No, she didn't want to spend the rest of her life without him. But now that she'd told him to leave, she had no idea where he was, how to find him.

She reached out to him with her mind, willing him to come back to her. She sighed heavily, letting her shoulders drop. That sort of thing only worked in fairy tales and romance novels. If she was going to contact Jarad, she was going to have to do it the old-fashioned way: in person.


Over the next couple of days, Ariel called everywhere she could think of, trying to contact him. She called his parents' house in upstate New York, where there was no answer, not even a machine. She called his house in California. When she heard Jarad's voice on the recording, she got so choked up she almost couldn't leave a message. There was no return call from Jarad, and Ariel began to give up hope he ever would call back.

With nothing else to occupy her mind, Ariel wandered the house like a ghost on a haunt. She knew she was driving Gran and Mrs. Thompson crazy, but she couldn't seem to help herself. One afternoon, Gran was in the foyer when Ariel came up beside her.

"What do you want me to do with these," Gran asked, referring to the long-dead roses that still occupied a place on the table by the door. They were still wrapped in the plastic they'd arrived in. No one had touched them for fear of what Ariel's reaction would be.

"I don't think my father would mind if we threw them out," Ariel said absently.

"Your father?" Gran asked. "What has he got to do with them?"

"He sent them, didn't he?"

Smiling indulgently, Gran shook her head. "What made you think that?"

Why had she thought they were from her father? Ariel didn't really remember anymore. So much had happened in the interim. She slid the card from the envelope and read it again. *See you soon, my little witch. I love you.*

She remembered seeing the words "little witch" and thinking of her father. Jarad must have come up with that name for her on his own, though she couldn't imagine why he would. He hadn't abandoned her in his absence as she had thought. And he'd told her he loved her. The smile that formed on her lips was bittersweet. She could imagine how hurt Jarad must have been to find her with Peter, after expressing that sentiment to her. She'd treated his suspicions as if they were totally unreasonable, after she herself hadn't wanted to speak to Peter, fearing the impression he'd get seeing her dressed as she was.

Ariel searched her memory of their time together. She couldn't think of one time she'd told Jarad she cared for him, that she welcomed his presence in her life in any way. Jarad had told her he loved her, and she threw that love back in his face. In her fear of being hurt, she'd done to him the one thing she most dreaded happening to herself.

In a bout of self-pity, she cried herself to sleep that night, wondering where Jarad was and whom he was with. The next morning she awoke, still on the sitting room sofa, achy from the uncomfortable position she'd slept in. Ariel knew she really must be in bad shape. She could swear she heard Jarad's voice.

Then she realized the TV was still on, tuned to one of the morning shows. She looked up at the set, her eyes widening in surprise to see Jarad on the screen. She drank in the sight of him, dressed in a navy blue sport coat with a paler blue shirt underneath.

She smiled, watching him, only vaguely aware of what he was talking about. He looked so handsome to her, so confident. Unlike many celebrities she'd seen on talk shows, he didn't fidget, he didn't say "um" every other word. It was the woman interviewing him who seemed flustered by him, stammering, looking away. She asked him the same question three times. Jarad had the good grace not to point it out to her.

The show went to a commercial. Something about the show's title flashing across the screen caught her attention. Live, Ariel mused. The show was taped live. She knew where the studio was— right around the corner from her doctor's office. As the commercial started to play, Ariel got up and clicked off the set. She knew what she was going to do. Jarad was in New York!

# Twelve

Jarad stepped through the doorway of the two-bedroom hotel suite he and Sam shared, tossed the room key onto the coffee table and headed to the hospitality bar for a beer. He downed half of it in one gulp, and was in the process of doing the same to the second half when Sam came out of her room.

"So how'd it go?" she asked, drying her hair with the towel around her shoulders.

Jarad removed the bottle from his lips long enough to answer, "All right."

"All right?" Sam said. "You aced it. You had that woman eating out of your hand."

Jarad looked at her over his shoulder, cocking a questioning eyebrow. It wasn't like Sam to be so disingenuous. "More likely she wanted to eat my hand," he said, "and a few other body parts besides. What are you so cheery about?"

"Nothing," Sam said, letting her annoyance show. "I'm trying to set a good example."

"Of what?"

"Grace under pressure. I think at least one of us shouldn't be drowning our sorrows in the nearest bottle." She took the beer from him, but at most there were only a couple of swallows left. She eyed it as if it were a snake about to bite her. "You've been doing a bit too much of this lately." She dropped it into the wastebasket, liquid and all.

Jarad sat on the overstuffed sofa, propping his feet up on the coffee table. "It's these damn interviews," he said. "You know how much I hate them. There's a guy from some magazine who's supposed to be here in an hour, then the gig tonight. Give me a break, Sam."

Sam did know how much Jarad hated that aspect of the business, but with the picture coming out next week, being in the public eye was one of those unavoidable realities. Pictures had to be promoted, and they were all doing their share, except for Billy, of course, who could hardly give interviews from a hospital bed.

"Give *me* a break," Sam said, placing her hands on her hips. "We both know that is *not* what is bothering you. You have been a colossal pain in the neck ever since you got back from Martha's Vineyard, and it's not because of some silly reporters."

"Don't start that again, Sam, 'cause I am not in the mood." He stood up, shrugging out of his jacket. He slung it over the back of the sofa and headed toward his room.

"Oh, no you don't," Sam said. "You are not getting off that easily. You may not want to talk about it, but I do."

"Talk all you want," Jarad said over his shoulder. "I'm going to take a shower."

Sam threw her hands up in frustration and gritted her teeth. Jarad could be the stubbornest of men when he put his mind to it. But she hated to see him suffering, especially when he wouldn't talk to her about it. There had never been anything between them they couldn't talk about. Until now.

She missed her friend, she missed his smile, his

sense of humor. She missed the way he used to tease her until she wanted to gag him. The Jarad she knew all her life was a kind, sensitive man. This Jarad that was in the other room, she didn't know at all. She didn't know how to get the other one back, but she had to do something.

She was waiting for him on his bed when he came out of the shower, wearing only a towel. Seeing her, he stopped short. "Do you mind, Sam?" he said, pointing toward the door.

"You forget I've seen everything you've got to offer."

"Oh?" Jarad raised a questioning brow. "When was this?"

Sam smiled coyly. "At Tommy Johnson's house that day the two of you got sprayed by that funny-looking cat and his mother bathed you in tomato juice in his backyard. His sister and I laughed." She drew out the last word.

"Very funny," Jarad said "But if you don't get out of here, you're going to see the grown-up version in about two seconds."

He should have known she wouldn't be bothered by his threat. She tossed him one of the hotel's terry-cloth robes. It hit him square in the face.

"I'm not going anywhere," Sam told him. "I wouldn't put it past you to barricade yourself in here the moment I'm out the door."

Grumbling, Jarad turned his back to her and put on the robe. Sam could be one of the stubbornest women in the world when she set her mind to it. He could think of only one woman who was more stubborn, and his thoughts about her were driving him crazy. Could it only have been a few days ago that he'd left her? He felt like he'd aged a year since then.

When he'd arranged himself to his satisfaction, he turned back to her. "Happy now?" he asked, leaning against the door frame, his arms crossed in front of his chest.

Sam shook her head. "How long do you intend for this to go on?"

"For what to go on?"

She cocked her head to one side. "Don't play dumb, Jay. It doesn't suit you. You know what I mean. How long do you intend to punish the rest of the world because some woman you met disappointed you?"

Now that Sam had jumped in with both feet, she waited for Jarad's reaction. The last thing she expected was for him to say, quietly, "You don't know what you're talking about, Sam."

"Then enlighten me," she said. "I've never known you to be too particular about what woman you were with."

Jarad was absolutely silent. The expression in his eyes warned her not to continue further in that direction. "All right, all right," Sam conceded. "So that isn't true. I don't understand you, that's all. When I called you that first time, you were in looove. You couldn't say enough good about her. The whole time you were in L.A. you were walking around with this goofy grin on your face. Then you go back for less than a day and you won't talk about her at all. What happened?"

Jarad shrugged. He and Sam had been through so much together, it was unfair of him not to tell her. Besides, he was spending so much energy trying to avoid talking about Ariel that it would be easier just to speak.

"I blew it, Sam, that's what happened. I drove up to her house and she was standing there with that bastard she used to go out with, and I went nuts."

"Whew," Sam said. "Is there a hospital somewhere I should be sending flowers to?"

"No," Jarad said, chuckling. "But almost. Somehow I managed to keep my hands off the guy's throat, but I did say a few things that were better left on the cutting room floor, if you know what I mean."

Sam shook her head, looking heavenward, imagining what a few of those things might be. "You accused her of sleeping with him, didn't you?"

Jarad nodded grimly. "Among other things. As you can imagine, she wasn't too pleased to see me."

"What is it with you men?" Sam exploded. "Always so quick to accuse and to blame, while you go off doing whatever you please?" Sam let out a heavy breath, knowing her outburst had more to do with her own love life than Jarad's.

Apparently Jarad didn't notice how quickly her bluster had run out. "Come on, Sam," Jarad interjected. "You didn't see her. She was standing there all tumbled, wearing nothing but—"

"But what?" Sam's eyes narrowed, fearing what she'd hear.

"My shirt. She was wearing my shirt. I must have left it there."

Sam had to bite her lip to keep from smiling. No woman wore the shirt of a man she didn't care for. "Maybe she was wearing your shirt because she missed you."

"Maybe," Jarad conceded. "I don't think it mattered one way or the other. She never got the flowers I sent her. After not hearing from me, she saw our picture in the paper and was convinced I'd forgotten about her."

"Oh, Jarad, I'm sorry. If I hadn't called you—"

Jarad shifted, shoving his hands into the pockets of his robe. "It's not your fault," Jarad said, shaking his head. "It's mine. I thought I was so clever, planning to go back and ask her to marry me. I didn't even call her, afraid I'd open my big mouth and spoil the surprise. I was so clever, the ring is still burning a hole in my pocket."

Sam sucked in her breath with her teeth against her lip. She had known Jarad was in love with the woman. She hadn't guessed the depth of his feelings. He'd never told her about his plans to propose. He'd probably wanted to spare her feelings, considering she'd recently broken off her own engagement.

"What are you going to do?" she asked quietly.

Jarad sighed. "I thought I'd give her a few days to calm down. After that I don't know." Jarad came and sat next to Sam on the bed. "I'll probably be wasting my time. She can be more stubborn than you are when she gets an idea in her head."

"I am not stubborn," she protested, until she realized he was teasing her. She supposed that was his way of ending the conversation. His smile was back in place, though it looked forced.

"I know I haven't been much fun to be around lately."

"No, you haven't," Sam agreed, nudging him with her shoulder.

"Give me a little more time to get my act together, okay?"

Before she could respond, the phone rang and Jarad turned to answer it. Sam went back to her room.

Sitting at her dressing table, she wondered if it was wise to give Ariel any more time to think. That's what had gotten Jarad in trouble in the first place. She also knew it wouldn't do her any good to point this out to him. As far as stubborn people went, the old saying definitely applied to Jarad: it took one to know one.

Sam put down the brush she'd been torturing her hair with during her musings. She was going to do something Jarad hated most of all. She was going to meddle.

Ariel slid into the black leather seat of the taxi that would take her from the airport to her apartment on East 68th Street. She fingered the glossy pages of the magazine bearing Jarad's picture on the cover. The words "Does He Have What It Takes?" appeared above an image of his handsome, determined-looking face. In some ways, at least, she could answer yes. A subheading asked, "Can this writer's son start something big with *Summer's End?*"

She wondered what Jarad's reaction would be to seeing her. That is, if she ever found him. Knowing what city he was in wasn't much help when the city was New York. She assumed he was staying in a hotel, which would make life easier, but with all the hotels in New York, finding him might still be like looking for the proverbial needle in a haystack.

She'd barely gotten inside the front door of her apartment when the phone started ringing. She made a flying leap across the sofa for the phone. "Hello," she said breathlessly, hoping it was Jarad.

"Are you Ariel Windsor?" a feminine voice asked.

For a minute Ariel was tempted to ask who wanted to know, but then she changed her mind. "Yes."

"This is Samantha Hathaway. Can I see you?"

"Sure." Ariel answered without thinking. Then she wondered why Sam would be calling her. Had something happened to Jarad? "Is Jarad all right?" she asked.

"In a manner of speaking. I'll be there in five minutes."

The line went dead.

Ariel stared at the receiver in her hand. "What was that all about?" she asked it. There was no use speculating. Sam would probably be there any minute.

Ariel barely had time to check her hair and makeup in the mirror when the doorbell rang. After the shock of hearing Jarad's friend's voice on the other end of the line, she wouldn't have been surprised if every hair on her head was standing straight up.

When she opened the door, Ariel was treated to a full view of Samantha Elizabeth Hathaway. Her picture in the paper hadn't done her justice. She was tall and slim—striking. Dressed in a stylish burnt orange blazer with a matching T-shirt underneath and jeans that couldn't have been tighter if someone had painted them on, Samantha was the most beautiful woman Ariel had ever seen in person. Sam removed her sunglasses, and Ariel saw that her amber-colored eyes complemented her flawless, almond-colored complexion and long auburn hair. "Ariel Windsor, I presume," Sam said.

Ariel swallowed the lump that had risen in her throat. "Pleased to meet you." Ariel stuck out her hand, feeling like an Elizabethan peasant summoned to meet the great lady of the estate. *This* was Jarad's *friend*? Remembering her manners, Ariel asked, "Won't you come in?"

Sam shook her head. "I've only got a few minutes," Sam confessed. "I wanted to invite you to the screening we're having tonight." Sam pressed an envelope into her hand, which Ariel assumed was an invitation. "Can you make it?"

"Jarad doesn't know you're here, does he?"

Sam wet her lips with the edge of her tongue. "No."

She knew in that instant that Jarad did not want to see her. Rather than discouraging her, it gave her added determination to see him. "What does one wear to a screening?" Ariel asked.

"I thought you'd never ask," Sam said, picking up the shopping bag at her feet. "I didn't know if you'd have anything to wear on such short notice, so I took the liberty of bringing you something." Samantha gave her the once over. "I'm sure it will fit."

"Thank you," Ariel said, wondering what the something Sam brought her would be. Whatever it was, she was sure it cost a fortune. The shopping bag was from a very expensive designer and the garment inside was boxed.

She wondered what Jarad had done to win this woman's loyalty and generosity. She knew none of this was done for her own benefit, but for his. She didn't want whatever happened between herself and Jarad to cause friction between the two friends. "Please don't tell him I'm coming," she asked.

"But—" Sam started to protest.

"I'd prefer it that way," Ariel insisted.

Sam shrugged before glancing at her watch. "I've got to run. I'll have a car here for you about seven." Before Ariel could say another word, Sam disappeared down the hall.

Ariel closed the door and whooped. She was going to see Jarad tonight!


Ariel looked out the tinted window of the limousine at the glass-enclosed theater where the screening of Jarad's movie would begin in less than an hour. The pink and blue neon marquee winked at her. Above that on the roof of the theater was a giant mock-up of a man and woman in a red convertible. The words "Summer's End" were emblazoned on the vehicle's side in large black letters. There was no doubt she was in the right place.

She was at once filled with dread and anticipation as she watched the advance of the chauffeur toward her door in the periphery of her vision. Once he opened it, she would have to get out and go inside. If she didn't want to make a fool of herself, that is.

All the bravado she'd felt earlier when she'd called the beauty salon and demanded an immediate appointment had coiled into a twisting knot of anxiety in the pit of her stomach. She couldn't imagine what Jarad's reaction to seeing her would be. Whatever it was, she would have to face it when the time came.

She stepped out of the car, straightening the royal blue dress she wore. If nothing else, Jarad's friend had excellent taste in clothes. The halter dress dipped into a deep V in the front, and was barely existent in the back, curving sensually over her lower back. The fabric was fluid and floaty and very feminine. The double hem ended well above mid-thigh. It was a bit more bare than Ariel would have liked, but the dress fit her perfectly, as Sam had said it would.

Taking a deep breath, Ariel started forward, the high heels of her sandals clicking on the pavement. She clutched her small purse in one hand, checked her hair with the fingers of the other. Once she told the women in the salon where she was going, they'd insisted on giving her "the works," including a fancy upswept hairdo, manicure and pedicure. They called in the makeup lady on her day off. They'd all seen her picture in the newspaper and were duly impressed. She only wished she was sure they had something to be impressed about.

The cluster of photographers outside certainly weren't impressed with her. Not one recognized her from her picture in the newspaper. Or they deemed her unworthy of the expenditure of any film. Either way, Ariel was glad to gain the entrance without calling notice to herself or enduring any prying questions.

Once inside, she surveyed the room. The space wasn't overly large, but it was packed with faces she recognized from the media and the entertainment industry. It was a heady atmosphere in which Ariel knew no one except a woman too beautiful for words and a man who, in all probability, didn't want to talk to her.

It didn't take her long to spot Jarad. He was standing amid a group of people, or amid a group of women, to be more precise. She drank in the sight of him, handsome in a double-breasted navy suit, the white of his collarless shirt accentuating the bronze of his skin.

As she walked toward him, he turned slowly to look at her, as if he felt her presence in the room. She finally understood what it meant for eyes to meet from across a crowded room. After their initial look of surprise, his eyes darkened with emotion, his expression seeming to grow more heated and intense the closer she got to him. By the time she stood in front of him, she felt flushed, excited and more than a little breathless.

She inhaled deeply, letting her breath flow out through parted lips. "Hello, Jarad," she said.

Jarad looked down at her, a smile playing at the corners of his mouth. He'd never seen her look so alluring as she had a moment ago framed in the open doorway. Every memory of her had washed over him in one powerful wave: their kiss on the ferry, her childhood sorrow and indignation, her siren's smile the night they'd first made love.

He remembered something else, too. Her father's words the night of Jenny's wedding. *If you love her, go after her. She isn't going to come to you.* But she had come to him. He felt humbled by that and very, very pleased. He raised his hand to cup her cheek. "What are you doing here?" he asked her.

She leaned into his gentle caress, rubbing her cheek against his hand. She had spent so much time believing he didn't want to see her that she didn't know what to say now that she was sure he did. "I missed you," she answered simply.

She hadn't noticed they'd drawn closer together until she felt her breasts pressing against the wall of his chest. Her hands went automatically to his shoulders. The hand on her cheek slid around to her nape, tilting her head further back. His other hand settled on her waist. In that moment, it seemed to her that it was just the two of them alone, apart from the glittering room around them. Going up on tiptoe, she pressed her lips to his, sighing as his arms tightened around her.

She parted her lips sweetly for him, yet there was nothing sweet about his kiss. It was full of passion and longing and need. There was something else, too, that Ariel had felt before but had never been able to identify. Love. Jarad loved her. She hadn't really believed it until that moment.

Hearing a sharp click and seeing a bright flash of red behind her eyes, Ariel pulled away, lifting startled eyes to Jarad.

He was smiling down at her. "It appears, Ariel Windsor, that you've created a scene."

"Me?" she asked, scanning the room full of avid faces staring back at her. A photographer stood a few inches away from them, poised to snap away should they do anything else interesting. She turned back to him, burying her face against his chest. "What did I do?"

Jarad threw back his head and laughed. Until she'd walked in the door, the whole evening had been as dry as stale toast. He'd wanted to hold the premiere in New York, far away from the usual Hollywood hype and hangers-on. Hollywood people were willing to do or say the absurd or merely sensational in order to attract attention to themselves. New Yorkers wanted to impress you with how detached and sophisticated they were. They spoke with urbane civility, even when they were ripping each other apart.

New Yorkers liked to think they'd seen everything, done everything worthy of being done. Yet throw them a surprise, something they didn't expect, and they became as avid as a pack of sharks in a feeding frenzy.

Ariel had drawn their notice from the moment she'd walked through the door. His wasn't the only male head to turn and watch her entrance into the room. He'd had to fight down the urge to take off his jacket and cover her with it. He knew he couldn't be the only man in the room whose body had come to life at the sight of her.

Then he'd heard someone whisper, "That's the girl from the newspaper." Several female heads had turned expectantly, apparently hoping something was about to happen to liven up the festivities.

"I'm sorry, sweetheart," he said, sobering, seeing the disgruntled look on her face. Taking her hand, he led her toward the back of the room. They turned a corner and they were in a darkened hallway which led to the theater where Jarad's movie would be shown.

With the door closed firmly behind him, Jarad pulled her into his arms, just holding her. His hands roamed over her bare back, then lower to cup her hips, drawing her soft body closer to his hard one. She felt so damn good to him, he groaned against her ear.

"Are you upset about the scene out there?" he asked her after a moment.

She shook her head, pulling back so she could look at him. How could she be, when she had caused it. "I love you, Jarad," she told him. "And if the whole world knows it, that's fine with me."

Jarad closed his eyes, breathing deeply. When he opened them, he asked her, "And when did you come to this conclusion?"

Smiling shyly, she looked up into his intense, probing gaze. "The day we went to Gay Head. You came up behind me and put your arms around me. I felt so warm and safe and cared for. I realized I wanted to make you feel the same way."

Taking her hand, he kissed the center of her palm. "I didn't think I was ever going to hear you say those words," he said quietly.

"I didn't think I was ever going to get to say

them," she countered. "I'm so sorry, Jarad, for all
the things I said. I—"

"Hush," he said, placing a finger over her lips.
"Neither of us was blameless. There's no need to
wallow in regrets. I think we'd both be better off
if we forgot the last few days ever happened."

She nodded her agreement as he laced his fingers with hers.

"Let's get out of here," he said.

She held up her other hand against his chest to
halt him. "Jarad, what about your movie?"

"I've seen it."

She cocked her head to one side, slanting a
glance up at him through the fringe of her lashes.
"I didn't come here to ruin your evening."

"Believe me, honey," Jarad said, laughing. "You
made my whole day."


Fifteen minutes later, they were in Ariel's little
apartment on the west side of Manhattan. She
turned from the task of locking the door to find
him standing directly in front of her. "Come
here," he said, a sultry command issued in a voice
deepened by his desire for her.

With a siren's smile, she walked toward him, sliding her arms around his neck. He lifted her, holding
her with his arms around her waist, her feet dan-
gling above the floor. He didn't set her down until
they stood before the queen-size bed in her room.

"Make love to me, Jarad," she urged him. There
was no coy flirtation this time. Her fingers went to
the small clasp holding the top of her dress together. She let the flimsy material slither to the
floor between them. Jarad sucked in his breath at
the sight of her, bare except for the scanty triangle

of lace covering her. She slid the panties down over her hips, letting them join her dress on the floor.

He reached for her, a growl rumbling in his chest. She felt it reverberate through her, too, as he brought her up against him. Her hands gripped his shoulders as his mouth claimed hers, his tongue imitating the act that would soon follow. His hands cupped her bottom, lifting her. She moaned, feeling his arousal so intimately against her heated flesh through the thin barrier of his clothes. But it wasn't enough. Her hands tore at his clothes, until he was as nude as she. She ran her hands over his perfect masculine form, pulling him closer to her, but she still wanted more.

"Jarad," Ariel called, sliding out of his embrace. She laid down on the bed, drawing him with her. "Now," she whispered.

In an instant he was inside her, filling her with such exquisite sensations that she cried out and clung to him more fiercely. He thrust into her deeply, eliciting moan after moan from her lips. She came apart in his arms, her back arching, her nails raking his back. He groaned his release against her throat. Together, they lay entwined, taking a long time to recover.

When he could speak again, Jarad looked into her passion-darkened eyes. "I love you, Ariel. I've loved you since that night you climbed over your balcony to get to me. I was watching you there in the moonlight, knowing I wanted to spend the rest of my life with you, wondering how I could get you to take me seriously."

"I did take you seriously," she told him. "That was the problem." She laughed, looking up into his twinkling brown eyes. "You scared the hell out of me. No matter how much I tried to push you away, you were so—"

"Persistent," he ventured. When she shook her head he substituted, "Stubborn?"

"Loving," she said, stroking the side of his face with her fingertips. "You were so loving to me that all I could do was love you back."

"Then come back to the coast with me tomorrow. They've booked me on some new talk show . . ."

Ariel giggled. He sounded as if he'd been told they were readying a guillotine. "I can't," she told him. "The first workshop is next week and I haven't planned anything yet."

She saw his disappointment and wanted to reassure him. "You don't have to worry about me going off the deep end if we're apart." She kissed his shoulder with a smile on her lips. All her doubts, her insecurities seemed so far away right now. "Just don't go showing up in any more newspaper articles without my permission."

"Oh, I can assure you you're going to be seeing my picture somewhere—right along with yours. Didn't you notice the number of cameras in the room. I think there was someone from one of the television stations, too. With any luck, we might make the news."

He was teasing her about the last part. He laughed when she covered her face in her hands and let out a little moan. "Could we really?" she asked.

He'd told her he doubted it, but she made him turn on the news anyway when it came on a half hour later. After the first commercial break, the newscaster came back on, wearing a broad smile. "And if you think movie people only did strange things in Hollywood, think again . . ." Ariel tuned out the man's voice, seeing herself on television.

The woman she saw looked pretty and sophisticated and in control. That was the opposite of how she'd felt. "Is that what I look like?" she asked.

Jarad smiled at her. "Better."

Then Jarad's picture came on the screen. "Is that what I look like?" he asked in a lilting voice.

She smacked him on the arm. "Worse."

They were portraying her as some mystery woman who'd whisked Jarad away from his own premiere. Adding to the air of drama was the fact that they'd slipped out the back door without telling anyone they were leaving. This was reported as the song "Devil with a Blue Dress On" played in the background. The reviewer spent as much time speculating about their whereabouts as she did praising Jarad's work.

"It looks like you've got a winner there," she told him, referring to his movie.

"I've got two," he said, his hand stroking her from shoulder to waist. Ariel felt a familiar heat begin to build deep within her. Her hands were as restless on Jarad's body as his were on hers. "I am going to miss you," he said.

"I'm going to miss you, too." She ran her fingertips up his muscled arms to rest on his shoulders. "Go do what you have to do. You know where I'll be if you need me."

"At the moment," he said, "I need you right here." Then he proceeded to show her exactly how much.

# Thirteen

Ariel stood at the railing of the wraparound deck of the Harbor View hotel on the southernmost tip of Martha's Vineyard. She stared down at the water below her. It was almost two weeks since she'd last seen Jarad.

That wasn't exactly true. She'd watched his appearance on the show he'd told her about. The host had insisted on asking about her, and Jarad seemed eager to talk about her rather than the movie he was supposed to be promoting. Her heart melted a little more when he blew her a kiss on the air.

So much had happened since then. Her workshop had gone so well that the program had offered her a position on their staff. She was still considering the offer. She wanted to talk with Jarad first before she made her decision.

And she'd finally talked with Peter. He'd confessed he'd taken the photographs of her and Jarad. He'd heard about Jenny's wedding and knew she would have come home for it. He'd planned to try to reconcile with her. Then he'd seen her and Jarad together on the ferry and taken her picture on impulse. He admitted he'd sold the photographs after he'd seen them together on the beach, to show her what life would be like with a famous man—like living in a glass bowl with everyone knowing your business. He'd apologized profusely, and Ariel forgave him. He was back with his wife where he belonged, although Ariel couldn't help but feel sorry for the woman.

The music from the party inside intruded on her thoughts. She really should get back inside. Gran and Charlie had been married that afternoon. Rather than hazard another reception at the house, they'd rented out the restaurant for the evening. Gran looked lovely in her pale peach gown and Charlie looked dapper in his formal clothing. Her whole family was eating and dancing up a storm with the 250 invited guests.

Ariel breathed in the salt air, resting her elbows on the railing. If she were honest with herself, she knew she'd come out here to escape. Her family kept asking her about Jarad, and she didn't know what to tell them. The man had a real aversion to telephones, and he wasn't on TV every night for her to keep track of him. The last time she'd spoken to him was two days ago, and the question on her mind was when she would see him, not where he was. All he'd say was "Soon."

Each day he'd been gone he'd had a single white rose delivered to her. She'd confessed to him her misunderstanding when the flowers had arrived at Gran's house. He'd been so indignant, it had been comical. At first she'd thought the roses were a sweet gesture. Then she'd thought he was crazy for being so extravagant. Then she'd come to depend on the daily reminder that he loved her. This morning it had arrived at Gran's house, just as she had convinced herself it wouldn't come.

She held it in her fingers now. She wanted him

there with her. She missed him. She couldn't listen to the radio because every love song reminded her of him. She couldn't go anywhere without thinking she saw him in the face of handsome strangers.

Only a few minutes ago, she'd seen a man on the dance floor that resembled Jarad. She'd walked up to him, tapped him on the shoulder, only to find an older version of Jarad staring back at her. She'd blinked, sure her eyes were playing tricks on her. The man stuck out his hand, introducing himself and his wife as Robert and Diandra Naughton, Jarad's parents. They had greeted her warmly, seeming to know a great deal more about her than she knew about them.

"Is Jarad here?" she'd asked his mother.

"We were hoping you could tell us that, dear."

At least she wasn't the only one whom Jarad failed to tell his whereabouts. She'd excused herself from them and come out here to be alone.

She sighed, looking up at the stars, which once again reminded her of a certain man's eyes. "Jarad, Jarad, Jarad," she chanted. "What am I going to do with you?"

"What do you want to do with me?"

Ariel closed her eyes, feeling a smile lift the corners of her mouth. "I could think of a few hundred things," she said wickedly. She looked up at him, taking in his dark countenance and the immaculate black suit he wore. All the love she felt for him shone in her green eyes.

He saw it there, feeling honored that this wonderful woman would look at him that way. She looked lovely in a floor-length gold-colored gown a shade darker than her skin tone. It was sewn over with tiny sequins that glistened as refracted light from the waves danced over it. "I've missed you, Ari," he said softly.

"I've missed you, too." She straightened and welcomed him into her arms. His hands wandered over her back, bare except for the crisscrossed spaghetti straps of her gown. He held her, knowing this wasn't the same woman he'd met that day on the ferry. She'd changed in some indefinable way.

The Ariel he'd first met wouldn't have dreamt of wearing such a daring dress nor, he suspected, would she have been able to carry it off. The woman in his arms was confident, feminine and sexy as hell. He only hoped he had something to do with her transformation.

Her hair was down, not in one of those fancy hairdos. He ran his fingers through her glossy curls, hearing her purr in response. After a moment, she pulled away from him, taking his hand in one of hers, holding the rose in the other.

"So what have you been up to since the last time I saw you?" she asked. "I hear the movie is doing very well. You must be very pleased."

"It's doing better than I expected. I think I have to give you some of the credit for that. All that publicity after the screening made for a payday at the box office. Did you see it?"

She smiled. "Only four times. It was wonderful, Jarad."

Set in a sleepy southern town, the story was about a young woman not living up to her potential and the drifter that comes to town and shakes up her complacent life. The stranger isn't what he seems, and through a variety of plot twists the pair end up falling in love. The title *Summer's End* was not only a description of the time of year in which the story took place, but also symbolic of the characters' end to youthful floundering, and a commitment to facing the future together. It was especially meaningful to her because so many of the themes explored reminded her of her own experiences with Jarad. "I cried," she confessed.

"Oh, sweetheart," he said, taking her back in his arms. He kissed her, slowly, tenderly, stroking her hair, the side of her face, her throat. Her arms came around his waist, splaying across his back.

When they separated, she was breathless. She picked a petal from her rose that had gotten crushed in their embrace.

"I see you got my flower," he said. He loved it that she would carry his flower with her when she didn't think he was there.

"What is it with you and white roses?" she asked. "How did you know they're my favorite?"

"I didn't. I sent them because of what they stand for." When she looked at him questioningly, he elaborated. "You'd know if you had an ounce of romance in your soul. True love."

"Ah, I've heard of that. The ruin of many a great woman."

"And a few men, if I'm any example. I love you, Ariel."

"I love you, too," she told him, going on tiptoe so she could kiss him. Her kiss was filled with all the urgency and passion they felt for each other. They pulled apart when they heard the sound of voices near them. Another couple passed by on their way around the deck.

"We'd better go inside," she said, taking his hand. If things kept up like this, they'd find themselves creating another scene.

"Before we do, I believe I have something that

belongs to you." Jarad put his hand in his jacket pocket. "Close your eyes and hold out your hand."

She did as he asked, sure he'd slip the silver and turquoise ring back on her finger. When he gave his okay, she opened her eyes. On her hand was a lovely onyx ring in a platinum setting. Surrounding the large black stone were at least two carats in diamonds. "Jarad, it's beautiful." She looked up at him. His face looked so solemn that it was almost comical. She could swear he looked a little pale.

"Jarad, what's the matter?"

"Will you marry me, Ariel?"

She shook her head in disbelief. It was too soon. She knew she loved him. She also knew that part of the reason for the misunderstandings between them was that they'd known each other such a short time. "We need time, Jarad. Together, I mean."

"I'm not asking you for a long-distance relationship. And I know you wouldn't be happy in L.A. Part of the reason I was gone so long is that I sold my house."

"You sold your house? Why?"

He looked heavenward, shaking his head, as if unable to believe she didn't know. "On the vague hope of finding an apartment on West 58th Street."

Ariel hugged him to her, this sweet, wonderful man she'd once thought she'd lost forever. "You'll still be ten blocks away," she said. "I live on West 68th Street."

"Honey, I don't care if we live in New York, Martha's Vineyard or Timbuktu. I just want to be with you."

Ariel smiled up at Jarad, replaying in her mind

all the wonderful times they'd shared together. Although their days together on the Vineyard were the most precious time of her life, she knew, in some ways, all of it had been like a fairy tale—a time apart from real life. Real life meant waking up each morning and falling asleep at night next to the same man and finding a way to keep on loving each other in between.

Neither one of them was perfect—they'd proven that already. But Ariel didn't need perfection. The man holding her, faults and all, suited her just fine.

"Yes," Ariel said. "Yes, I'll marry you, Jarad."

Jarad whooped and picked her up with his arms around her hips. He spun her around and when he released her, she slid down his body sensuously. "What made you think of the onyx?" she asked him, studying her ring from its vantage point of her hand on his shoulder.

"Onyx is supposed to be a witch's stone."

She made a face. "I'm no witch."

"Yes, you are," he said, tilting her chin up to him. "You cast your spell on me and I went down for the count."

She laughed at Jarad's mixed metaphor. "Come on," she said, taking his hand. "I want to show off my fiancé to my family. They've been pestering me about you so much, I might as well put them out of their misery."

Five minutes later, Ariel wished they'd made a beeline out the back door. Her family, in their excitement, made so much noise that the guests at the surrounding tables wanted to know what was going on. The commotion reached Jarad's parents, whom she'd forgotten to inform him were there. Charlie insisted on announcing their engagement to one and all, and ushered them to the dance floor for a trip around the room. When the others joined in, she and Jarad slipped out the door, up to his suite on the second floor.

Ariel was truly speechless when Jarad opened the door to his room. There were white roses everywhere—on the dresser, on the nightstand. There was a basket of roses by the door. He picked one up and handed it to her, as she'd lost the other one in all the excitement downstairs. She inhaled its scent deeply as she looked up at him.

"You are a crazy person," she told him.

"I'm crazy about you."

From the heated look in his eyes, she knew Jarad planned to show her exactly how crazy he could be. She stepped into his arms, a suggestive smile on her lips. "Let's be crazy together," she said.

Later, they lay in each other's arms, sated, content and finally happy. Ariel snuggled against Jarad's chest, absently running her fingers along his collarbone.

"You know," she said. "I never realized how many busybodies there were in my life until I met you. I think my father is the only one who didn't have some hand in trying to bring us together."

Jarad opened his eyes and looked down at her. "Are you kidding? He threatened me with bodily harm if I let anything happen to you."

Ariel's mouth fell open. "He didn't."

Jarad nodded. "He did."

"When we have kids, we are not g—"

"Kids?" Jarad asked. "Who said anything about kids?"

Seeing his startled reaction, she continued, teasing. "Yes, we'll have a little boy first. One with dark hair and eyes like his father's. I may have to beat off the little girls with a stick . . ." Ariel trailed off laughing.

"Followed by a little girl, I suppose. One with sea-green eyes like her mother's. No thanks. I'll spend the rest of my life making threats to pimply-faced adolescents. Maybe Steve can give me some pointers."

"I was thinking . . ."

"Oh, no! We're in trouble now."

"I was thinking, maybe we'll be lucky and have twins, one of each. Then the baby factory is closed." Ariel moved one hand from his shoulder to make a horizontal slashing gesture.

With one hand on the small of her back and the other at her nape, Jarad pulled her closer. Resting his chin against her temple, he said, "Aren't we getting a bit ahead of ourselves here? I want to spend a couple of years with my wife before the troops invade."

Jarad was right. They'd have plenty of time to decide these things. A lifetime in fact. She opened her mouth to tell him that.

He placed a silencing finger across her lips. "Why don't you do us both a favor. Shut up and kiss me."

That was one direction Ariel could follow for the rest of her life.

# Epilogue

"Heads up!"

At Jarad's call, Ariel looked up to see a multi-colored beach ball headed straight for her. She caught it, bringing it down to her lap. Jarad appeared a moment later, winking at her as he took the ball from her fingers. "See you later, Schweetheart," he said, in an imperfect Bogie impersonation.

When he'd gone, she'd turned to Jenny, who was sitting next to her. "I swear, that man gets worse each year." Jenny grunted in response.

Ariel lifted her sunglasses and looked at her cousin. "How are you doing?" she asked.

"Fine," Jenny said. "Considering my stomach is bigger than that ball."

Ariel let her sunglasses drop to the bridge of her nose. Jenny was due to deliver in less than two weeks. "It's not that bad." She looked at the ball being tossed between Jarad, Dan and the kids down at the water's edge. It was hard to believe Jenny's son was nearly three and her own twin girls were almost two. It seemed like only yesterday they were all babies in their mother's arms.

Absently, Ariel rubbed her stomach, forgetting the book she'd laid there, knocking it to the sand.

When she leaned down to pick it up, she felt a wave of dizziness wash over her. She sat back quickly, not noticing the acknowledging looks that passed between the women around her.

"Here we go again," Diana said.

"What?" Ariel said, looking around.

"Nothing, dear," Gran said. "Look, there's Steve and Charlie."

The two men bore trays of hamburgers, chicken and ribs, barbecued on the massive grill Jarad and Dan had built for Gran a couple of summers ago. They'd told her the youngest generation of men married to Ludlow women was staging a revolt. All that fish was fine for the ladies. The men wanted meat.

Jarad joined her a minute later. He dropped one little girl in her lap. He plopped down in the sand next to her with the other.

"Careful," Jenny said as Diandra squirmed on her mother's lap. Ariel's little girls were cursed with their mother's flyaway curls, and Ariel had to comb their hair ten times a day to keep it in pigtails. Unfortunately, neither of them enjoyed having their hair combed. Ariel looked up at Jenny, wondering if she knew. Jenny merely smiled noncommittally, turning to adjust her son's bathing suit, which was beginning to slip down.

"Leave the kid alone," Jarad pronounced, taking Diandra from Ariel and sitting the little girl on his lap next to her sister, Diana.

He tickled both girls until they tumbled from his lap into the sand. When he picked them up, the backs of both their heads were filled with sand. "You are washing their hair tonight," Ariel told him.

"Yes, dear," he said, affecting the voice of a henpecked husband. Seeing the others starting to fill their plates, he asked her if she was hungry.

She shook her head, sticking out her tongue. The mere thought of food made her queasy. "Feed the girls, okay?"

He looked at her closely, but said nothing. He got up and the girls followed him, leaking sand from their hair. Ariel put her face in her hand, laughing.

An hour later, most of the food was gone, consumed in large part by Jarad and Dan. "I'm going to have to put you on a diet," she told Jarad, playfully smacking his still-flat stomach. "You're getting fat."

"I am not." He was so indignant that she laughed.

"Girls," he called. "Don't go so far in the water." All the adults were sitting on the beach. Jenny's son, Daniel Jr., had fallen asleep curled around his mother's stomach.

The twins turned and, as if of one mind, ran and attacked their father. They jumped on him, trying to tickle him as he'd done to them. Jarad scooped them up, looking into the two identical faces he and Ariel had created. They had her golden brown complexion, her black-as-midnight hair, but they had his eyes, a warm dark brown that sparkled in their little faces.

Jarad sighed. "I guess the curse of the Ludlow women is over."

Four pairs of feminine ears pricked up. "The curse of whom?" Diana asked in an imperious voice. She took her namesake grandchild from Jarad's grasp, while Gran took Diandra on her lap.

"The curse of the Ludlow women?" Jarad asked as if he'd added the word "Duh."

"Charlie," Gran said with warning in her voice. "What is he talking about?"

Charlie was up from his seat in a flash. "You know I do feel like a swim. How about you, Steve?"

"I'm right behind you, Charlie." The two of them hurried off toward the water.

"Wait up," Dan called. He wasn't exactly sure how much complicity he bore in this situation, but he wasn't going to wait around to find out. His wife was very pregnant and very grouchy and he wasn't taking any chances.

Jarad looked as if he were about to bolt, too. But the women weren't having any of that. "Tell us about this curse business, young man," Gran said, leaning close to him.

Jarad recounted what Charlie and Steve and Dan had told him. His story was greeted with varied reactions by the women. Diana sighed and huffed dramatically. Gran said, "The man is touched. I've married a crazy old fool." Jenny laughed so hard she nearly knocked D.J. from his perch on her belly.

Ariel looked at him as if he'd just declared himself to be Napoleon Bonaparte. "And you believed that?" she asked when he finished recounting his story.

"Then why does your father call you little witch?" It was the only thing he could think of to say in his defense.

Ariel sat up, putting her feet in the sand next to him. Wrapping her arms around herself, she leaned down close to his face. "My father called me little witch before I was born. My mother's due date with me was Halloween. I had the good sense to be born two weeks later.

"And don't worry," she continued. "Children's

eye color isn't set until they're three years old, sometimes later. My eyes were brown when I was a baby, too."

Ariel spoke in that clinical voice he hadn't heard in a long time. She'd given up her job when the girls were born, and he wondered if she was ready to go back to work. She'd been restless lately, snapping at him in a way she hadn't since before they were married. She'd wanted to work part-time, but with twins it had been impossible.

Her reason for wanting to work had surprised him. She didn't want to have to come to him for money. She'd always been independent, and she refused to be totally reliant on him. So he paid her an exorbitant consultant's fee for the last film he'd made. The money went directly to her, and that seemed to satisfy her, financially at least. She still felt guilty for taking money she hadn't earned.

Ariel stretched languidly. "I for one am ready for a nap," she announced. She stood, stepping over Jarad's feet to collect the girls.

"We'll watch them," Gran and Diana said, almost in unison.

Ariel shrugged. "I'll see you guys later," she said between kisses to her daughters' cheeks.

When she was out of earshot, Gran said to Jarad, "Maybe you could use a nap, too. You're looking a little peaked there, boy."

"Maybe I will." Jarad stood, but sleep was the farthest thing from his mind. He tried to keep his lascivious thoughts from showing on his face. He knew he'd failed when Diana said, "Make sure she sleeps."

"Yes, ma'am," Jarad said before taking off after his wife. He chased her into the house and up the stairs. They were both laughing when they landed on their bed side by side. He scrubbed his hand over the outside of her thigh, the small rise in her belly.

Playfully rubbing the mound he felt, he said, "And you accused me of getting fat."

"That's not fat. That's our baby." Ariel held her breath, waiting for his reaction.

Jarad was perfectly still for a moment, closing his eyes and biting his lip. "Our baby," he echoed tightly.

She didn't know what to say to him. She wasn't sure what he was feeling. "Jarad, I . . ." she began.

"How far along are you?"

"Almost three months."

"Three months," he boomed. "Baby, why didn't you tell me?"

"I thought you'd be angry with me, which you are." She tried to get up, but he pulled her back.

"It's not that." He exhaled a long breath. Having the twins had been hard on her small body. There wasn't a stretch mark on her, but internally, where it counted, it had taken her a long time to heal.

After that, he hadn't wanted to put her through the ordeal of pregnancy and birth again. His girls were enough for him. He hadn't been sure she could conceive again. A year ago, she'd stopped using birth control, and there was nothing he could do to dissuade her. Ariel knew that deep down he wanted a son, and she was determined to give him one.

After so much time had passed with nothing happening, he'd given up hope. He'd thought she wanted to go back to work, in part, because she'd given up, too. He viewed it as their own little miracle that they were given another chance.

He bent and kissed her stomach worshipfully. "Thank you," he said.

Ariel looked down at her big, strong husband, and there were tears in his eyes. She sat up, putting her arms around him. "You big softy," she accused. "Will you be disappointed if it's another girl?"

He shook his head, his brown eyes intense, his voice solemn. "I could never be disappointed, as long as I have you."

His words filled her with such warmth that she felt tears brewing in her eyes. "You're going to make me cry," Ariel protested.

He pushed her back against the pillows. "The only way I'm going to make you cry is with pleasure." He lay down beside her, wondering how he'd missed the signs of her pregnancy. Her breasts in his hands were already swollen. He bent his head to sample one tender peak. "That is okay, isn't it?" Ariel nodded, smiling.

As he continued to make sweet love to his wife, he decided he didn't care what anybody said. She was a witch. First, she'd bewitched him and made his life a living hell. Then she'd charmed him and turned it into a paradise.

He couldn't wait to see what she'd do next.

Dear Readers,

I hope you have enjoyed reading about Ariel and Jarad. Their story is close to my heart as I spent many, many summers on the island of Martha's Vineyard soaking up the sun and scribbling in one of my various notebooks. Although Ariel is not me, some of her experiences were based on my own adventures on the island. Yes, I did climb the mountainside at Gay Head, terrifying my own mother and about twenty onlookers. The next time we went back, the area was roped off to prevent other would-be daredevils from repeating the stunt.

The island has changed in so many other ways since the days of my youth. Gay Head recently took back its Native American name of Aquinnah, meaning "the land under the hill." The Flying Horses no longer gives out a brass ring, though it is still the oldest continuously operating carousel in the United States. The beach in Vineyard Haven was so overrun with seaweed the last time I went there that it was impossible to swim. Yet, in my memory, the island is the same place it was twenty years ago—simple, charming, and, like true love, perfect.

I would love to hear from you. You can write to me at P.O. Box 233, Baychester Station, Bronx, NY 10469 or E-mail me at DeeSavoy@aol.com. And who knows, if you find yourself on the island of Martha's Vineyard one summer, I may see you there. Just look for the woman on the Paradise Island towel, frantically scribbling in her notebook.

Best regards,
Deirdre Savoy

## About the Author

Deirdre Savoy started writing romance as a teenager on the beaches of Martha's Vineyard. The island provided the perfect setting for her first novel, SPELLBOUND.

A graduate of the Bernard M. Baruch College of the City University of New York, she has worked as a secretary, a legal proofreader, an advertising copywriter and a news editor of a popular Caribbean-American magazine. Currently a first grade teacher, she lives in Bronx, New York, with her husband and two children. She enjoys reading, dancing, calligraphy and wicked crossword puzzles.

# Coming in January from Arabesque Books . . .